ADVANC
THE SIN

"A sizzling tale of closeted corruption, McCarthyite intimidation, ruined lives, state-sponsored pornography, a professor-student love affair, and down-and-dirty politics under the moss-draped oaks of the Sunshine State."
—Elliott Mackle,
author of *Captain Harding's Six-Day War* and *It Takes Two*

"What Stockett's *The Help* did to bring alive the individual stories of race in the South in the early 1960s, Farris's *The Sin Warriors* does to illuminate the personal and political battles surrounding sexual orientation during the same era—a truly unforgettable read."
—Thomas Serwatka,
author of *Queer Questions, Clear Answers*

"Julian Earl Farris exposes with a passion the cruel inequalities of Florida's past. He does not forget to tell a story, a touching story rich in historical details, in the process."
—Sandra McDonald,
Lambda Literary Award-winning author of
Diana Comet and Other Improbable Stories

THE
SIN
WARRIORS

THE
SIN
WARRIORS

A NOVEL BY

JULIAN E. FARRIS

LETHE PRESS
MAPLE SHADE, NEW JERSEY

Published in 2012 by Lethe Press, Inc.
118 Heritage Avenue • Maple Shade, NJ 08052-3018
www.lethepressbooks.com • lethepress@aol.com
ISBN: 1-59021-274-6
ISBN-13: 978-1-59021-274-5

Set in Hoefler Text, Calisto MT, and Myriad.
Cover and interior design: Alex Jeffers.
Cover artwork: Ben Baldwin.

LIBRARY OF CONGRESS CATALOGING-IN-PUBLICATION DATA

Farris, Julian E.
  The sin warriors : a novel / by Julian E. Farris.
    p. cm.
  ISBN 978-1-59021-274-5 (pbk. : alk. paper)
 1. Gay college students--Fiction. 2. Gay college teachers--Fiction.
3. Legislators--Florida--Fiction. 4. Florida--Social conditions--20th century--Fiction. I. Title.
  PS3606.A7457S56 2012
  813'.6--dc23

                                        2012017516

DISCLAIMER

While this novel is inspired by true events occurring fifty years ago, it is a work of fiction. Names, characters, places and incidents are products of the author's imagination or are used fictitiously. Any resemblance to factual events, locales or persons living or dead is entirely coincidental.

PROLOGUE
THE UNIVERSITY, DECEMBER 1958

"WE LOCATED PREVATT."

"Outstanding. Have you primed him?"

"He's primed and ready. Told him his dismissal was all a mistake."

"And the student?"

"Primed and ready. What about Warren?"

"He's ready. He'll cooperate. We just need his deposition."

"And the Jew? What about the Jew?"

"Cohen's next. Let's move it."

—⁕—

ELLIS COHEN KNEW the tactic. The late night call. The anonymous voice summoning the victim. He had readied himself. "Do you have a subpoena?" Cohen asked.

"Will we need one?" the voice asked.

"You will if you want to interrogate me."

"It's to your..."

Cohen broke in to finish the statement, "...advantage to cooperate?"

Silence on the other end.

"Tell you what. I'll spare you the subpoena. Yes, I'll be delighted to cooperate."

"Fine," said the voice. "Be here in thirty minutes."

"No. Tomorrow. I'll let you know when. And don't call me again like this," Cohen said, gently placing the phone on the cradle and turning off the light.

COHEN SAT IN the lobby of the Rosemont Hotel. They had kept him waiting for an hour. Another tactic. Keep him waiting. Build up anxiety, then pounce. Except he was ready to pounce.

As usual, the room was empty except for the table in the center, the straight chairs on either side and the lone light overhead. Cohen recognized Senator Billy Sloat seated at the far end. Mayes, the committee's legal counsel, and Henson, its chief investigator, held positions at the center. Except for file folders and note pads, the only object on the table was the recorder.

Mayes glanced at Senator Sloat, cleared his throat and began. "Would you state your name, occupation and residence please?"

"Ellis Cohen, Professor of English, State University, United States citizen."

Mayes stiffened, paused, glanced again at Sloat and continued. "Do you swear that the deposition you are about to give..."

Cohen interrupted. "I don't swear, Mr. Mayes, except on rare occasions, and I will take an oath only in a legitimate procedure."

Mayes sneered. "You are suggesting that this investigation is illegitimate?"

"Your procedure is questionable. You wanted my cooperation in your inquiry. I'm prepared to offer my cooperation. What do you want to know?"

Caught off guard, Mayes hesitated, looked again in Sloat's direction, then plunged ahead. "Are you now or have you ever been a communist or have had associations with known communists, Dr. Cohen?"

Cohen laughed. "My God, man, you sound just like Joe McCarthy, a bit rough around the edge, but not a bad imitation."

"Will you answer for the record?" he demanded.

"No."

"No, you have not been, or no you will not answer for the record?"

"No, I will not answer for the record."

"Are you homosexual?" Mayes asked.

"That is really of no concern to you."

"Oh, but it is. Homosexuality is a felony in this state, punishable with prison."

"No, Mr. Mayes, a homosexual tendency is not a felony, only the act itself is a felony, and that is unfortunate."

Suddenly Mayes was energized. "Oh, so you condone homosexual acts. And your students? Do you encourage their engagement in such acts?"

"I encourage them to be who they are, not to hide behind pretense."

"As a teacher, Dr. Cohen, you have an obligation to set an example. Your association with known homosexuals and communists is well established. Moral turpitude and subversion are grounds for dismissal," he threatened.

Cohen looked directly at Sloat, then at Mayes. "Since my associations are so well established, it appears that further cooperation is unnecessary."

Mayes glanced again at Sloat, sensing his impatience. He cleared his throat.

"I will ask you once more. Are you a homosexual?" he demanded.

Cohen's response was direct. "No."

"But you know others who are."

"Well, of course, even some who are closeted. For all I know, you could be. Are you, Mr. Mayes? Have you ever in your life had such tendencies?"

Mayes's eyes widened. His face flushed. Blood rushed to his cheeks. He waited a moment for his rage to subside. Sloat shifted in his chair at the question.

"There are serious allegations about you and your association with certain individuals," Mayes said. "You can make this easy or difficult."

"For whom? For me or for you?"

"For all of us, Dr. Cohen. Just give us the facts," he insisted.

"What facts would you prefer? The truth or what you construe as truth?"

"The truth truth," he shouted.

"Oh, that truth. Not the half-truth, the partial truth, but the truth truth. Well, Mr. Mayes, the truth is your so-called investigation is a pathetic abuse of power. If it weren't for the lives you have ruined, I would pity you for your arrogance, your ignorance, your bigotry, your cowardice." He stopped abruptly, then leaned forward, speaking directly into the recorder. "But put this in the record. My great disappointment is Dwight Thurgis. He is pitiable. Politics is rife with scum like you, but the president of this university has made himself your academic whore. And that *is* the truth! Now if you want anything else from me, get a subpoena," he said. He rose from his chair. He looked directly at Billy Sloat, turned, and left the room.

OUTSIDE, THE OCTOBER air was brisk. Cohen walked along the commons and, reaching the pond, plopped on the bench next to the path. Back there he had maintained an air of defiance. But the truth was there seemed no recourse other than to resist. The university was supposed to be a refuge against ignorance. Now it was the instrument of ignorance itself. How incredible, he thought, that this could happen in this country, in this time, in this place and that there was no protection under the law, no recourse except to resist.

CHAPTER 1
MORGAN COUNTY, FLORIDA 1915

IDA WAS DREAMING again. It is two years before the end of the Civil War. The other plantation slaves gather to witness the union of her mother and father—something akin to a marriage. The man and woman place their brooms on the ground, the owner raising his arms to silence the crowd now pressing in on the nervous couple.

They join hands and jump across the brooms, then backward and over again as the brooms are raised higher while onlookers watch to see who will fail to clear the brooms; but both clear the brooms easily; then Shaw, the generous owner, bestows his surname on her parents.

The dream shifts abruptly. The plantation is in ruins; twenty-three years have passed; Shaw is standing next to the bed where his wife bleeds from the difficult birth; Ida is holding the infant Annabelle but all at once the infant is a young woman of eighteen or so, and it is Ida, now, who delivers Annabelle's only child of another premature and traumatic birth—Billy Sloat.

———

DOWN AT THE spring, the other boys shed their clothes and plunged into the seventy-two degree water. Billy Sloat watched from the distance, saw their bodies glistening in the early afternoon sun, uneasy at their nakedness.

"What you wait'n for, Billy?" one shouted. "Come on in."

The ten year old averted his eyes, pretending not to see them.

"What's wrong with you, Billy?" Josh called from the spring. Billy hesitated before finding a response.

"I ..." he struggled to say, "I don't want to swim."

5

But he did want to swim. It was Josh's nakedness that halted him. Billy surveyed Josh's hard, confident body cutting through the icy spring water.

"Come on, scarecrow," one of the others yelled.

"Come on, sissy," another teased.

He retreated to the safety of the bank. There, he stole another glance at Josh, then turned away, trying to deal with his discomfort and his confusion, shuffling his bare feet along the dry, sandy road.

The Florida summer humidity pressed upon him, the afternoon sky thick with clouds, smelling of rain, and heat, unrelenting, from the sun parching his already tanned skin. He stopped abruptly. A water snake slithered into the brush and down toward the creek. He picked up a stick from the side of the road, hurling it at the snake, which slid into the water.

On down the road he came to Ida's cabin, separated from the main house by fifty feet. Ten years of neglect since her brother's sudden departure had taken its toll. It was a small clapboard shanty with a wood stove and an outhouse in the back. In summer, the screenless window in the tiny kitchen was left open, bringing some relief from the sweltering heat. A back door led to the hand pump and the outhouse. In winter the wind whistled through the open cracks of the wooden planks. The boards that formed the floor, like the ones that enclosed the cabin, were bare and loosely fitted, exposing the dirt below. Outside the ground was barren except for patches of dollar weed that provided the only break from the dry earth.

Through the kitchen window, Billy saw Ida at the stove.

"Ida, I come to see if Owen wants to come out for a bit."

"Ask him yourself. Owen," she called without looking away from the kettle, "Billy wants you."

Owen eyed Billy from the open kitchen window, watched him kicking sand with his bare feet, observed his impatience. There was little diversion in the backwoods of Morgan County. When school was in session, it was different. But in summer, in the country, Owen was Billy's main distraction from boredom, and he knew not to cross him.

BILLY AND OWEN wandered through the woods toward the creek.

"Owen," Billy said, "you can try my slingshot—see what you can hit." Owen took the slingshot, picked up a stone, aimed at a tree and released the sling. He missed.

"Damn, Owen, don't you know nothing about how to aim a slingshot? Gimme that thing," Billy said. He spotted a bird up in the tree, took aim and hit it dead on. The bird fluttered and fell to the ground. Owen grasped the bird, held it against his bare chest, as if this could bring it back.

"That's how you use the shot, Owen. Aim dead on at the target. That's how, you dumb nigra."

Owen wanted to holler back at Billy's insult, scream at him for killing the bird. But he diverted his eyes and buried his anger.

OWEN NEVER KNEW his father. That was something he had in common with Billy. Ida had told him his father abandoned them prior to Owen's birth. But there was something not right about it. Like something she was holding back each time he asked her.

The death of Billy Sloat's father the year Billy was born was still the topic of Morgan County gossip ten years later. They found his body in the woods a hundred feet or so behind Ida's cabin. The attack had been brutal, the face bashed almost beyond recognition, sections of the skull cracked by a sharp object, exposing part of the brain. Why anyone would want to kill him was a mystery. He had been a deputy with the Morgan County Sheriff's office just under two years. He was unreliable, arrogant and lazy. Except for his death, he likely would have been fired. Still people speculated. Was it something that caught up with him finally? Was somebody out for revenge? Who would know? Who would even care?

Certainly not Billy's mother. As far as Annabelle Shaw Sloat was concerned, her husband's death wasn't much of a loss at all. It was never a good marriage. She had endured his drunken stupors and disappearances days at a time when she was pregnant with Billy. In spite of him, she and Ida were survivors, their twenty-eight-year bond as strong as family blood. Billy was never allowed to forget that. Never.

THE FOLLOWING YEAR might have been like any other in the backwoods of the former plantation, but the summer of 1916 marked the turning point in their lives. Billy watched the Ford barreling down the sand road toward the main highway a mile away, vanishing in a cloud of dust. "Who was those men, Mamma?"

She wiped sweat from her forehead and the back of her hand on her dress. "We are having a stroke of luck. Won't be keeping this place no more, be moving on, son."

"Moving?" Her words disturbed him. "Where? This is home," he protested.

"Not for long," said Annabelle. "Railroad's buying us out. They're going west beyond Tallahassee."

"What's gonna happen to us?" It didn't make sense to him. Where would they go if they left here?

"Don't worry, Billy. We'll git a nice place in Monroe. You won't never again walk down a dirt road for school. We will live like civilized people, Billy, like civilized people again."

"And Owen and Ida? They comin' too?"

"Well of course they're coming. Why wouldn't they?"

He watched the road's settling dust in the distance.

"Answer me, Billy. Why wouldn't they?"

He shook his head. "Just wonderin," he answered with a frown.

THE MOVE WAS quick. Two men showed up one day in an open flatbed truck, hemmed in on both sides with rickety wooden boards. In less than an hour, they had loaded the few remnants of belongings. Billy wandered through the house still littered with worn out pieces of furniture.

"Ain't we taking these too?" Billy asked.

"It's junk, Billy. Just junk. We'll be buying new. Now let's git moving."

BY THE END of summer, Annabelle Shaw Sloat had begun her civilized life in Morgan County's only town—Monroe or Mun'ro as the locals called it. The house was not large, but compared to what was left of the former plantation house, it seemed like a mansion, with its clean, well appointed rooms shimmering with sunlight.

Annabelle floated from room to room, arms arched over her head like a ballerina, eyes closed as she twisted and turned, coming to a halt before Ida, whose apprehension about the new arrangements was unmistakable.

"Well," said Annabelle, "now what's wrong, Ida? You look like you swallowed a green persimmon."

"This ain't gonna work. You should see the looks I get when I venture down the street to the store."

"What kind of looks?"

"You know what I'm talkin' about. Like we don't belong here—Owen and me."

"Never mind that," Annabelle insisted. "This is our home, Ida, and like it or not, they'll just have to get used to it. Besides, where is a place for you and Owen in a small town like Monroe? It's not like Tallahassee, where colored people have their own part of town."

"But..." and before Ida could finish, Annabelle cocked her head in defiance and said,

"This discussion is over, Ida. Your place is here. Hear me? Now, let's have tea." She closed her yes, twirled again, arms raised and said, "It's such a lovely afternoon, isn't it?"

BILLY AND OWEN were shooting marbles in the dirt below the dining room window. Billy scowled, raising his voice in a high-pitched whisper. "It's such a love-ly afternoon, let's have tea, shall we?"

Owen giggled. Billy's scowl grew darker. "What's so funny, stupid?"

—✺—

THE EXPENSIVE CLOTHES his mother bought him for his eleventh birthday hung on Billy's scrawny frame, making him an easy target.

Dressed in green knee pants and a striped flannel blouse, with its large sailor collar, double cuffs and pearl buttons that his mother had ordered from the Sears Roebuck catalog, Billy walked the four blocks toward the corner store. Rounding the corner, he saw them. The gang of three. For a second, he thought of turning to head back toward home, but he knew they would take this as a sign of coward-ice. He slowed, measuring each step with caution.

Josh was leader of the pack. He moved to the center of the walk, blocking Billy's path, his eyes darting back and forth at the spectacle before him.

"Well looky here, if it ain't momma's boy, all dressed up in his Sunday outfit," he drawled, glancing back at the other two. "We ain't seen you at the spring since you moved to town. Where you been? Where's your little nigger friend?"

Billy tried to manage a smile as the three approached, wiping grime from their half worn-out coveralls. Josh gave a forceful push, sending Billy scrambling on the sidewalk, blood oozing from the scrapes on his knees.

"Aw," mocked Josh. "Looky there, the little sissy done tore his pretty new pants. Poor Billy. Here," he offered, "lemme hep you," he said, smearing traces of blood on the frilly shirt.

Billy hobbled to his feet and, running now, cursed the new home in Monroe, stumbled again to the sidewalk, scraping elbows and knees. When he reached the house, Owen took stock of the torn knee pants and the blood-smeared blouse as Billy limped up the steps to the porch. "Billy," he called, "what happened? What's wrong?"

Billy glared at him. "You," he snapped, "you're what's wrong!"

THE FOLLOWING SATURDAY, Annabelle sent them to Wiggins' grocery. Billy did the buying. Owen did the carrying. Cora Duncan and her friend ambled down the narrow walk, two schoolgirls chattering aim-lessly, arms loose around each other's waists, not looking left or right. Owen, his vision blocked by the loaded bags he carried, bumped into Cora who lost her balance and fell headlong to the sidewalk.

Billy snarled, "Damn you, you clumsy, stupid fool, just look what you done." He helped Cora to her feet. "Sorry about that, Cora. This dumb nigger never looks where he's goin."

—⁂—

THE OPENING OF the Biograph Picture Show in the summer of 1918 was a milestone for Morgan County. It was the only movie house east of Tallahassee and west of Jacksonville. People from three counties crowded the hundred-seat theater's opening to see D. W. Griffith's 1915 film, *Birth of a Nation*. Billy Sloat was among them.

His attention was fixed on the images flickering across the screen, carpetbaggers swooping down upon the defeated Southern Confederacy, mobs of Negroes raping white girls—total anarchy—and the white hooded vigilantes rising up to vanquish and vindicate.

Outside the Biograph, intoxicated by the pictures, he leaned against the wooden electric post to catch his breath, overcome with the images still replaying in his mind.

After a few minutes, he started down the now deserted street toward home, and someone called to him.

"Billy, wait up."

He stopped abruptly until the sixteen year old caught up with him.

"Well?" the older boy asked, waiting for a response. "Was that something or what?"

"Lordy, that sure was something," Billy said with amazement.

"Well, Billy, you ain't seen nothing yet. There's something special happening tonight."

"Like what?"

"Well, it's kind of a secret," he said, arousing Billy's curiosity. "Can you keep secrets?"

"What kind of secrets?"

"How old are you?"

"Turning thirteen. Why?"

"That's old enough."

"Old enough for what?"

"There's a special gathering tonight in the woods. Meet me here at midnight if you're interested."

"What kind a gathering?"

"Recruitment," was his only answer.

ANNABELLE SHAW SLOAT was sound asleep. Billy eased out of the house then rushed down the street for his rendezvous and the secret midnight gathering. In the woods, his heart raced at the ghostly vision of white hooded figures setting fire to a cross. Lordy, Billy thought. I ain't never seen nothing like it. It's just like in the picture show.

CHAPTER 2
DAVID AND STEPHEN

IT WAS 1944. In Jacksonville, Florida as in many other towns and cities across the country, it seemed as though the war would never end. David Ashton's grandmother sipped the warmed-over coffee and winced at the bitter taste of chicory as she watched the two eight-year-old boys from the kitchen window. Over make-believe roads etched from the heavy sand, the toy cars, too large for their small hands, careened around sharp corners, zigzagging right, and left, then right again.

Greta Hofmann noted the time. Four o'clock. Time to come in. Yvonne would be home from work soon. Dinner, then homework. Playtime over. There was a moment when she hesitated to halt their play. The child had been through enough already, hadn't he? She was not indifferent to his needs. She loved him, after all. But with all that had happened, she would not allow her feelings to come between her responsibility to protect him, and his need for protection.

David shook sand from his car. "Got to go. Want to spend the night?"

Stephen nodded.

"Grandma," David shouted, "Can Stephen come back later?"

"No," said Greta. "Not this time."

"But it's Friday."

"I said no. Now go wash up before your mother's home." She slammed the window shut. David knew the final answer was no. "See you tomorrow?" he called as Stephen shuffled toward home.

"Yeah, tomorrow."

IT WAS A small private school run by the church, no more than two hundred boys, grades one through four. The sisters from the convent were assigned a particular grade. Sister Margaret's assignment was David and Stephen's third grade.

During penmanship drill, David raised his hand to be excused. He held up his finger, indicating number one. Sister Margaret gave a disapproving glance, turned again to the blackboard. Recess was five minutes away. He could wait for recess. She saw David again hold up his hand, indicating number one, now waving with a sense of urgency.

"Put your hand down," she ordered.

David's urgency gave way to a warm stream down his legs as the others marched from the room. He felt a slap from Sister Margaret. "Get the mop and clean it up!"

Afterward, David sat at his desk, the stain from the accident soaking through his trousers, too mortified to move or to speak. When everyone had gone, the two boys walked quickly from the room, not wanting to spark more annoyance from Sister Margaret.

—⚍—

WALTER ASHTON THOUGHT he had reached closure on the conflicting pull he had struggled with for most of his adult life. He adored his son, and that had been the one reason he had stayed in the relationship with Yvonne. But the marriage only aggravated his lack of self-respect. It had never been a satisfactory solution to his dilemma, though he had thought so at the time. He had met Yvonne the year she and her mother, Greta, had left St. Louis to settle in Jacksonville. Within a year they were married and the following year, David was born. Five years later, with the Japanese attack on Pearl Harbor and the country's entry into war, when other men were either drafted or volunteered, Walter Ashton had been exempted through his appointment as Vice President of Jacksonville Operations for Seaboard Shipyards, considered vital to the war effort. The position enabled him to stay with his family and to provide generously for them.

For the better part of a year, what began as scattered absences became regular weekends away when he claimed he was called out of town to look into management issues, then with increasing frequency, a week away at a time on other pretexts of corporate problems. But

Yvonne was not stupid. Even when her husband was home, there was an unmistakable aloofness, and when she attempted to engage him, he would respond with repeated excuses. She had reached the end of it. She would force the issue. She would confront him.

He had arrived home late, offering his usual apology, telling her he had to leave for an unexpected appointment. Greta, unnoticed, listened from the kitchen.

"Who is she?"

He waited for her next assault.

"Answer me," she demanded. "I want to know."

"Are you sure?" he warned her. He watched her with an easy detachment, took a deep breath, and said without a trace of emotion, "You're half right. But it isn't *she*."

He braced himself for the rage he knew was imminent.

At first, his response did not register with her. Then the impact of his words struck her full-force. She was prepared to cope with his infidelity, but not this—her disgust smothered by her bitterness.

"My God," she screamed, "how could you...? I can destroy you for this."

"Yes," he said, lowering his voice to a whisper. "You can, and I would deserve it, but where would that leave us? I lose my position with the company, and we're both left without any resources whatsoever. Is that what you want, Yvonne? Would that satisfy your anger? Go ahead, ruin me."

"You bastard. How could you do this to us? I hate you," she cried.

"Of course you do. Who could blame you? But this isn't just a choice. I would never intentionally hurt you. You have to believe that."

She felt a surge of nausea, fought the urge to vomit, tried to focus on him in spite of tears blurring her vision. At that moment, she wanted to kill him. She reached for a pen on the desktop, scribbled something on paper and tearing it from the note pad, thrust it in his hand.

"Sign it," she demanded.

He read the lines. "Is this really necessary?" he asked helplessly.

"Sign it and date it," she insisted.

He read the note again:

> *I am a practicing homosexual*

"Now, get your things and get out. And so help me God, if you ever try to see David again, I *will* destroy you." But he was already destroyed. "Now!" she screamed.

DAVID HEARD THE commotion in the living room. Roused from sleep, he padded into his parent's bedroom and watched his father pack his things. "Where are you going, Daddy?"

Walter kneeled in front of David. "I have to live in a different place for now," he told him.

"Why are you leaving? Don't you love us anymore?" David asked, his voice breaking.

His father held him close. "Of course I love you. I always will, but things are different now with your mom and me. Sometimes not being together is best."

"Can I go with you?" the eight-year-old pleaded.

"Not now, not this time, but we'll be back together again, you'll see." He gave David a kiss on the forehead, bent down for a final hug, then snapped the luggage closed and David watched him leave. Afterward, the only contact he had with his father were the lavish presents he received on each birthday.

ON HIS ELEVENTH birthday, David would enter the lobby of Seaboard Shipyards, fix his eyes on the marbled walls, study the directory for the executive offices to find his father. On the third floor, a receptionist asks why he is there. To see his father. She returns to tell him that his father couldn't see him. He leaves and never goes back there again to see his father—the only connection the gifts each birthday.

—∞—

STEPHEN'S FATHER WAS a shadow father. Between them was an emotional void against which Stephen sought refuge with David in the fantasy world they shared.

Like Walter Ashton, Scott Smith was another of those left behind during the war. A heart murmur prevented his participation. Not that he minded. He considered the wild enthusiasm of his contemporaries for the war irrational. He was no hero. He was satisfied to be exactly where he was.

Stephen could not please his father. The man appeared incapable of feeling. He offered no acknowledgement of the boy, only a detachment from Stephen's presence. Stephen had brought his report card home, his first with all A's—sure his father would be pleased, even tell him he was proud of him as his teacher had. His father gave it a passing glance, nodded and continued reading the afternoon paper.

And there was the fire. Stephen and David had gathered discarded Christmas trees, dragging them inside the empty garage behind the house. They had set up camp in the make-believe forest, readied themselves for the long night ahead. The small campfire they set had ignited the dry, brittle branches into an inferno that the firemen barely managed to contain. When the fire was over, Scott Smith assured the firemen it would not happen again. While David got it good and hard from Greta, Stephen waited for his father's rebuke that never came.

Then there was the late-night quarrel that woke him from sleep. He eased out of bed, opening the door barely an inch to hear the insults his parents hurled at each other. He heard his mother's voice, but it seemed not hers at all, shrill, uncertain, her voice yet someone else's, a stranger's voice, his father's voice a menacing growl like some wild animal. He had never heard his father's anger. Their voices frightened him.

Scott Smith hurled his words back at her. "What did I expect? A wife. I wanted a wife, not a family. Not being tied down—stuck in one place. You never asked me."

"I never thought I had to. It's because of your father!"

"Leave him out of it," he demanded.

"Never leave that behind, can you?"

"I did already, God damn you, Evelyn. What else do you want?"

"For you to stop...taking your father's rejection...out on your son," she called out as he stormed from the house.

Stephen pushed the door closed. Back in bed, he huddled beneath the blanket, covering his head in the darkness that hid him.

—◆◆◆—

DAVID WAS KEPT away from his father by court order, although the divorce was not final. Only with his mother's permission could he see his father, but Yvonne would have none of it. This was the one plea from David she would not grant, no matter his insistence.

David's tie to Stephen was another matter entirely. When the boys were together, they were happy kids. That's what mattered. How could she deny David that?

For Greta Hofmann, that was precisely the problem. She had not left her Prussian values in Germany or back in St. Louis. Her daughter's permissiveness would ruin him. Children required discipline, didn't they? What would come of a boy raised by two women and no discipline? A family consisted of a man and a woman, didn't it? A father, a mother—and of course a grandmother. But Greta knew Yvonne would never look for another husband. Her Catholic upbringing and her devout faith would never permit it.

An annulment was out of the question. Her husband's disclosure and the consequences of losing his job ruled that out, and Yvonne would be denied the sacraments of the Church if she remarried after a civil divorce. So Greta had accepted the role of disciplinarian. Someone had to. One fire in the family was enough.

—⁕—

ON DAVID'S NINTH birthday, the two boys walked the mile to the Palace Theatre. *Snow White and the Seven Dwarfs* was playing once more. They arrived early in the morning for the first showing, sitting close to the front, then for the second consecutive showing sitting farther back, and for the third high in the balcony, as though each vantage point gave the illusion of seeing the repeated scenes from a different, revealing perspective. Each time they cried when Snow White was offered the poisoned apple and rejoiced each time the handsome prince appeared. Especially when the handsome prince appeared.

When they left the theatre, it was dark. They took the shortcut through the dimly lighted park, around the pond and down Market Street to David's house. And David's grandmother was waiting for them. David knew from her pinched mouth what was coming. She gestured toward the wall clock, waving her hand erratically.

"Get in here. Now," she ordered, and spinning around toward Stephen, shouted, "and you...get yourself home."

Yvonne said nothing, did nothing to prevent Greta's rage.

Stephen made the slow trek back to the shadow house alone.

———∞———

IN SPITE OF everything, Stephen could not win Greta Hofmann's approval. She understood his need for her acceptance, how hard he tried, but her duty was to her grandson. With the break-up of the family, if indeed it had ever been a family given Walter's revelation, it was her responsibility to protect David. Stephen was a bad influence.

There was the incident when Stephen, David and Alice, the five year old from next door, played doctor, patient and nurse. They had set up the doctor's office inside the empty garage at David's house; Alice had brought one of her mother's discarded dresses. Both Stephen and David were astonished when she removed her own clothes to put on the long white garment.

She had no pee-pee, just a curious flat place where the pee-pee should have been. David asked if she would like to see his, and once it was exposed, she just snickered at the funny thing dangling there. At that moment David's grandmother burst into the makeshift doctor's office, outraged at her discovery, screaming her disapproval as the doctor, the patient and the nurse burst into tears.

It was Alice's mother who, against Greta Hofmann's objection, declared this a non-event, merely an educational experience requiring no special attention, no need for a trauma. But David's grandmother remained unconvinced. If she ever caught David like that again, she would take the scissors to him "—and cut it off," she said.

———∞———

A HALF-MILE FROM David's house, Reeder Creek twisted its way through the dense canopy of oaks, maples, and a scattering of palmetto. The two boys sat very still, gazing intently into the shallow water, nets in hand, poised to swoop down as minnows swam by. David spied one, flung the net into the stream, and came up with the catch. "That's three for me against your two," David boasted, dropping his catch into the Mason jar of water.

After several hours, when they had grown tired and it was time to go, they released the small fish back into the stream. As they inched their way through the park, David caught sight of a cat flinging something in the air, then catching it again with its paws. A *bird*. He darted ahead, grabbed the cat and, forcing its mouth open, released the bird from the cat's hold—a baby Cardinal. He held the fledgling in the cup of his hand as Stephen examined it. "His wing looks broken."

"Let's take it home and keep it 'til it's better and he can fly away. We can feed it worms and give it a soft place to sleep," David said.

When they brought the bird to David's house, Greta greeted them at the back door.

"It's useless. The wing is useless. Nothing can be done. We have to finish it off," she announced with authority as her grandson looked on helplessly.

"No Grandma," David pleaded, "please, just give it a chance. I *know* we can take care of it until it's well."

"It's no good, David. No good. You have to do the right thing."

She followed him as he carried the injured bird to the back yard and placed it under the tree onto the grass. The neighbor's cat watched. David cast another glance at his grandmother, looking for some sign of reprieve. He glanced at Stephen, then back to Greta, and the cat waited, and waited as cats will do.

Greta gave a commanding nod. "Do it."

CHAPTER 3
MOVING ON

NINETEEN EIGHTEEN WAS a good year and a bad year. The Great War to end all wars had come to a close with 320,000 Americans dead and wounded, and the great influenza epidemic would claim 548,000 victims in the country by the year's end. But it wasn't such a bad year for Annabelle Shaw Sloat.

The railroad connections in Monroe had been an important supply link for the war effort. With some of the money from the sale of her land to Great South Railway, Annabelle Shaw Sloat had purchased shares in the company and her investment was paying off. God had blessed her perseverance. She had not only survived; she was a rich woman.

But God had not seen fit to bestow any particular blessing on Ida. Her present and her future remained unchanged. She was a world apart from the young girl who had taken on the task of raising Annabelle when her mother died. There would be nothing beyond what had been and what could not be. She accepted that reality for herself. What was hard was knowing Owen had no future in Monroe, Florida—or anywhere else.

Ida gazed out the window over the sink. She had lost any sense of time. The dishwater was cold to the touch now. She would still be standing trancelike there but Annabelle interrupted the moment.

"Ida, is something wrong?"

No response.

Something is wrong. "Ida, look at me. What's going on?"

Ida gave a quick tug of her shoulders, attempted a smile but turned away, peering blankly out the window.

Annabelle led her into the living room, pointed toward the over-stuffed chair. They sat without speaking. Annabelle reached for Ida's hand.

"Talk to me, Ida. For a week now you've hardly said a word. What's bothering you? What can I do to make you happy?"

"It ain't you. You done so much already. Owen has learn't to read, thanks to you. It's just..." Annabelle waited for her to finish.

"Just what, Ida?"

"Just I don't see much coming of it. Ain't no school for Owen no-where here. Heard they's just one in the whole state."

Just one in the whole state. Of course nothing coming of it. Nothing. Not for Owen. "I know, Ida. Don't you know it's crossed my mind? I've thought about that, the two years since we've been here." She waited for some reaction, but Ida stayed quiet. "And Owen's such a smart boy," she added, searching for words to fill the oppressive stillness of the room. "He learns fast. You can be proud of him."

"I am proud of him," she said, folding her hands tightly, but avoiding Annabelle's eyes. "It's me. I feel so helpless."

Helpless. She turned the sting over in her mind. "Well," Annabelle protested, "you're not helpless, Ida. You're not."

Another silence.

But of course she's helpless. How could she be otherwise? This black woman and her child whose only future is defined by the town limits of Monroe, Florida (their prison actually and no chance for a reprieve) just stuck here, in this place, in Morgan County, in Monroe, Florida for life.

"Maybe it's time we do something about all that." Annabelle took a deep breath, summoning her courage. How would Ida take to this? How would she take to it herself? "I've been thinking, Ida...about...for a long time...maybe you and Owen...going...to...to Pennsylvania?"

The words jolted Ida. *To Pennsylvania.* She jerked her head abruptly. "Pennsylvania? How would we make it? I got no money, no education, nothing to offer. What would a fifty-four-year-old colored woman do in Pennsylvania?"

"There're schools for coloreds up north, Ida. And I have means."

Ida was shaking now from Annabelle's pronouncement.

"Listen to me, Ida. With my railroad connections, I can get you in with someone. You'll have work and a safe place to live. I'll see to it.

It won't be easy, I know. But you can make it, Ida. You will. I'll help you. There's money enough to get you by. It's a chance Owen will never have here. An opportunity. An education. Think about that, Ida."

Now they were both silent. She could see that Ida was weighing the offer. Annabelle pushed back from the desk and paced the room. It would be hard to give her up. The bond was stronger than race or blood. Both had known hard times, Ida more than she. It was Ida, after all, who had taken over raising Annabelle after Annabelle's own difficult birth and her mother's death. Annabelle felt the pull. She wanted Ida not to go, and knew there was no other way.

And it was Ida who had borne that other burden, unspeakable, at the old plantation the year Annabelle was pregnant with Billy. As much as Ida tried to erase it from memory, Annabelle knew how the event intruded through dreams, unannounced and unexpected, how Ida would awake in a soaking sweat, how much she loved Owen and yet, even in his innocence, how he was the constant reminder of the night when the intruder, drunk, broke into the cabin, and afterward, when they had dragged him into the woods, as he screamed when the ax handle crushed his skull in retribution.

"You blame yourself for what happened," Annabelle said. "You were not to blame. You were the victim. We were both victims. No one can hold us to account for that. There is no shame in it. No guilt. It was justice, Ida. We have to put that behind us. Now you can do something for Owen and for yourself. Do it," she insisted. "Get out of this prison."

Here now was a risky juncture in their lives, an irrevocable risk that must be taken. Annabelle took a key from her desk drawer, unlocked the chest, and removed money from the box inside. "Here, Ida. This is for you, and there's plenty more when you need it."

Ida frowned, shook her head, blurted out her frustration. "I cain't take your money." She wrestled with ambivalence, wanting to go, yet afraid to leave. "They ain't nothing for me outside Monroe."

Annabelle closed her eyes and saw Ida in that alien place, so different from the only life she had known here in the backwoods of North Florida. Of course it's a gamble. Against security here, an uncertain future. But it was, nevertheless, a future, however uncertain, wasn't it? And they were survivors, weren't they? What other choice was there for this black woman and her child with no future?

"Owen will need his mother," she whispered. "*That* is something for you beyond Monroe." Annabelle looked into deep, dark eyes peering at her through tears Ida could not hold back, eyes lovely and sad. "It's only right, Ida. It's Owen's one chance. With no schooling here, he's got no future. So take this," she pleaded, forcing the money into Ida's hand. "I will miss you, Ida. Yes I will."

EARLY ONE MORNING, Billy watched Owen carry the cardboard luggage to the front porch, place them on the steps and wait for his mother. Annabelle wrapped the last of the sandwiches, tucking them snugly in the cloth handbag which she held out to Ida.

"This isn't much of a lunch, but it will tide you over till Atlanta," and before Ida could respond, Annabelle called out to Owen. "Come here, son. Give me a proper hug. You take good care of your mother. O.K.?" she said, extending her arms toward him. Owen nodded, accepting her gesture quietly. She held him close, not wanting to let him go but finally offered a reassuring smile, and turning to Ida, she said, "This is the right thing, Ida, you'll see. And one thing to remember—I'm always here—not going anywhere."

She watched them walking toward the Greyhound bus depot until they were out of sight. And then she cried, and wondered if she would ever see them again, and if they would make it, and whether she was sending them away now to their execution.

How could she know that this journey to a new beginning would change Owen's life in the most unexpected way. How could she know then that years later he might return to confront an incredible challenge, a legacy beyond anything a small Negro boy from the backwoods of Morgan County, Monroe, Florida, could imagine.

CHAPTER 4
CALLING IN THE CHITS

THE CONFLICTING EMOTIONS Billy felt over Owen's departure five years earlier hung on. At the time, he was elated, thinking that he wouldn't have to listen to any more of the endless slurs from Josh and the gang at Morgan County School about the cute little nigger who lived with him in his mother's house. But Billy never did fit in. Owen had been his claim to superiority. With Owen gone, he had become accustomed to the new slur—Mamma's boy.

She just wouldn't leave things alone. The week of graduation from Morgan County School, Annabelle had rented the social hall of Monroe Baptist Church, inviting the sixteen graduating seniors and their dates to celebrate Billy's graduation. Only eight came and within an hour, all eight had left. And Josh never showed. He was probably somewhere screwing Cora Duncan. Josh got everything he went after. He could screw any girl he wanted, even Cora Duncan if he wanted. And who did Billy Sloat screw? Nobody. He was turning eighteen and he had never screwed a girl.

Donnie was the last to leave the church. Billy had noticed him sorting through the rack of church pamphlets against the wall. What was he up to?

"Well," Billy said to him, "you must've had a good time, still hanging round. Don't you got nothing better to do?"

"Maybe. Depends." Donnie offered Billy a smile, waiting for his response.

"What you staring at?"

Donnie was staring at the pockmarks on Billy's thin, wiry face. He felt a connection—the scars written on Billy's face and his own scars etched in his hidden nature, which defined his otherness. They were both outsiders, in their different ways.

"I like you Billy. I can be your friend," he said, taking a step toward him. He saw Billy stiffen and step back, and heard the panic in his voice.

"I don't need nothing from you. Keep away from me, I ain't like you," Billy shouted and bolted from the room.

HE WANDERED THE deserted streets, avoiding home and the litany he knew was waiting from his mother, unable to shake Donnie's wispy voice offering—what? At once he remembered a hot summer day and Josh's hard body cutting through the icy spring water, and recalled then his own confusion as he fixed on Josh's nakedness that had aroused something unsettling, something unwholesome within him.

Eighteen and never gotten screwed.

—∞—

NINETEEN TWENTY-NINE WAS not a good year for most people in Monroe, especially for the owner of the local ice company. He lost everything in the October crash, including the icehouse. But it was a good year for Annabelle Shaw Sloat. Aside from her investment in Great South Railway, she had never put much trust in something as confusing as the stock market, and so with cash on hand, she bought Jim Everett's ice company, and Billy Sloat became an entrepreneur on his twenty-fourth birthday.

Six years earlier, after Billy's graduation from high school, Annabelle had used her connections with Great South Railway to land him a job as railroad conductor with the line. Working the trains, he had discovered a life far different from what he had known in Monroe, particularly the hordes of blacks who had begun their migrations north to seek opportunity and a better life, change that both alarmed and reviled him. And then came the October crash of 1929 followed by the Great Depression, and his railroad traveling days were over.

As the depression deepened, he ingratiated himself among the Monroe families with cheap ice delivered door to door in a brand-new ice wagon. He even provided generously to the families too poor to pay, like the Simpsons.

When he brought the ice wagon to a halt in front of the Simpson house, Mrs. Simpson stared blankly at him. "How many pounds of ice today?" he shouted from the street. She continued to stare. "How much?" he repeated.

"Cain't today. Cain't no more actually," she said.

"What you mean, Mrs. Simpson? You gotta have ice or everything in the icebox will spoil."

"We got no money for ice, Billy."

What did she mean, no money for ice.

"Well you damn sure got to have ice," he insisted. In spite of his wiry frame, he carried a twenty-five-pound block up the steps, into the house and placed it in the ice-box. Turning to the woman, he said, "Someday, you'll be able to repay me, you'll see."

Down the next block, he brought the ice wagon to a halt in front of Cora Duncan's house. He glanced in the rear-view mirror, spit on his hand and slicked the strands of loose hairs along the side of his head. Satisfied with his appearance, he skipped up the steps to the house, knocked briskly on the door and waited for Cora Duncan's appearance.

"Yes?" the girl's voice answered from behind the closed door.

"It's me, Cora—Billy," he called, attempting to conceal his anxiety.

"Oh, yes, Billy," she said, opening the door and offering a conde-scending smile. "Momma said thirty-five pounds will do."

"I was wondering, Cora, if you might like," he hesitated, "I mean— go with me to the Biograph on Saturday night?" he asked, his head shaking with anticipation.

"Thanks, but Josh and I already have plans for Saturday. But thanks, anyway, Billy, and oh—the back door's open, just leave the ice in the box," she said, brushing past him as she descended the steps.

Josh. The encounter fourteen years ago still clear in his mind—the green knee pants, the blouse spattered with blood, Josh's eyes like razors, Owen waiting on the porch as he limped, step by step, toward the front door of his mother's very respectable house on a very re-spectable street in very respectable Monroe. Yeah, Josh the he-man.

Back at the ice wagon, he dragged the block of ice toward him, hoisted it over his bony shoulders and, entering the kitchen through the back door, shoved it in the ice compartment of the box, and glancing around the spotless kitchen, spit on the floor as he left.

—⁊⁊—

THE ICE STORM in the winter of '33 was a catastrophe for Morgan County and an unexpected opportunity for Billy Sloat, now approaching his twenty-eighth birthday. On the East Coast, from Jacksonville to Miami, the cold was more an inconvenience, a rare outburst that would last a day or so and be over. But the rolling hills of the panhandle more resembled Alabama than Florida, and while cold winters were not uncommon, ice storms were.

The success of the icehouse enterprise had been gradually eclipsed by the increasing prevalence of electric refrigerators for those who could afford one. But the ice storm dealt a brief blow to the recent innovation. Power lines were down for a week, rendering electric iceboxes useless, and Billy seized the opportunity. He had sixteen-hundred pounds of bulk ice stored in the icehouse cooler. For those too poor to pay, he donated free ice. For the affluent who owned electric boxes, he provided cheap ice and everyone offered gratitude.

Three years later, just before his thirty-first birthday, Billy was ready to call in the chits.

"Momma, I been thinking...bout goin into politics...how it might be time for it."

"Politics?" she said with surprise.

"Gonna run for the state senate." He cocked his eyebrows. "What you think about that?"

Was he crazy? Politics? What has gotten into him? "Don't we have plenty going on here without you getting mixed up in politics? Why would you want to go into politics, Billy?"

"I want to be somebody. Accomplish something."

"But you are somebody. What would I do here if you got mixed up in Tallahassee politics? Just look what we have. Isn't that something of an accomplishment?"

"Ever since I quit the railroad, I've spent five years running a stupid ice company in this damn place. You call that accomplishment? What kind of future is that? There's more to living than Monroe and I'm goin' for it. I'm gonna be somebody—somebody important," he said defiantly. "I would like your blessing, but one way or another, I'm gonna do it."

She saw the determination. She had lost Ida, and now Billy would leave her. There was no doubt in her mind that he could win, no doubt he could even be governor one day if he set his mind to it. But politics! She placed her hands against his thin, almost gaunt face, eyes deeply set. Then with resignation, she gave up.

"I think you'll make a fine senator, Billy, a really fine senator if that is what you want. I know you will."

WHEN THE VOTES were counted, Billy Sloat had beaten the incumbent by a two-to-one margin. He had taken aim and hit his opponent dead-on.

The night of his victory, friends and foes alike gathered to celebrate the extraordinary accomplishment. He caught a glimpse of Josh and Cora—Mr. and Mrs. Josh Sykes now. Cora Duncan-Sykes squeezed through the crowd, taking Billy's hand and, giving a wink, said, "We are—I am—so proud of you, Billy." He studied her momentarily. She was twenty-eight now. Wonder how many times Josh screwed her before they got married? Where was that girly charm now? Across the room—Josh, cornering Cora's young sister. He tried to remember Josh's firm body cutting through the icy spring water years ago, sensuous muscles glistening in the sun. Hard to imagine—that body so gone now. He then winked back at Cora, and gently removed her hand from his. Tallahassee was the next stop. Morgan County was behind him. He didn't need them any more—just their votes.

SLOAT WANDERED THROUGH the long corridor of the senate office building searching for his office assignment and rounded the corner at the end of the hall. Four men locked in conversation blocked his way until the fat one with jaws that, Sloat thought, resembled a pig's face, gave a quick, superfluous smile.

"Well, the iceman arrives," he bellowed. "Billy Sloat, welcome to the senate chambers. How's the ice business in Monroe?"

Sloat's eyes narrowed. It was contempt at first sight. He recognized the senator from photographs in the newspapers—Johnson Taylor, the bellicose liberal from St. Petersburg.

"Could be better, but helped git me here," he answered, offering his own shallow smile. "Hard work and persistence pays off in the long run."

"Hard work or luck?" Johnson quipped.

"Maybe some of both."

"Well it's all relative after all, isn't it Billy? Your good luck and Jim Everett's misfortune, not to mention your mother's good fortune with the railroad. Speaks volumes for your success, wouldn't you say?"

Sloat offered a forced smile. "Well you certainly know a lot about my success."

"Indeed, you are one lucky man," he mocked. "A small town boy with little education, and look where you are. The newspapers got it right. Small town boy makes good."

"Yes, you are right on that. When opportunity presents itself, you run with it."

"Buy a lot of votes with that ice, can't you?" Taylor blurted.

"Damn right. Helped get me here, didn't it?" he offered with a confident glare, and nodding at the other three witnesses to the encounter, Billy Sloat made his way to his office cubicle at the end of the corridor. Yes, Monroe was behind him. Nineteen thirty-four was off to a good start.

CHAPTER 5
END OF THE GAME

IN 1945, THE ninth year of their lives, three events changed everything for David Ashton and Stephen Smith.

The president and the war had been two permanent aspects of their existence. Both had been forever—the president and the war.

Late afternoon on April 12, Stephen and David sat with rapt attention staring at the glowing dial of the radio, listening to Silver's galloping hooves as the Lone Ranger pursued the outlaw. Then abruptly the sound stopped, followed by a brief silence and then an announcer's trembling voice.

"We interrupt this program to tell you that President Roosevelt died this afternoon at 4:35 PM."

It was the year of the president's death, the year the war ended, and the year of the tingling nerves. The end of fantasy and the end of childhood.

DEATH AND WAR were just stories told over and over again on the radio, in the movies—only stories. Death was nothing more than images projected on a screen in a darkened theater, heroes of their favorite Westerns pursuing the outlaw, guns blazing, the outlaw tumbling from the horse, good always prevailing over evil. Always. Even the one bite of a poisoned apple was merely a brief interruption in the life of Snow White until the handsome prince would return to bring her back.

And war was a game to be played. One day David was the German and Stephen the good American. The German of course always died only to return as the American. And so the game continued on and on, a favorite game, but a game nevertheless. But the president's death was something else again. Muffled cries from strangers in the audience punctuated newsreel images of the funeral procession that flickered across the screen.

The president was like the king. He was always the president, the king, and yet the president-king was dead, the confusion compounded within the space of a month when the same people filled the theatre to witness the end of the war in Europe, which always had been and yet was no more. The end of the game.

In that year, not long after *Snow White* at the Palace Theater and just months before Stephen's ninth birthday, the third and most confusing event of all changed their lives beyond anything the boys could imagine: the tingling nerves within Stephen's body.

THE CRAMPED CLASSROOM combined with the relentless summer heat that persisted into late September had a suffocating effect as Stephen sat motionless during the penmanship drill. Sister Margaret, wandering around the room, stopped at his desk. Stephen did not look up but stared straight ahead, his breathing short, his head throbbing, a dull nausea slowly taking hold. "Now what?" she demanded. "Take your pen, this is not recess."

David knew something was not right. Stephen's glassy stare frightened him. He was breathing in short gasps, beads of sweat forming on his forehead. *What is happening?* Again the Sister gave the command, but this time Stephen fell forward. And then the Sister also knew that something was terribly wrong.

IN THE WEEKS that followed, Stephen experienced degrees of weakness and a tingling sensation in his legs, spreading to his right arm, which had grown weaker from the paralysis. He sat on the examining table. His mother stood beside him. The neurologist shook his head and uttered the dreaded word.

"Polio. It appears to be polio. We need to hospitalize him to confirm the diagnosis."

Evelyn Smith remained motionless, not yet fully accepting what she had heard. The doctor was uttering something, but the only word she could hear was the pounding repetition of the word *polio*. He was trying to tell her something, but all she heard was that word.

STEPHEN SAW THE panic in his mother's face and was terrified. What did he do to cause this? Something was wrong.

THE DOCTOR READ the panic in the boy's eyes. He rested his hand on his head, moving his fingers through the shock of golden hair. Such a beautiful child. This could be his own child here in this room, the same hair and eyes, but thankfully he was not. He was someone else's child.

STEPHEN'S MOTHER WAITED in the hospital room for the doctor, like a prisoner awaiting the final judgment, her mind a pendulum of confusion and numbness. Where was he? Why this? Why us? When he came at last, her eyes remained locked straight ahead, her mouth dry, the prisoner preparing herself for the sentence.

"Well, Mrs. Smith, I've news—some good, some not so good. Good news is this *isn't* polio," he said. "Still, there's no certainty about recovery."

Not polio? Is that what he said? Not polio? "I don't understand. If not polio, then...what?"

"Guillain-Barré."

Guillain-Barré. She repeated the strange, alien words.

"Not a disease. A syndrome. Guillain-Barré is rare. It mimics some of the same effects as polio."

Not a disease. Not polio.

"The body attacks the nervous system and affects the muscles, which become useless, the patient sometimes becoming completely paralyzed. Or the effects can be less severe," he told her, "resulting in varying degrees of recovery. The two conditions are often confused. No evidence that it's contagious. So that is..." he paused briefly taking a breath, "if not the best news at least a better prospect. Recovery can occur within a few weeks or over many years." Another pause. "Or not at all."

For a moment, Evelyn Smith felt the rush of blood through her head and then relief. She would not allow any self-pity, uncertainty, or doubt. Here was a thread of hope. However thin, she would not let go of it. It *wasn't* polio. It was a reprieve.

Stephen's uncertain journey from innocence to awareness had begun, his release from the hospital the beginning.

—⟶⟵—

THE BRACE HE wore stabilized his right arm, the upper arm at a right angle to his body and the lower forearm pointing directly forward, mimicking a salute, announcing to the neighborhood some unspeakable transgression, a sign of unwholesomeness, something to be shunned as much as feared—except from David.

"Why do they make you wear that?" David asked.

"It's because of the nerves," he answered.

"What are nerves?"

"They're inside me, and something killed them. That's what caused the tingles. Sometimes people grow new nerves, but I have to wear this brace till then."

The brace and the dead nerves puzzled David. He did not understand what caused the nerves to die in Stephen's body. He missed Stephen and the games that were lost to the dying nerves.

—⟶⟵—

THE HOUSE IN which Stephen, his mother, and his shadow father lived was like the other tract houses that lined the street, each exactly the same, except for a different color paint on this one, the trim on that one, front porches differentiated by a swing or rocking chairs of different configurations, potted plants on one, bare banisters on another, but otherwise a sameness that announced at once conformity along with difference.

Each house stood alone, row after row, separated by an alleyway not more than twelve feet wide that allowed air to circulate and provide relief from the heat of the long, humid summers. In the evening, families sat on the front porches, talking, singing, waiting for the night to cool so that finally they could sleep. Windows left open, a cacophony of radios singing against the stifling heat of the night, effecting a kind of communal sharing, in a way comforting, each household linked by the smell of food cooking, of voices heard telling of good times or bad, but an unspoken acknowledgement of something commonly shared.

Along with the rumors.

Rumors at first whispered, then repeated freely. The contraption the boy wore revealed what anyone could plainly see in spite of the mother's denial. The boy had polio, didn't he? That wasn't something you could ignore. He could infect anyone. The mother's denial, her attempted assurance that it was something else, something more benign, could not convince them. Everyone knew it *was* polio. Stephen and his family did not belong now. They had become outcasts. It was not safe as long as they were here.

At first there was the isolation, former playmates forbidden contact with Stephen, and then increasing hostility festering like a boil. One morning when his mother stepped outside onto the porch to retrieve the morning paper and the milk delivery left by the door, the bright red paint against the green of the house spelled out the word. *Polio.*

It was only the first of expressed frustration, and finally rage from neighbors who regarded themselves as decent people determined to protect their children. But what hurt more was David's absence. Greta Hofmann did not consider herself a heartless woman, but she decreed there would be no contact. She was determined to keep her grandson safe.

DAVID SAT NEXT to the empty desk that had been Stephen's. He knew what would happen if his grandmother found out, but he made up his mind. After school, he would see Stephen whether she liked it or not.

Outside the house, he called to him. There was a long stillness until Stephen peered out through the living room window and, realizing it was David, stumbled clumsily onto the front porch.

David's eyes darted over the shiny brace which reflected the afternoon light.

"Can I touch it?" he asked tentatively.

"Sure," Stephen replied, "It don't bite."

David examined the sharp angles of the brace, felt the coolness of the metal. "It's kind of pretty," he said. "Does it hurt?"

No answer.

"Guess I have to go. Would you like me to come back, listen to the radio? Anything?"

Stephen's face was expressionless. "Whatever you want."

"All right then," said David. "Later."

Stephen watched him, waiting there until David reached the end of the block, until David turned and was out of sight. He touched the brace that imprisoned the useless arm, paused momentarily and entered the house alone. Games over.

CHAPTER 6
CHALLENGES

STEPHEN, HIS MOTHER, and his shadow father searched for refuge somewhere away from the row upon row of houses proudly lining the street with their sameness. There were few housing options in 1946. All through the war, housing had been scarce. In January, they had found a place near the school for special students, twelve miles away, much smaller than the only house Stephen had known, but at least a house in a neighborhood of poor, recently settled immigrants too weighed down with their own misfortunes and by their own circumstances to waste any attention on a misfit.

The day the moving van loaded the last piece of furniture, David was there.

"Don't go," he cried. He turned to Stephen's mother. "Don't take him away." He turned back to Stephen. "I love you, Stephen. Please don't leave me." He grasped his friend's usable left hand, holding fast. If he could not go with him, he would hold him back. Stephen was frantic now. He held tight to David. But Stephen's mother separated them, and next the mover's truck rattled away, farther away down the long, narrow street, until it seemed only like a toy truck vanishing in the distance and they were gone.

—∾—

THE COUNTY HAD one school to accommodate someone like Stephen, children affected with a range of disabilities, some with palsy, some with attention disorders, one blind, another deaf, one who continually stared at Stephen's brace, offering a drooling smile. Stephen was, as they believed, the only *polio* child. The arrangement consisted of one large room in the basement of the red brick building called

County Grammar, a world apart from anything that he had known or could have imagined. Yet somehow, here among others with their own deformities, he felt safe, just another misfit, his lifeless arm supported by the contraption he was forced to wear.

The first year in the special needs class was intended as transition to regular classes where he would be placed with ordinary students. He would have to relearn penmanship with his mobile left hand. It would require months of grueling and frustrating physical discipline, resulting in a scrawl of letters on paper that was radically different from the controlled lettering demanded of him by Sister Margaret.

The second year was integration with normal students—no longer regarded a threat, not feared, merely ignored, his presence tolerated with indifference. Nothing more. But he was used to that. Lost within that mix, he felt more isolated than ever.

At home he attempted various ways to gain attention from his father. If being good commanded no acknowledgement, then bad behavior might demand some response. But in the end, his father would merely signal a dismissal as he would at any ordinary occurrence, like leaves falling from the trees in autumn, or rain falling after the humid heat of summer afternoons, events merely repeating in endless cycles, ordinary events requiring no particular attention, just detached acceptance.

Once, Stephen had hurled the photograph of himself, his mother and his father against the wall, the glass in the frame shattering. His father surveyed the remains for a moment and then without a trace of anger glanced over to the boy to say, "You might want to clean that up before your mother gets home. I don't think she'll like it."

Years later, Stephen would wonder which was worse—to be feared or ignored?

—⁂—

FEBRUARY GAVE WAY to brisk, windy March days, signaling the arrival of spring. Stephen fixed his eyes on the fresh green of leaves against a cloudless sky underscoring the change. Then something strange happened. He had spent two and a half years with the brace that supported his useless arm. Now he was watching the fingers of his right hand *moving*. It was the kind of movement he had once seen in the dark of a theater as Frankenstein's monster came to life, hands trembling from what had been a lifeless body.

As spring gave way to summer and summer to fall, the recovery, though gradual, was consistent. The physical healing had begun, and to some degree an emotional healing as well.

In 1949, on Stephen's thirteenth birthday in December, his special gift from his mother was a set of free weights and a bench. On his fourteenth birthday he celebrated with a noticeable set of biceps accompanied with significant pectoral development, his young body responding rapidly to the increased regimen as he pushed himself ever harder. By his fifteenth year, except for some lack of coordination, there was little outward evidence of the previous seven-year struggle with the syndrome. Standing before the mirror, he studied the new contours of his naked body, a body more like that of a swimmer, firm yet graceful.

The tenth grade, his first year at Franklin High in September of 1952, provided a new start. The school was located on the opposite end of the county, miles away from the neighborhood where he had grown up. He had no friends there. No one knew about his years of isolation. He guarded his anonymity, and with it shame he could not shake.

That same year he failed typing class, his fingers not yet entirely coordinated to readily stroke the keys. His typing teacher just thought him clumsy. His physical appearance masked a lack of coordination and other residual effects. Only he was conscious of these and he was determined to master them—and if not master them, suppress them, to pass as any ordinary person, no longer the unclean outcast.

THE FOLLOWING YEAR, the Smiths bought their first house. Initially, his father had resisted. Buying a house meant putting down roots. He resented being tied down, but Evelyn Smith was adamant. In the end, Scott Smith surrendered. They were back in the city. The house was a good mile from the old neighborhood and within walking distance of Jefferson High where Stephen would begin his last year of high school.

The move occurred during the summer. The anticipation of his senior year at Jefferson High produced both optimism and anxiety.

JULIAN E. FARRIS

How many of his former peers would he encounter? It had been over eight years. Some would have moved on. Others might have remained. What would they remember?

And Oak Street. Its row houses lined one against the other, the narrow spaces between each house allowing shared secrets between the inhabitants from the open windows on hot summer nights. He walked that street. It had changed from what he remembered. There was a shabbiness now that permeated each of the houses, a decay that ate away at houses abandoned and forgotten by the previous tenants and now ignored by new occupants seeking only a tentative stay before moving on, only to accommodate still other inhabitants whose time would be brief and temporary, an endless cycle of human rotation.

Blocks farther away, he walked down Market Street to find the house that had been David's. There on that same corner was an empty lot. He walked over to the edge, bent down to grasp a handful of sand, allowed the sand to escape between his fingers, then turned and walked back toward his new home, not looking back.

CHAPTER 7
THE PORKBARREL GANG

BY 1953, THEY were known as the Porkbarrel Gang, an elite power group of rural legislators formed to forestall the rising influence of urban liberals who were changing the political dynamics in Florida. Billy Sloat was their unchallenged leader.

He bragged about his track record in steering public projects to his end of the state. The Morgan County Medical Clinic was the only clinic between Tallahassee and Jacksonville, and no one was turned away for lack of money, not even the blacks. After all, like it or not, they had votes. He made sure that they had access through a special entrance at the rear of the building. And when his nemesis, Johnson Taylor, objected to the highway project linking Monroe and Denson forty miles south, Sloat was quick to point out how construction jobs were good for the state economy. And he made sure it was just as good for him as well, a little payback for all his good works.

He was clever at dispensing reward or punishment to secure his position and advance his agenda. During his nineteen years in the senate, he won re-election with little opposition. The folks in rural north Florida counties had no reason to let him go.

As senate president, his political influence was second only to the governor himself. He commanded respect, not from the love of his fellow senators, but out of fear. The guise he projected was that of a simple, good-natured old boy from the rural backwoods of north Florida, but it masked a cunning, astute Billy Sloat whom friends and enemies alike knew to avoid when he did not get his way. You did not cross Billy Sloat unless you were bent on political suicide.

A newly elected and handsome young fledgling from central Florida had no intention of doing that. He tapped on the open door to Sloat's office. Sloat looked up from the stack of proposed senate bills on his desk, cocked his eyebrows and motioned him in.

"Hope I'm not disturbing you. Just wanted to introduce myself. I'm..."

"I know who you are. What can I do for you?"

"Well, then I guess you already know..."

"...that you don't have much experience in politics, and yes, it's a minefield here with all those south Florida liberals jockeying for control. You'll learn quick or they'll eat you alive. But you haven't answered my question. What can I do for you?"

"You just did. It is a minefield out there," he said, pointing toward the long corridor outside Sloat's office. "I would deeply appreciate your guidance in helping me navigate it. Your political reputation is legend."

"Meaning?" Sloat said.

"That you don't take kindly to opposition."

"What else have you heard about me?"

"Your insatiable interest in football, your partiality to State University and its team, your disgust with liberals and," he paused cautiously before continuing, "that you're...somewhat racist."

Sloat cocked his left eyebrow, gave a twitch to his mouth. "You want advice from an ignorant uneducated racist like me?" he said with a trace of acrid venom. "That's how they brand me. Well, I'm no racist and I don't need a college education to know what's right and what's not. It's about decency, about order, about family. I never had family to speak of, but I do respect what it represents."

"I'm listening, Senator."

"Then here's some advice," Sloat began, leaning toward him across the littered desk. "Don't ever compromise your convictions, son. Never betray your convictions like those liberals do, never, even when they prove to be wrong. If you believe something is right, stick to your conviction. Be consistent. That's what character is about. Consistency." He said this as a preacher might to some wayward sinner in need of salvation.

"You seem...so sure of yourself. Mind if I ask—and I mean no disrespect, but..." and before he could finish his question, Sloat cut him off.

"Listen, boy, you're ambitious, seem reasonably intelligent, and you're a nice looking guy," he said, holding the man's uneasy gaze. "Learn to use your God-given assets. They can serve you well in this business."

The young senator blushed, not sure how to respond to Sloat's attention. But he welcomed it, nonetheless.

Sloat relished the reverential awe from the newcomers, and this one was no exception. He would season him in the ways of political maneuvering and in return accept—no demand—unconditional loyalty.

"I got a mission to fulfill. Know what it is, son?"

He waited for Sloat to continue but guessed Sloat already had his answer.

Sloat eyed the young blond, his squared jaw, an almost perfect nose jutting from the prominent forehead. For a moment he imagined Josh standing there, hanging submissively onto his benevolent wisdom, patiently waiting for a benediction. He got up from his chair and walked over to the young senator. "To safeguard our honored traditions, son. Like ol' time religion—good enough for daddy and good enough for me."

He couldn't remember having a father, but what of it?

"Power is what it's about. Without it, you're nothing. Use it, along with any other assets God gave you. I do, by God, and no liberal governor will git in my way," he said, placing his arm around the young senator's shoulder, giving an affectionate squeeze. "Now let's grab some lunch. Tell me about yourself. You're not married, I see" he said, looking at the senator's hand. "Any girlfriends?"

"A few. Nothing serious. And you? Never married?"

Sloat offered a wicked smile. "Like FBI Director J. Edgar Hoover. Married only to my job."

WHEN SLOAT WAS told of the governor's fatal heart attack, he was in a committee planning session. Members of the committee, stunned by the news, waited as shock gave way to the realization of a different momentum for the Porkbarrel Gang. All eyes were riveted on Senator Sloat. As senate president, he was next in line and would now complete the unfinished term of the liberal governor for the next two years. His eyes shifted from each of the men seated at the table opposite him. There was an uneasy stillness in the room. He studied their faces. The governor's death was a mandate after all, wasn't it? Not through the usual maneuvers of political expediency. No. Not at all. But from God Himself. He had been given an unexpected opportunity, a political arsenal, and he would use it.

"Gentlemen," he said with a forced and quiet humility, "let us have a moment of silent prayer for our departed colleague."

BILLY SLOAT WASTED no time in his first year as acting governor. He created special task forces, assigned key allies to chair special initiatives, derailing any opposition. Allying himself with the newly elected senate president, Sloat commanded unchallenged obedience from any potential renegade legislator and tightened his grip on liberal politicians of the state's urban south.

The constant harping from the news media and objections from even friendly colleagues served only to strengthen his resolve, the insults intensifying his will.

"I can't understand you, Billy," the junior senator from central Florida protested. "Why in the name of God would you support that crooked son of a bitch as senate president, and the rabble he panders to?"

"Well see here, son, as that rotten scoundrel FDR once said, they may be sons a bitches, but they are *our* sons a bitches."

The more the liberal press hurled insults and members of the legislature expressed doubt, the more he took pride in his leadership of the Porkbarrel Gang. Billy Sloat was on a roll.

—∞—

MAY 1954. GOVERNOR Sloat sat at his desk, rocking back and forth in the leather chair as he contemplated which bill he would sign into law and which he would banish with the stroke of his pen. Just then his aide burst into the room. "Governor," he shouted, his voice cracking with urgency, "the court in Washington has ruled on Brown vs. the Board of Education."

Sloat's eyes widened, his jaw tightened. He knew the outcome.

"They've ruled against *separate but equal*," he blurted, waiting for the governor's reaction.

Sloat was unusually quiet, allowing the announcement to fully register, his expression difficult to read. "Well, no surprise there," Sloat muttered, "just the beginning, only a matter of time till the whole damn state is dictated to by that Washington court. We knew this was coming. Time now to show those sons a bitches a thing or two."

He rolled his eyes toward the ceiling and saw himself, a boy of thirteen at a midnight gathering out in the woods in Monroe, the white-hooded vigilantes marching around a burning cross, and the picture show, the three-hour epic of *Birth of a Nation*, the images still clearly embedded in memory. The film had inspired him, had fed his resolve that one day he would join the cause for white supremacy. This was his moment, his mandate with destiny. He welcomed the challenge. Not the Supreme Court, not the NAACP, not every nigger in the South would stop him.

Just then the secretary's intercom broke his concentration.

"It's your mother again, governor," she announced.

"Tell her I cain't talk now. Tell her I'm busy. Tell her I'll call her. Hell," he barked, "don't she know a governor's got work to do?"

—⟋⟍—

FEW AT FIRST shared Sloat's visceral reaction, since the court had ordered segregation to be phased out over time but "with deliberate speed." The state legislators were more concerned with the growing power shift from the rural to the urban areas. Brown vs. the Board was initially regarded as at best a nuisance, the court not to be taken seriously. Throughout the state there was an unusual calm, but one not to last as events of the following year played out. And Sloat would discover that he had other problems to contend with. Reelection. As his acting governorship came to an end, his campaign to hold the office found him not just in a tight race, but also at the turning point of his political career.

He sat alone, glued to the television. The ashtray was littered with half-smoked cigarettes, the room reeking of tobacco smoke. The early returns from rural precincts had been good. But as the night progressed, he watched as returns from the southern half of the state shifted the results toward his Miami opponent, Marvin Rudge. By midnight, he had conceded the race to Rudge. No longer the acting governor, in keeping with procedural rules, he would be returning to the senate, lining up the necessary votes to resume his leadership as Senate President.

—◆—

GOVERNOR RUDGE SHUFFLED through the proposed bill that Sloat had introduced through committee to create a state bureau of investigation. The initial calm that followed the Supreme Court's desegregation ruling had ended. By January 1955, a sense of urgency was spreading throughout the state, fueled by the growing protests of civil rights activists. Sloat's bill would empower a state bureau of investigation to fight crime and subversion against civil order.

What bothered the new governor was the word *subversion* in the proposed bill. Sloat had a devious way of circumventing opposition by including in his sponsored legislation feel-good elements. *Crime and subversion*. Well, the governor thought, who wasn't against controlling crime? But subversion? Whose subversion? What subversion? This was yet another attempt by Sloat to create obstacles to the Court's Brown decision. The last thing the state needed was a vehicle to wage war against the Supreme Court of the United States. Governor Rudge would exercise every option of his office to oppose such a bill.

But Billy Sloat was ready for the challenge. Now as senate president, he opened the legislative session with the introduction of his bill. It was all he could do to control his anger toward his nemesis, Johnson Taylor, the senator from St. Petersburg. That intellectual snob was nothing but a pompous, attention-grabbing prick. Sloat braced himself for the display he knew was coming.

Taylor got to his feet, waited for the room to quiet, cleared his throat and began his rebuttal. "Mr. President, I say once more, in the presence of my colleagues, this bill, if passed, will give unprecedented authority to an investigating committee that, left unchecked, could lead to witch hunts and subvert liberal dissent." The words *witch hunt* elicited a stir in the chamber. Taylor allowed the reaction to reach a crescendo, then turned again to Sloat. "We do not need this legislation," he shouted.

Pandemonium rocked the senate chamber until Sloat pounded the gavel to restore order. "Senator Taylor," he sneered, "what do you have against preserving the order and safety of the citizens of this state?"

Taylor fired back. "What price, Senator, would you have the citizens of this state pay for such order and safety?" More shouts among the restless lawmakers.

Sloat sensed that the debate had gone sour. His eyes darted around the senate chamber, and the shift in support began to sink in. He would maintain his usual self-confident demeanor, offering his infectious smile to conceal his acknowledgement that his opponent had killed his bill before it ever arrived.

CHAPTER 8
DÉJÀ VU

THE SLEEK 1953 Packard convertible screeched around the corner and came to an abrupt stop in front of David's house. Greta Hofmann watched suspiciously from the second floor window as David hurried toward the curb and climbed over the closed door, squeezing in next to Barbara, pressing her tightly against Mike who tapped the steering wheel, keeping time with Bill Haley and his Comets blaring from the radio. The rear seat was a compression of bodies, one male sandwiched between three girls.

Greta glared her disapproval. It wasn't just the car that Mike's father had given him. It was the extravagance of Mike's father, a car costing more than some houses that people could afford to buy. Her grandson was compromising his life with this wild assortment of spoiled, ungrateful rich kids. He needed direction. What teenager didn't? But Greta's attempts to develop character, to instill in David a semblance of purpose were thwarted at every turn. Yvonne allowed him free run with irresponsible adolescents whose own parents not only indulged but encouraged reckless behavior, behavior which spelled trouble. Incomprehensible that Mike's parents would allow seven teenagers without adult supervision at an isolated lake house thirty miles away on Lake Santa Fe. When she had made clear her objections to Mike's father, he had dismissed her in a patronizing gesture of gratitude for her concern. The kids deserved some fun, didn't they? In three weeks, they would begin their final year of high school.

As the car roared away, tires squealing from Mike's heavy foot on the accelerator, Greta caught David's smile as he waved back to her and the car vanished around the corner.

—ᴍ—

DAVID PLACED THE water skis in the twenty-foot Chris-Craft while Mike filled the gas tank.

"Grab that cooler of beer from the dock," Mike called "and let's take her for a spin around the lake, old buddy, just you and me." David concealed his reluctance, placed the container in the storage compartment in the stern of the boat, and took the seat next to Mike. The beer thing posed a divide in their friendship. If Greta had the slightest inkling about the beer, or that Mike's father not only permitted but even provided it, without a doubt, that would rip the connection with Mike, no question about it. That he was sure of. And he couldn't say he would blame her actually.

Mike opened the throttle full-blast and the Chris-Craft skimmed effortlessly over the clear shimmer of the lake. Soon they were out of view, alone now, sun, water and speed complementing their seclusion from the others as the boat pounded the lake's surface. Approaching a turn ahead, Mike cut the wheel suddenly and sharply to the left, throwing David against him.

"Damn, Mike, slow it down. You trying to kill us?" David shouted over the roar of the engine. Mike answered the protest with an enticing smile, running his hand through David's hair, a gesture, David sensed, of Mike's satisfaction that they had escaped for now the company of the others, a gesture not particularly welcomed, but he couldn't exactly say why.

Zigzagging through a maze of cypress knees protruding from the lake's shoreline, Mike brought the boat to an abrupt halt a half-mile at the other end from the lake house. David threw a questioning look. Mike ignored the expression, tied the line around a cypress stump, dropped cutoff shorts and plunged naked into the water, the sun reflecting over ripped muscles and a tanned body.

"Coming?" he called to David, rolling on his back, arms outstretched as he floated on the surface, beckoning David from the boat in what seemed almost to David like a seduction. Was it? They were just good friends, just football teammates at Jefferson High, weren't they? Just friends after all.

WHEN THEY ARRIVED back at the dock, the others were waiting. "Climb in," Mike commanded, pointing to the rear of the Chris-Craft. Sam and the three girls eased into the boat as David climbed out.

"Coming, David?" he called. David shook his head, ignoring the disappointment on Mike's face. He walked over to join Barbara sunbathing on the dock.

"Hold on, then" Mike bellowed to the four. "We're going to have one hell of a ride." And for the next hour, they took turns falling from the skis and righting themselves again as the boat skimmed across the water.

David and Barbara watched the activity from the edge of the dock. She studied his expression, a detachment from all that was happening around them. The sun sparkled from the water's edge and she squinted against the glare of the late afternoon light, attempting to read his distance.

"Hey, where are you? You're awfully quiet," she whispered, trying not to sound intrusive, but curious nonetheless. He kept his silence, replaying the incident with Mike at the secluded end of the lake. There was something that unnerved him and he couldn't place it. Why had he not accepted the invitation? What was that sudden, spontaneous rush he felt for a moment? They were, after all, just good friends. Wasn't that it? He shook the thought away and offered Barbara a forced smile.

"Nothing," he murmured. It's nothing. Now it's my turn for questions. Why didn't you want to go skiing with the others? Is it that time of month?"

Barbara felt her face flush. "David, that's private! No, I'm just not up to it, that's all," she protested.

AFTER SUNSET, WHEN they had finished grilling burgers outside and Mike was captivating the others with a replay of his touchdown that won the team's countywide unbroken record for the season, David wandered unnoticed down to the boathouse. On the distant side of the lake, lights from the several houses blinked like fireflies in the darkness. He settled back against the wooden planks, staring at the night sky, the silence interrupted only by the faint bursts of laughter from the direction of the lake house.

It was nothing, he had said to Barbara, nothing. But that was a lie. His ambivalence about Mike was persistent, at once seeking his approval and yet uncomfortable knowing he already had it. What after all did they really have in common besides the team? Was it Mike's father who stirred his resentment? A father who obviously loved his son, who trusted him, who was always there for him at every game, who expressed pride in his son's achievements, who would never abandon him, no matter what. He remembered that eleventh birthday when he had gone to see his father in the shipyard building where he worked, that moment when the receptionist had asked why he was there and told him that his father wouldn't see him, how that was the last contact, or lack of contact, between them, except for the gifts each birthday, and his mother's insistence that it was only his father's attempt to pacify a guilty conscience, her refusal to discuss his father's departure, the circumstances of the failed marriage and...

And then he heard Barbara's footsteps, breaking his solitude.

"Want company?" she asked, and not waiting for a response knelt toward him.

"Sure," he said, taking her hand to steady her as she edged in beside him. When he attempted to disengage his hand, she held on, her fingers encircling his. He looked at her quizzically and thought he saw in her eyes an expression of something resembling—what? It made him uncomfortable. She was beautiful, smart, genuine and clearly attracted to him. Why his reluctance? Was it Mike? She was Mike's girl and Mike was a friend. Would he betray a friendship with Mike in exchange for an opportunity with his girl? Was that it? He did like her, a lot, but as a friend. There had been other opportunities with other girls that he had passed up. Why did they have to complicate everything by getting serious? He was just weeks away from eighteen and one more year in school, then college, then what? Not marriage. Not even close to it.

"You all right, David?" she asked, letting go of his hand. He saw now a different expression—concern, confusion, like that of a mother who had surprised a child in a private moment. "Are you?"

"Sure. Why wouldn't I be, all right, I mean?"

"I don't know. You just...since you broke off with Susan...I don't mean to pry..."

"Then don't." The reply was quick and sharp.

His clipped response stung and she turned away. He had not meant to hurt her. "I'm sorry, Barb. I really am. You're the one person in my life I wouldn't lose for anything," he said, taking her hand again.

"Like that friend, Stephen, you mention so often?"

Stephen. He turned the name over in his mind, replaying a distant moment etched in his memory. The movers carrying the last of Stephen's things to the waiting truck, the sudden slam of the truck's bay like an explosion, the sun's reflection on the brace strapped to Stephen's useless arm, and holding fast to him until the mother separated them and they were gone.

"Yeah," he said finally, "like Stephen too. The three of us would have had a lot in common. Growing up as we did without a father." He swallowed hard, pressed the memory away. "Know something? You're my best friend—really do love you, Barbara," he said.

"I know you do, David, in your own way. And that's enough for me."

They sat there, looking out into the dark, allowing the moment to settle. Then Barbara nudged him, took her hand from his and began tickling him.

"Well, Daddy David, it's probably time to get the others and head back, don't you think? Wouldn't want to rile Greta, would we?"

—⚉—

THE FIRST WEEK of the new school term at Jefferson High was a chaotic push of students in the narrow hallways as they searched for their homerooms. Stephen located his locker, placed his book sack inside, snapped the lock and maneuvered through the sea of bodies. Suddenly, he stopped cold.

Within the crowd, he caught a familiar face. Gone was the child's look he had known. Yet in spite of the chiseled jaw and the athletic neck, the cleft chin and the dimples in the cheeks were unmistakable. Stephen blinked hard, as if he had seen a ghost, and blinked again to convince himself that what he was witnessing was real.

David froze momentarily, stepped back a foot or two, his eyes darting up and down, taking in the same shock of golden hair and radiant blue eyes that returned his gaze.

The two young men studied each other in disbelief.

"Stephen?"

The other nodded dumbly, stood there, mouth agape. "David!"

Ignoring the bodies bumping against them in the corridor, David felt a sudden rush, as if adrenalin had been pumped into his veins, and he embraced him, this friend, at once changed and yet still the same, not changed at all.

"Stephen—Stephen," he repeated, his thick dark hair waving as he shook his head in amazement. "I can't believe this. God almighty— look at you!" They stood there, like Greek statues that had come to life, oblivious to anyone. "I never...I thought..."

They maneuvered between the shuffling of other students, David, lost for words, arm resting over Stephen's shoulders, trying to process the incredible encounter. What would have provoked curious stares from their peers was ignored with benign indifference. David was the exceptional youth, the all-round and capable athlete—football, field and track—and a straight-A student as well—accepted, admired, the all-American boy.

AT THE END of the first day of school, after everyone had left, they found a picnic table in a secluded place beneath the canopy of an oak. They threw their books on the table and grinning ear-to-ear launched into conversation, their talk hurried, non-stop, punctuated by bursts of details and a replay of the eight-year absence. So much had changed. Reeder Creek Park where they played had gone to seed, and the Palace Theater was relegated now to second-run films. And where David's house once stood, now was only an empty lot. What had happened during those eight years? Stephen wanted to know.

"It was pure spite," David told him. "My dad grew up there. His dad built the house and left it to him. After the divorce settlement, my mom had it torn down and sold the lot."

"Why?" Stephen asked. "Why would someone do a thing like that?"

"Like I said, pure spite. Same reason she refused to let me see him, I guess. Whenever I asked her about my dad, she just said some things were better left alone," David said, and then added, "strange thing, though—he never forgets my birthday. Isn't that weird?"

Stephen thought about David's remark, and said, "Yeah, that's weird. What do you make of it?"

"Don't know. Doesn't make sense."

"And Grandma Greta?" Stephen asked.

David smiled, shook his head. "Still with us, barely. Grandma take-over. She means well, but doesn't get it, probably never will at her age. And you? What about the brace and the dead nerves?"

Stephen looked away, keeping his silence, then turned again to David. "Don't...don't mention that, David."

David sensed that he had touched a raw spot. "I only wanted...I only meant...I know how hard it was for you."

Stephen stopped him. "How could you know, David? How could anyone? It wasn't just the *brace* and *the dead nerves*. Worse was the rejection—my dad, the neighbors, the kids in school—the isolation." There was an awkward pause in the conversation, and Stephen could see the regret registered in David' eyes. "I'm sorry, David. I know you mean well. It's just something I have to put behind me. Right now, I'm just damn glad to be here—to find you again. I never thought I would. Who could have thought it?" he asked, trying to reassure him.

"You're right," David agreed. That's behind us now. You're going to love it here at Jefferson High. I'm going to make sure of that!"

For a long time they sat quietly as if to trade each other's thoughts. Only the sound of passing cars and the wind rustling through the trees punctuated the silence.

CHAPTER 9
RELATIONSHIPS

IN THE WEEKS ahead, David brought Stephen into his circle of friends, the who's who within the hierarchy of Jefferson High. He was included, but more as an intruder, an unknown entity, unlike members of the circle whose bonds had formed over years from junior high and now high school. Out of deference to David, they acknowledged Stephen but also withheld unconditional acceptance.

From the first encounter, Mike Summers despised him. He and David had a special relationship. What did David and Stephen have in common? Nothing. David was Mike's closest friend. They were star athletes, teammates on varsity football, admired not just within the inner circle but throughout Jefferson High. But more than that, Mike Summers hid a deeper, uncommon attraction for David that he could not explain, an obsession that at once excited and yet bothered him. Stephen was a threat.

IT WAS A late Friday afternoon in April. David sounded the horn in three short taps, and Stephen slid into the Chevy, closed the door, and they were off.

"O.K. So tell me where we're going," Stephen quizzed him.

"A special place. Just relax, find something on the radio."

David coveted the weekends when he and Stephen would escape the inner circle of David's friends, just the two of them. The three-year-old Chevy offered a boundless freedom that they otherwise wouldn't have had. The second-hand car had been a gift from his father on David's seventeenth birthday the previous year, a gesture of atonement for his absence—wasn't it? Gifts that promised what?

Absolution? No matter. It wasn't a Packard convertible, but it was freedom.

Each weekend, accessing another adventure that the Chevy provided, David and Stephen distanced themselves from the inner circle. The winter had been colder than usual but was followed by a comparatively warm spring. The single road linking the city to the far-flung beach gave way to scrub palms and uninhabited countryside, and then, after the better part of an hour, David pulled off the beach highway and stopped the car in a grove of sea oaks, palmetto and sand dunes.

They climbed over the dunes and onto the long deserted beach. Finding the preferred location, they deposited blanket and ice chest filled with Cokes and, shedding shoes, scavenged the beach for driftwood and the fire they would make once night came. Stephen took the Polaroid from the knapsack, held the camera at arm's length, motioned for David to close in, and heads together, wide smiles, David, his dark eyes peering out from under dark brows, and Stephen's sunny blondness, his eyes reflecting the late, clear afternoon sky, the Polaroid froze the moment.

David examined the camera. "That's some toy," he said. "Where'd you get it?"

"It's my dad's," Stephen said.

"He lets you use it?" David asked.

"Doesn't know I have it."

"Will he mind you taking it?"

He grinned at David. "Only if I break it."

"Race you to the inlet," David said, offering Stephen a friendly challenge.

Jogging down the beach, David saw that Stephen was falling behind. He slowed unnoticed, allowing Stephen to gain on him and then to reach the inlet first.

After the race, they were walking back when Stephen said without looking at David, "You didn't have to do that, you know."

David acted surprised. "Do what?" he asked.

"Let me win. You don't have to protect me," he said, casting a glance at his friend.

Back at the campsite, they plopped down on the blanket. David reached into the ice chest he had packed and retrieved a Coke. "Want one?" he asked, holding one out for Stephen. When they recovered from the race along the beach, David said, "About your dad..."

Stephen asked, "You mean the Polaroid?"

"No," David said, "if things are different now?"

Stephen hesitated. He rolled the moist, cool green bottle between his hands, thought about David's question. "I came to hate him. Nothing I could do could make him love me. Now, I just feel sorry for him," he said looking at David. "It's awful not being able to love." After a while Stephen asked, "And what about your dad?"

"Like I told you before, I never saw my dad after the divorce. Once, when I was eleven, I went to his office to see him, but he wouldn't see me. Right after that, he left the city, stayed out of our lives, never tried to see me. Whenever I asked my mother about what happened, she would just change the subject. But," he added, "he sure isn't stingy with the gifts. Guess that's meant to make up for the absence."

"Do you miss him?" Stephen asked.

David nodded. "Yeah." He paused. "Yeah, I do."

They sat there, wordless now, listening to the ocean, the breaking waves, the seagulls circling overhead. It was a good feeling, David thought.

"Hungry?" David asked.

"Yep," replied Stephen.

"Hope you still like Spam sandwiches," he said, reaching into the ice chest.

Later, they watched the sun sink in the western horizon. To the east, the ocean was calm, and as the darkness descended, it took on an onyx hue.

For David this was a special place. No lights. At night, stars so intense they looked artificial, like lights strung against a pitch-black sky. He had been here often alone. Now he was sharing it with Stephen for the first time.

The fire had begun to burn itself out, just a warm red glow of embers that no longer competed with the sky and stars. No sound now except the gentle surge of waves wetting the dry beach, then retreating with the ocean's endless cadence.

They lay there side by side staring into the night sky. Then, after the prolonged silence, David whispered, "Look at all that," pointing into the darkness, "a patch of the universe, and us only a speck in it. Just think! A lot of those stars aren't even there any more, can you imagine? Just their light cutting through space, light-years away." He turned toward Stephen, propped himself up on one arm, studied Stephen's face for a moment, and said, "Here's a question for you. If in the beginning was God, and God made light, what was *before* God?"

Stephen turned toward him, grimaced for a moment, contemplating the question. "Jesus, David, that's pretty deep stuff."

"Well what do *you* make of it?" he asked.

Another silence, then he said, "I don't. Wherever God is, or was, God doesn't know me and I don't know God. We parted a long time ago."

David settled again on the blanket. He thought about the tingling nerves that had died in Stephen's body but had been resurrected, thought about this unexpected and welcomed reunion, thought about how content he felt right now. There was a momentary quietness, and then David said, "I wonder sometimes if, when we die, we might come back, like on some strange planet out there."

He looked at Stephen, studying the familiar features, barely discernible in the deepening night. "Hard to believe," he continued, "we're the only intelligent life in all of this, isn't it? Wonder sometimes if earth isn't just the insane asylum of the universe, all of us sent here, just misfits, to return again and again until we're whole, ready to connect with whatever intelligence is out there. What do you think, Stephen?"

But Stephen could not find words for what he was feeling. His arm had brushed against David, who had not moved away. Against the coolness of the night, he felt the warmth from David's body, felt his own stirring hardness as David turned toward him, their faces now separated only by the warmth of their breathing. Their lips brushed lightly, tentatively. David took hold of Stephen's hand, but Stephen turned away to hide his embarrassment.

"It's O.K. I'm there too," David said. They settled back, letting the moment to pass, gazing into the darkness in awkward silence. They lay there, their heavy breathing subsiding, Stephen pressing close in, his head resting securely on David's shoulder. Finally he drifted into sleep. David stared into the darkness, overwhelmed by a completeness he had never known. They had crossed, not a line, but a precipice that had separated them and that David vowed would never separate them again.

—◊—

MIKE SUMMERS NEVER felt compelled to mask his feelings with anyone he disliked, let alone Stephen. He made no attempt to disguise his contempt, and David began to distance himself from Mike's deepening hostility.

Stephen bore some responsibility for the group's reluctance to accept him. However unintended, he exhibited an air of aloofness, as though he himself could not fully offer them his own unconditional acceptance, an acceptance he desired but that was never within his reach. As much as David attempted to bring him within the circle, Stephen maintained his distance. Inside the circle, he was still the outsider. Except with Barbara.

Barbara Hampton acknowledged him, not as the intruder, not as David's friend, but on her own terms. She sensed something fragile beyond the aloofness he projected. She was curious about this stranger that David had told her so much about.

Soon after meeting, they found themselves sitting together outside Jefferson High, waiting for David and Mike to finish football practice. Stephen gave her an awkward glance and looked away.

"Hey you," she said, breaking the silence, not taking her eyes off him.

He returned her gaze, gave a tentative smile, but she could sense his uneasiness.

"Ask you something?" Barbara said.

"What?"

"Your opinion," she said, leading him on.

"About what?" Now she had his attention.

"The group," she replied.

He hesitated. "They're all right," he said without conviction.

"Just all right?" she persisted.

"They're David's friends."

"And me? Am I just David's friend?" She reached for his hand, brushed it with her own. He thought for a moment about a response, looking now directly at her.

"No," he said. "You're mine too."

She gave a reassuring smile. She knew what being an outsider was like. Others in the inner circle had grown up together, had known each other over years of childhood, belonged to respected and influential families. Barbara's father was killed during the war, one of thousands who died in Normandy. Her mother struggled to make ends meet, the meager support that came monthly from her husband's death benefit, barely enough to sustain them without the additional income from her job as a stenographer in the law firm of Fisher and Fisher. While they were not poor, they were cautious in what was spent for anything beyond basic needs.

There was something beyond Barbara's beauty that made her so appealing. She was unlike the girls in the clique whose status was marked by expensive, designer-brand clothes they wore, or the pricey vacations they took with their families. She was taller than average and to a stranger could have been taken for a model, an actress, a celebrity. But she was wholly unaffected by her looks, and it was this that generated an unspoken resentment from the other girls. If not for Mike, they would never have welcomed her into the group.

She was smart too. She was a formidable presence on the debate team, yet in spite of that, she concealed a shyness that suggested a lack of self-confidence that the other more sophisticated girls projected.

It was this hidden lack of self-assurance and not merely her uncommon beauty that attracted Mike to her, her unassuming sex appeal that generated heat inside him, aroused in him a desire to dominate her, to compel obedience, to command submission. And she saw Mike with his well-to-do family as a way out of her middle-class status. They had become a steady couple within the inner circle for over a year.

And then there was David. She could just as easily have been *his* girl. She would have liked being his girl, in fact, but he had never hinted at that kind of interest. Other than Susan, he hadn't dated anyone. His focus was football and academics. She and David were just friends.

That's all. Wasn't that enough? David was Mike's friend, and Barbara was his friend. If there was anything else, she knew David wouldn't act on it. She loved Mike, but she loved David too. Whatever it was, she still loved him, if only from a distance.

Despite her ongoing relationship with Mike Summers, she did not hide her disapproval of his arrogant display of hostility toward Stephen. Her acceptance of Stephen and David's closeness was unconditional and without any need to say it, Stephen understood. Next to David, Barbara was his closest ally, and the bond would deepen in the months to come but bring unexpected and unimaginable consequences.

CHAPTER 10
UNEXPECTED TURNS

IT WAS AFTER football practice late Friday. David and Mike were the last ones off the field and into the locker room. Mike cast quick glances as David exited the shower.

"Say, buddy. Dad's not using the lake house this weekend. What say we grab some brews and chill out for a change?" Mike asked casually.

"Can't this weekend, got plans," David said, without further explanation.

"Stephen?" Mike said, trying to conceal his resentment. David glanced at him but said nothing. "Just thought, you know, you and I, we could use some time to ourselves."

Mike continued stealing glances as David finished dressing.

"Got to run now. Some other time," David said, not looking back as he left the locker room. Mike frowned. He was not pleased. Not at all.

—⚭—

AS THE END of school approached, David had completely withdrawn from the exclusive clique. Though he still saw Barbara now and again at school, whatever free time he had, he spent with Stephen. He welcomed the evolving closeness without any reservations whatsoever. It surprised him how natural it felt, no expectations, just the anticipation of being together, time shared with no one outside themselves.

It was not the same for Stephen. He struggled with ambivalent feelings, at once wanting to accept this gift he had been offered and reluctant to receive it unconditionally, afraid to lose what he had found. Soon now, when the year ended, they would go their separate directions, with David already contemplating a myriad of choices after graduation, and Stephen left with only limited options—feelings he managed to conceal from David.

THE LAST PERIOD of the day was phys ed class. Stephen entered the locker room and stopped abruptly at the sight of Benny Simpson forced into the corner by two guys haranguing him, their voices echoing off the tiled walls.

"What is it, little girly boy? Want some action, little girly?" they mocked.

Stephen saw the expression on Benny's face, and backed away, unseen by the two who pushed Benny against the open locker. That was the first encounter Stephen witnessed. Two days later was the second.

Stephen and David were coming down the steps when they caught sight of Benny Simpson shoved against the building by the two Stephen had stumbled upon in the locker room. One held the boy while the other smeared lipstick on his mouth. David dropped his booksack and bolted across the grass, grabbing the two, forcing them to the ground, his face red with rage. The two scrambled to escape his anger but David blocked their retreat.

"Want some fun?" he bellowed. "Come on," he shouted, fists clinched. "Let's have some fun, assholes."

The two looked up and saw his fury. David cast a glance at the boy. "It's Benny, right?" he said. The boy nodded. David towered over the two sprawled on the ground. "These assholes want to apologize, don't you?" his words a command not a question.

"Sorry..." they whimpered.

"No," David snarled, "Say it like you mean it."

"We're sorry, Benny, really sorry," the larger bully offered.

"Now get the hell away from here," David ordered. "Lay a hand on this kid again and I break your head," he said as the two fled.

"You O.K., kid?" David asked. Benny nodded a response. But that was the last that they saw of Benny Simpson. He did not return for graduation.

—⁓—

EARLY IN MAY, David and Stephen had driven to the Okefenokee Wildlife Refuge, the largest landlocked swamp in the eastern United States, hundreds of square miles teeming with an amazing and awesome variety of wildlife. The swamp came alive in the spring, gators sunning along the banks of the canals, the savannahs occupied with thousands of birds again migrating north. Okefenokee was the name the Indians had given the swamp, meaning *land of trembling earth*.

David paddled the kayak with ease through the tea-colored water. A gator on the bank rose on all fours, slid ominously into the water and disappeared.

As they navigated the narrow canals that snaked through the swamp, David pointed toward the open savannah. "That plain ahead is actually layers of peat that trembles under foot," he explained. Turning the bend, they saw another gator slide from the bank. Massive knees from the cypress trees rose like giant cathedral spires from the canal.

"The water's so dark," Stephen observed, the sky and towering trees reflected from its mirror surface.

"It's tannic acid from decaying vegetation. Nothing bad, just nature purifying itself with no help from any human being," he told him.

Nature purifying itself, Stephen repeated to himself. This day was overwhelming. Out here just the two of them and the endless silence except for the sounds of wildlife humming about them, and the trembling earth. At this moment he was purified.

AGAINST THE OBJECTIONS of his grandmother, David had made arrangements for the overnight cabin. At dusk, when the park closed, they sat on the open porch listening to the approaching night, an owl's hooting, crickets chirping, frogs singing aloud, the mating sound of gators now invisible in the deepening night.

Stephen instinctively reached for David's hand but quickly caught himself and withdrew. Back in the city, he had thought often about the end of school, the beginning of the separation that he knew was inevitable, when David would leave for the university and he would again find himself alone, unsure of what was next.

"Well, David," Stephen half whispered, "I'm proud of you, really happy for you—not just one but two scholarship offers. So which one is it? Georgia or Florida?"

There was the athletic offer from Georgia and the veterinary scholarship at Florida.

"Not football," he answered. "I'd like to be a veterinarian, fix broken wings. How 'bout you?"

"There's a small college in North Carolina. I can work part-time on campus and camp jobs in summer and figure out the rest later." He felt a rush of regret at that moment now that the year's end was fast approaching.

INSIDE THE CABIN, the brightness of the full moon illuminated the darkness. David's heart raced. The two stood motionless, no sound except the sound of their breathing. This time, there would be no retreat. Slowly, deliberately their hands fumbled in the dark, shirts, then jeans tumbling to the floor. They closed in upon each other, David's hands cradling Stephen, pressing against him, and Stephen responding now with equal intensity. With both hands, David held Stephen's face. There was a quiet acknowledgement as they accepted each other fully, offering their innocence, with unquestioned abandonment.

—⚉—

MIKE WAITED OUTSIDE the classroom for Barbara to finish practice for the upcoming debate on the court's recent hearing on racial segregation. She could tell as she approached him that he was agitated.

"I don't like it," Mike growled. "What the fuck does David see in that creep?"

"Watch your tongue," she scolded him. "Why are you so bothered about David's social life?"

"Because, Barbara, David is my buddy. I don't like what's going on," he scowled.

"Just what *is* that, Mike?" she demanded.

"David's not been himself since that creep showed up. There's something weird about that guy. I don't like it. You tell me what's going on."

"Well," she began, "for starters, they like each other"

"More than *like*, maybe?"

"Meaning?"

"Meaning there's something unnatural. Meaning there's something sissified about the guy. Meaning David is being dragged into something and doesn't realize where it's headed."

"And just where is that?" she asked, her voice betraying a growing irritation.

"Go figure," he said sullenly.

"Well, super stud," she mocked, "I'm so impressed with this new talent you've cultivated about character. If I didn't know better, I'd say there is a tinge of," she paused, raising her eyebrows, "jealousy, maybe?"

"Fuck you."

"I don't think so."

—⁓—

IT WAS STEPHEN then, not David, who was their target. Comments, whispers, sentiments like Mike's, the unwanted fugitive who did not belong, and David, so naïve, who couldn't see what was happening, couldn't see where this was leading, Stephen who was alienating him from the group.

During the coming weeks, Stephen sensed the chill that had settled in from the other guys, no longer subtle but overt. After phys ed class, he had gone into the shower and Mike followed.

"What are you staring at, faggot?" Mike snarled.

Stephen's face went white, the word stinging in his ears. At Franklin High, he had endured insults from the phys ed teacher who demanded he throw the ball like a guy, not like some girl. But faggot. All at once he hurled his fist into Mike's jaw, knocking him against the shower wall. Mike got up slowly, deliberately, wiped the trace of blood from his mouth and said nothing, did nothing in response to the blow, just stood there with a snarl of a grin, then turned and walked away.

IN THE WEEKS that followed, Stephen distanced himself not just from the group but now from David as well. In the school cafeteria, he would leave abruptly whenever David approached him. Phone calls seldom returned. Other plans already made. More time on the books. Complete detachment.

David's anxiety gave way to desperation. How could something so good have gone so wrong? What had happened? He waited outside long after everyone had left the campus. When he caught sight of Stephen sauntering down the steps, he moved quickly to block his way. He said, "We have to talk," his voice betraying his panic.

Stephen nodded, following him to the spot under the tree where months ago they had shared each other's thoughts in silence.

"What offense did I commit? Why are you shutting me out? Tell me."

HE HAD TO shut him out, didn't he? There was no alternative, was there? If there was, what was it? Mike had the answers. "It's not you, David," he whispered, head bowed, looking away.

"Then what is it? Things were so right. What happened?" he pleaded. There was no response. "Look at me, Stephen. Look at me."

Stephen heard him plead, but looked away.

"That night—on the beach—I made a promise to myself. I promised I would never lose you again. And the night in the cabin. I've done some shameful things in my life, but not that night. I know you felt the same. Tell me you didn't feel it."

Now Stephen, without flinching, fixed his eyes on David. He swallowed hard, summoning his courage. "I felt it then," he admitted. "I don't feel it now."

"Don't do this," he pleaded.

Stephen's face was expressionless. "Get a life, David," he droned, and turning—without looking back—left David there, wounded from the rejection.

STEPHEN'S MOTHER WAS again rearranging furniture in the living room. She did this several times during the year to break the routine of a marriage she tolerated because the alternative was unacceptable. She maintained the semblance of family, of marriage for her son's sake. Security was preferable to divorce. Marriage was security. Even in 1954, divorce was not an easy option.

She didn't notice Stephen until he called to her.

"Hi Mom," he said. "Breaking up the boredom again?" his voice a monotone as he moved past her.

Something was wrong. She watched him move toward the stairs.

"What's the matter, son?" she asked, but he didn't answer.

He climbed the stairs to his room.

"Stephen!" she called. No answer. "Stephen?" she repeated. No answer.

HE CLOSED THE door gently so as not to face the inquisition. Once in his room, he noticed the Polaroid snapshot wedged into the side of the mirror, two carefree faces outlined against the dunes and the sea beyond them. The loss that he had initiated then came upon him hard—to protect the one person in his life whose love he had accepted and now discarded. Or was he trying to protect himself?

OUTSIDE THE ROOM, his mother stood tentatively, hand poised against the door but then withdrawing. She listened for some movement in the room, turned and descended the stairs to resume the rearrangement of the furniture.

—∞—

WITH THE END of school and graduation, Stephen abruptly headed to North Carolina to find a place near the four-year college that he would attend in the fall. He hadn't a clue about a major. He would take the summer camp job and worry about the rest in the fall. What he could not foresee was the labyrinth of experiences waiting for him beyond North Carolina. For now, he was driven by the need to shut out the last year of Jefferson High. Yet the memory of the beach and the swamp would sneak in without warning, rekindling aching feelings about his loss.

—∞—

AS FALL APPROACHED, David began planning the transition to college. Stephen had already left for Carolina and David had accepted the reality that the separation was final. By the end of summer, he had made arrangements for the dorm at State University and had begun packing things for the campus. Barbara helped him load boxes in the Chevy. She was unusually quiet.

"Something's bothering you," he said, taking the box from her and dropping it in the crowded trunk of the car. "What is it, Barbara? You can tell me."

He had never seen her so detached, so disconnected.

She caught his stare briefly, then glanced away. "What is it, Barbara?" he insisted. Another silence.

"I'm pregnant." She looked directly at him, holding his surprise at her revelation.

"Pregnant?" he repeated in astonishment. "Who's responsible?"

"Both of us," she muttered.

"I mean *who is the father?*"

"Who else," she said as a matter of fact. "Mike doesn't want it. His father knows someone just across the state line who can take care of this. Mike's future is football. Marriage is the last thing he needs to distract him from his future. I'm not to worry. His father will pay for the arrangements."

David's rage was a furnace inside him. "That son of a bitch," he blurted, pounding his fist into his open hand. "What do *you* want, Barbara?" he demanded.

"I'm scared, David. Mike drove me up there. It was disgusting—just a shack in the woods, the room was filthy...I don't want the abortion, but I don't see any other options. What other options are there, David?"

He shook his head. "Do you know how dangerous an abortion would be? The rate of infection, not to mention the thing itself?"

"Yes, that and more. It's not raising a kid alone that bothers me. My mother did pretty well with me after dad died. But I was legitimate. What would this kid be without a legitimate father?"

David held her close. He searched for something to say that would reassure her. He could feel her trembling. In place of the proud, confident Barbara he had known for so long was a frightened little girl. He ran his hand through her hair, and all at once she could not hold back her tears.

"Hush, hush," he whispered. "Everything's going to be all right. You're not going to have an abortion. You're going to marry *me*."

"MARRY?" YVONNE SCREAMED at him. "My God, David, have you lost your mind? She's not your responsibility. I can't stand thinking you'd do something stupid like this. Marriage is a sacrament between a man and woman—not some convenience. I forbid it."

"Forbid?" he repeated. "Just as you forbid me seeing my father? Well, I'm eighteen, and I don't need your permission."

"I'm your mother, and I will not allow you to throw your life away on a tramp."

"Stop me," he called over his shoulder as he was leaving.

She was almost hysterical now, clenching her fists and waving her arms wildly. "If you do this, don't come..."

But in his anger, he had already made up his mind not to come back.

THE WEDDING WAS quiet. In spite of objections from Greta and from his mother, David was unwavering in his decision to stand by Barbara, to shield her in this difficult moment. It was the test of his loyalty and his friendship. How could he abandon her? She would not have an abortion at the hand of a butcher. He would not abandon her and that was final. He postponed his first year at the university, taking a teller's position at a local bank to earn extra money that Barbara would need once the baby had arrived. He would do this to help her during that first year in adjusting to her new challenge. What else would a friend do?

Except for the birth of Barbara's child, it was an uneventful year. Among their friends, they were regarded as the ideal couple, their marriage the typical storybook marriage, not the slightest trace of anything out of the ordinary.

David had his own space in the house, and no one but Barbara's mother and Mike Summers and Mike's father had a hint that the ideal couple were merely two friends who had arranged a solution to an unexpected problem. As far as anyone knew, Barbara was the perfect mother and David the proud father. This was the true test of friendship, neither having any expectations from the other.

The following fall of 1955, David was ready for the next phase of his life. Barbara remained with her mother and David was off to the university, embarking on his future in veterinary medicine. He had already begun to heal broken wings.

CHAPTER 11
THE UNIVERSITY

THOUGH PROFESSOR WILLIAM LEE could not know it at the time, the fall semester of 1955 was the beginning of what would be the irrevocable turning point, not only in his career, but in his life.

He had grown up in the thirties in Pine Bluff, Arkansas—a typical Southern small town isolated by its distance from Little Rock. There was a public library, but the selections were limited, mostly what one would expect in the backwoods of a small Arkansas town, the collection ranging from mediocre to profound. The more challenging collection largely went unnoticed, except by William Lee.

He was different from the other boys his age. They liked fishing, hunting, shooting guns and sneaking cigarettes. His interest was books. When the other boys struggled with basic grade-level assignments, he was challenged by Maugham, Hemingway, and Fitzgerald, his imagination fired by the intricate conflicts so meticulously constructed. His intellect marked him as an outcast. Once after school, waiting for the bus, a classmate accosted him.

"Why you puttin' on airs. Think you're better than us?" he asked.

"No, just different," he said, wanting to avoid another confrontation. Why, he wondered, was that so wrong—to be different? He counted the days until graduation and his escape.

The scholarship to Oxford had provided his exit from Pine Bluff and his entry into a new and rigorous challenge of advanced studies in England's most prestigious university. Graduating early from Oxford at the end of his third year, well beyond others in his class, he was offered another scholarship to Washington and Lee for his masters, and then, two years later, having completed a doctorate by his twenty-sixth birthday, he was ready to launch a distinguished academic career. But December 7, 1941, changed everything.

After the attack on Pearl Harbor, World War II was no longer a distant war separated by two oceans, and for William Lee the survival of Western civilization itself seemed at stake. He didn't want to wait for the draft, but he faced a dilemma. On one hand, he must conceal his homosexuality in order to enlist. On the other hand, if he enlisted and somehow was discovered, he would face a dishonorable discharge, which would not only destroy his career but wreck his entire life as well. He could, of course, admit his sexual nature and therefore avoid those alternatives. After all, it would be society and the country rejecting him for who he was, not he rejecting the country.

But there was a youthful idealism that he shared with others willing to postpone personal futures for a commitment to a common cause, one that demanded the sacrifice of convenience in exchange for a greater good. He weighed the consequences of avoidance, or commitment in spite of the risks, and his idealism won out. William Lee enlisted.

With his fluency in German and French, he had been assigned to a military intelligence unit and soon found himself back in England at an allied base just outside London. The assignment was unlike anything he could have imagined. Throughout the day, he would pore over reams of German intelligence reports, and at night, unable to sleep, listen to the drone of aircraft miles away over London, the pounding of bombs from the German planes heightening the excitement. He had never felt more alive and more committed in his life.

Lee had been with intelligence operations barely a month when the captain introduced him to the new arrival assigned to be his assistant. Ronald Jackson was a tall, lanky kid, just over twenty-two and recently out of college. In spite of his lack of experience, he was exceptionally bright, had a superior fluency in German, and, in addition, a cockiness that Lee found at once engaging but also annoying.

He was impressed with the young officer's self-confidence as he plunged straightaway into the data, not waiting for direction, just tackling the translations with abandon. But Lee also resented his assertiveness, especially his unrelenting insistence that they slow down, as he would say, and loosen up.

"Lighten up, man," Ronald Jackson taunted him. "You're going to give yourself a stroke."

"No, you're going to give me a stroke. I don't have time for your small talk," Lee growled. "We've got a job to do here."

"Hey," he said in his usual abruptness, "tell you what. We'll go into town, buy you a beer. Like to get to know you."

It was already nineteen-hundred hours, and it had been a grueling day. Lee nodded at Jackson. "O.K. Let's do it." That night began their friendship.

They shared the room in the officer's quarters, and during the next six months the bond between them grew fierce. For William Lee it was the high-point of his young adult life. He had debated with himself about postponing his future for this. The debate was over.

THE FOLLOWING YEAR, they were assigned to different units, Lee to Scotland and Ronald Jackson to a base in Iceland, the only connection now the letters they exchanged and the assurance that once the war was over they would be together again.

After the war, Lee accepted an appointment to the humanities faculty at State University in Florida, and a year later Ronald made good on his promise. For the next seven years, they would find a quiet acceptance in the liberal academic community of a university town. For Lee, those were the most satisfying years of his life—and the most disappointing when the relationship ended and Ronald Jackson moved to California. After seven intoxicating years, Lee was alone.

ON THE FIRST day of classes in the fall semester, Lee paused momentarily, took a deep breath, opened the door and marched into the crowded classroom. In spite of his background and achievements, he always felt a surge of excitement but also a kind of stage anxiety meeting his new captive audience for the first time. He was, after all, not only a teacher but a performer as well. The first day was always act one.

Afterwards, after introductions, he would relax, repeat the name of each student and look around the room, committing each face to memory as each voice responded. And at once, he caught his breath when David Ashton half raised his hand indicating his presence. From that moment, captivated by those incredible brown eyes set under dark lashes and accompanied by an entirely disarming smile, Professor William Lee knew he had spotted the pick of the litter.

Later in the morning, Lee stopped by the campus bookstore to check on the textbooks he had ordered for the course, a routine he had always observed since the semester when no books had arrived due to a misplaced order. He edged toward the humanities aisle, stopping abruptly, heart skipping a beat. The young man from the morning class was standing there, book open, eyes scanning the page before him, lost in concentration. Lee studied him carefully. Even in the jeans, the well-formed buttocks and thighs were apparent, the broad shoulders accenting the six-foot frame. *You dirty old man,* Lee thought, but quickly brushed the thought aside. He was merely Socrates admiring one of his handsome students.

Feigning an air of casual interest, he approached this paragon of beauty. "I'm afraid you might find portions rather tedious," he said in a self-deprecating tone.

David glanced at the man standing there, then responded with a generous smile. "Professor Lee," he uttered with surprise. "David Ashton, from your humanities class," he said, offering his hand. "I was just glancing through your text. Really impressive."

"Well, thank you for the flattery. I'm afraid not everyone shares your enthusiasm, dear boy. It's not your typical classroom text. I attempted to orient it around my erstwhile travels which, I suppose like so many photographs people take on a trip to Europe or wherever, some may find dull, but be that as it may, I'm eight dollars less poor than if I hadn't done it," he answered.

David laughed. "Well I haven't paid for it yet, but I can't ignore the poor, can I?" he laughed. "Anyway, I'll reserve judgment for now. Looking forward to your class, sir," he offered as he walked toward the cashier. Lee's eyes followed him. Yes, indeed. He was, too, looking forward to the class.

—◊—

WILLIAM LEE WAS not the only one captivated by David's presence. Norton Brell arrived in class early to get a seat across the aisle from David. David was everything that Brell was not. Brell was tall, a little over six feet, but unlike David, his frame was thin, his skin waxy like paper stretched over protruding bone. In some respects, his face resembled that of a weasel that had assumed human form—thin facial features, eyes that darted back and forth as if to spot some unseen danger.

But what Brell lacked in physical attractiveness, he made up with intelligence and an uncommon talent in photography. The recognition he earned in amateur exhibits set him apart from his competitors. Photography was his life. He had no interest in music, books, film, or sports. Photography was his escape from the endless patronizing he endured from others.

David settled into his seat, placed books underneath the chair and, glancing over at Brell, smiled. "Hi, I'm David," he said casually.

"Norton Brell. First year at the university?" He affected an air of casualness to conceal his nervousness.

David nodded. "And you?" he asked.

"Second year," Brell replied.

"I noticed your camera first day of class. Never saw one like that. What is it?" David asked, interested in what was obviously a serious and expensive instrument, not just an ordinary camera.

"It's a Leica M3," Brell said, "launched last year with the Summicron 50mm f/2 lens. He seemed impressed with David's curiosity.

"Going into photography?" David said.

"Well I suppose I'm already into it, not professionally of course, but that's my long- range goal. And you?"

"Right now veterinary medicine if I survive all the pre-reqs," he said. "This is my first humanities. Not quite sure what to make of it. Different from the usual high school stuff."

"Well," Brell responded, "Lee will be a trip. For sure, you won't be bored."

And so was the beginning of a relationship that would have ominous consequences.

—⌘—

NORTON BRELL WAS right. William Lee was anything but boring. His lectures were more vivid than any movie, the characters from history forming an endless stream of experiences. Sometimes David would close his eyes as Lee's voice thundered across the room, bringing to life from the ancient past the men and women whose own stories resonated so clearly with his own. David's fascination with his professor went beyond the relationship of student and professor. Of all the classes, Lee's was the door to unique encounters he experienced for the first time: the *Iliad* of Homer, *The Symposium* of Plato, the trial of Socrates and the hemlock he was compelled to drink at his execution, punishment for insulting the citizens of ancient Athens, but most of all of Alexander the Great and his beloved companion, Hephaestion. Alexander, conqueror of the ancient world, who lay upon Hephaestion's lifeless body, lay there over a night until friends, by force, dragged him away. He could connect with Alexander and his relationship with Hephaestion, associating the moments between himself and his own beloved Stephen, and when he relived those moments, he would suppress a silent cry at his own loss.

It was during one of the classes when they had been reading the *Iliad* that a student questioned Lee about the relationship between Achilles and Patrocles.

"Were they homosexuals?" the student asked without hesitation. There was a sudden stillness across the classroom, punctuated by a collective embarrassment at the sound of the word, all eyes focusing intently on Lee in anticipation of his response.

Lee paused momentarily. It was a delicate subject, given the fact that homosexuality was a felony in the state, carrying a prison term upon conviction. How to respond in an intelligent way without dodging the issue.

"In the ancient world, in Greece and in Rome, one did not divide groups into heterosexual and homosexual," he said in the most casual manner he could manage. "Sexuality was merely a component of one's makeup. The issue was not whether one was homosexual or heterosexual. The question was one of behavior. The emperor Hadrian, for example, ruled the mightiest empire of his day and yet had a companion, a lover if you will, and was quite open about it. It was how one treated others that marked the acceptance or lack of acceptance, for the most part. Of course, there were always those who frowned upon any same-sex relationship, but all in all, that was not an overriding issue."

The student glared, eyes widening, a deep smirk on his face. "So the Romans weren't depraved deviates? Then what caused them to fall?"

Lee could sense the tension in the room, students shifting awkwardly in their chairs waiting for the next response.

"Well," he replied, "it took four centuries before Rome was finished. Perhaps it was more than their sexual mores that was responsible for the collapse. Otherwise it was a slow process, wouldn't you say?"

"Tell you what I think," the student shot back. "The Bible says it's a sin, an abominable sin, worse than murder even. It says men who lie with men should be put to death."

"And do you believe literally every word of the Bible or just the parts that we are told to believe?" he asked.

"I believe every word is the word of God and God speaks to us through His word," he insisted.

"And is it God's word that demands death to children who sass their parents or that prescribes the number of slaves a man can own?" he asked, his voice controlled, his demeanor calm.

Agitated now by Lee's rebuttal, the student sprang from his desk, kicking the chair aside, assuming an adversarial stiffness as he confronted the professor. "I won't be subjected to such filth," he shouted, glancing around the room, his voice ricocheting from the walls. "The rest of you can stay," he said, staring at Lee, who offered no response, "but not me," and he was out of the room, slamming the door as he left.

Lee shook his head and was quiet. Then smiling, he said to the mortified students, "Please complete Book Sixteen of the *Iliad* for our discussion next time. Class dismissed."

David remained in his seat after the last student had left. Lee smiled. "Well, that was quite an unexpected exchange, don't you agree?"

David said nothing. He did not need to. Lee knew he had his unwavering approval.

CHAPTER 12
EXTENDED FAMILY

As the semester progressed, David found himself part of the se-lected few invited to Lee's house for Saturday afternoon broadcasts of the Metropolitan Opera, good food, and stimulating conversation. Opera was an entirely new experience for him. Even though the lyrics were incomprehensible, he was captivated by the voices, the music, and especially by Lee's presence.

Whatever fantasies William Lee entertained, his professional relationship with the young students he found so stimulating and so untouchable was impeccable. They were a welcome distraction from the breakup with Ronald two years earlier, a disruption still unsettled. He was attracted more to their youthful enthusiasm and their idealism, which no doubt would vanish once they were out-side in the real world and away from the sheltered cocoon of the university. Meanwhile, he would fantasize about them, but remain passionately distant. His real passion remained—food, books and music, and the pleasure he experienced in cultivating the same tastes in his students.

—⁂—

Norton Brell was careful not to be noticed. His fixation on David was at once something intensely satisfying and at the same time a mixture of anticipation and anxiety.

Brell stalked David, catching his movements with the eye of his camera, and photographs of David lined the wall of his darkroom.

Brell noted his prey's daily routine: after David left the dorm in the morning, he had his class schedule, then spent the afternoon in the library, and afterwards worked out in the gym. One day Brell waited inconspicuously outside the gym, careful not to be seen watching for David to leave.

When he caught sight of David descending the steps toward the sidewalk, Brell rounded the corner where he had been waiting and feigned surprise at the "coincidental" encounter with his target.

In a controlled, casual voice, he said, "David, what's happening?" He glanced down at the gym bag, "You work out regularly?" He did not wait for an answer. "I hired a trainer once, thinking that it might do me some good, but it didn't work."

"Maybe you had the wrong trainer."

"I don't know," he said dropping his head, "It was so intimidating, I'm not exactly what you'd call the athletic type. Some people just aren't cut out for it," he said in a self-deprecating tone, "like me, for instance."

"Tell you what," David said, "give it another try. Meet me here Saturday morning."

Brell hesitated, "Oh, I don't know, it would probably be a waste of your time. Like I said, I'm hardly the athletic type."

"Trust me," David said reassuringly, "you *are* the athletic type," he said with emphasis. "See you Saturday morning at nine. I won't take no for an answer. O.K.?"

"Well, I guess," he said pausing, "O.K. Saturday, then."

"Great, looking forward to the challenge," he said with a smile as he walked away.

Brell studied his movement with a warm sense of accomplishment. *Saturday for sure.*

—⁂—

ZACK CONNER ARRIVED at the university on his twenty-third birthday. He had spent four years in the Marine Corps and was anxious to move ahead with his education and then pursue his working career. During his years in the Marines, he had made few close friends and never entered into anything like an intimate relationship, let alone a permanent one.

Any serious relationship would have been unthinkable because frequent assignments to different bases discouraged long-range commitments, and also because it would have proved too risky. Instead, he took advantage of free weekends and would drive miles from the base to the nearest city, cruising bars, maintaining anonymity, and making contact safely with guys who knew not to ask too many questions or attempt to pin him down.

In this way, he kept his military life apart from his private encounters. It wasn't what he wanted, but it was the only practical way to avoid detection and ensure that he would complete his military obligation without any unpleasant incident that could lead to a dishonorable discharge. The stint in the Marines demanded a circumspect detachment from too personal an association with other individuals in his company, and that was the way it had to be.

At least he had no difficulty in hooking up with other guys. Standing just over six feet, his body was hard, a byproduct of the physical demands of the Corps, and his face formed a firm, almost classical profile. He never sat alone at a bar for any length of time. But in spite of his success in making contact with other guys, he missed not having an ongoing relationship, and at twenty-three, it began to seem as though he never would.

Now in civilian life, he focused on his studies. He had no interest in joining a fraternity or participating in social activities typical of entering freshmen. His single goal was his education. He breezed through his courses with little effort.

Socializing consisted of an occasional movie with acquaintances, sometimes a beer at one of the local student hangouts, and indulging his passion for bodybuilding. At first, he tried the gym in his dorm but realized that the sparse equipment and the isolation were not for him. So he joined a gym off campus. Saturday morning was his first visit.

In the men's locker room, he caught sight of David and Norton Brell changing into workout gear. The contrast between the two made David's body stand out in a way that excited Zack. He took his time changing, listening intently to the conversation between the weasel-like individual and the well-defined six-foot frame now pulling his gym shorts on. *Christ almighty.*

"All right, Norton. Let's hit it," David said as Brell followed sheepishly.

The following Saturday, Zack made a point of arriving at the gym at the same time, sharply at nine. He waited in the locker room for the unlikely couple, but half past the hour, he realized that his assumption had been wrong. They were not going to show. Disappointed, he wandered out into the workout area, began his routine but with little enthusiasm, forcing himself to focus on his workout.

Moments later he stood before the mirrored walls, concentrating on his controlled movement as he raised the barbells slowly then lowered them to the starting position, the repetitions beginning to burn his biceps. And then he saw them, the unlikely pair maneuvering around the rows of exercise machines.

It was clear that the prodigy wasn't at all interested in the physical ordeal that his trainer was subjecting him to. It was also clear that the guy had a keen interest in his trainer's body, from the way his eyes studied the trainer as he raised and lowered the weights.

Finally, Zack made his move. He placed the loaded barbell onto the rack of the incline bench next to the adjacent bench that the two were approaching. After several repetitions, he made an audible grunt as he faked an attempted final effort that indicated difficulty in controlling the weight of the barbell. David quickly rushed over, providing assistance to the struggling weightlifter.

"Thanks, man," Zack said earnestly, extending his hand. "I'm Zack—Zack Conner."

"David Ashton," he said, returning the greeting. Neither of them noticed Brell's glare and his annoyance at this interruption. It was the beginning of a new bonding and the dissolution of the other. In subsequent workouts, Brell grew less attentive to David's instruction and ever more resentful of Conner's intrusion. Finally, he discontinued the sessions entirely.

The workouts had been the initial link in David's newfound friendship with Zack Conner, but by late fall, they were discovering mutual interests outside the gym, especially music.

"Someone I'd like you to meet," David announced, "someone very special," he added.

Zack frowned. *Someone special. Here it comes. Knew this was too perfect.*

And it was. One weekend and Zack was captivated. William Lee had made another conquest.

OVER THE INTERVENING months, as the Christmas break approached, Zack Conner began to feel something deeper, warmer about the relationship. David had become the focus of his life, the boyish innocence, the masculine strength, coupled with a vulnerability that awakened in Zack something he had never felt before, something more than just the sexual attraction. He began spending his entire free time with him, even though there had not been the slightest indication that David felt anything beyond a casual friendship.

Still, with the developing friendship came a trust. David had told him about his failed relationship with Stephen, but insisted he wasn't gay, and Zack could sense that David was not ready to let go. First loves were often like that, weren't they? Zack was just grateful for being able to spend time with David, and he came to enjoy the meetings they shared with William Lee—the music, the conversation, the occasional dinner. Of course he would like more. Who wouldn't? But he was content to take whatever he was offered.

As their friendship took hold, Lee's usual weekend invitations involving other students were less frequent, and eventually only the three of them shared time together. For David, this was a welcomed distraction from Barbara and her baby. Lee provided the solidity to the evolving relationship. Under the surface of what appeared sometimes as a flippant, superficial personality was a genuine complexity of character. Lee welcomed David and Zack's company and was reminded of the years he had spent with Ronald, the only person he had ever loved. There was something refreshing in seeing two young men so completely at ease and enjoying each other's presence, whether or not anything would ever come of it.

One Saturday night, having finished dinner, the three settled down for the usual evening of music. Lee had selected Richard Addinsell's *Warsaw Concerto*, which David had come to like immensely, its passionate nostalgia set against the Battle of Britain in the 1941 film *Dangerous Moonlight*. Afterwards, David said to Lee, "I don't understand how you can be so indifferent to that music."

"Oh, it's not that, dear boy. It's dramatic, to be sure, and it's not without skill, in fact it has a gracefulness of its own. But Rachmaninoff it isn't, though Addinsell borrows directly from his second piano concerto. I rather like it, actually—brings back memories of my own war-time experiences in England." He said this not in any pejorative way, just a matter of observation. It was one of Lee's attributes that made David appreciate even more the man's encyclopedic knowledge, which he possessed without the slightest trace of snobbery or affectation.

"Anyhow, my friend, if the music speaks to you, enjoy it." he said.

Turning to Zack, he asked again about his experiences in the Marines, told him more about his own time in the Army during the war and the difficult choices he had made, especially the part about being gay.

"I don't suppose it was very different for you either," he said to Zack.

Zack cast a tentative look at David, searching for the right words. "Growing up in my hometown, you had to hide, deep inside the closet. There wasn't an alternative to hiding who you were. In the Marines, the frequent moves between bases made things easier. You never had to worry too much about anyone discovering any secrets because you never got too close." He glanced again at David as he said this.

DAVID RETURNED THE glance, but said nothing. He had had no sexual contact with anyone since Stephen. In spite of that encounter, he wasn't gay. Of course he wasn't. Not that it bothered him. But the thing with Stephen was—what? He couldn't say exactly. Except that he was trying to figure out what secrets might have been hidden in his own closet for so much of his life—and now there was this awkward attraction he had begun to feel toward Zack.

THE ROOM WAS suddenly quiet, not a strained silence, merely a stillness enveloping their thoughts until Lee ended it. "Mozart anyone?" he asked, placing the record on the turntable. What bothered Lee most, now that Ronald was no longer a part of his life, was the absence of any family connection whatsoever—no siblings, no other surviving relatives, his mother and father both gone, and his acceptance of the fact that he never would have a family. Except for Zack and David, he was alone. They had become his family.

Soon there would be another addition to the extended family—and not without consequences.

—∽—

DAVID COULD HARDLY believe how quickly his first semester at the university had slipped by. The intellectual stimulation—the new direction his life had taken—was exhilarating. He had barely given thought to Barbara and the baby, their contacts limited to the letters they exchanged randomly. But his visit at Christmas marked an uncomfortable turn in what had been his youthful commitment in helping Barbara during the tenuous circumstances of her pregnancy. At eighteen months, Daniel had learned to call David by name, and it was obvious that Barbara was proud of the child's precocious development, and pleased that David was home for Christmas. Now, David sensed that perhaps this was becoming something more than a marriage of convenience.

In his own way, he loved Daniel, and when the child called his name, David felt a connection. He could imagine himself with a son like Daniel, whom he would love and never abandon, as his father had abandoned him. But this child needed a father, a need David could not fulfill, and the realization of this stirred conflicting emotions. For the first time, he acknowledged the responsibility he had assumed by marrying Barbara, and this in turn awakened guilt, that he was betraying loyalty to Barbara, his friend whom he had wanted to protect.

Daniel pulled at David's leg, calling his name, and David attempted a grin. Barbara noticed his uneasiness. "David, are you all right? Is anything wrong?" she asked, trying to interpret his reaction to Daniel's persistence.

"Yeah, everything's great," he told her, attempting to convince himself that he believed it, then abruptly changing the subject. "How's your work with the law firm?" he asked.

"Good," she answered without much enthusiasm. "Mom and I are fixtures. Really good," she said, taking hold of Daniel who indicated his displeasure with a spontaneous cry. "I think he's really glad to see you," she said, contemplating David's awkwardness.

—∽—

STEPHEN'S THIRD SEMESTER in North Carolina at Ridley College was over as quickly as it had begun. He sailed through the required courses with ease. It was the drama class that demanded a concentration that he had not anticipated. He lost himself in the class improvisations with others as they sharpened their acting skills, and later, cast in the role of Peter Trophimof, the young idealist in Chekhov's *The Cherry Orchard*, he suddenly knew that his future was the theater. In those moments on the stage, he was someone else, a person in another time and place.

The night of the play, just before the performance was to begin, he peeked out from behind the curtain to locate his father and mother. He would make them proud of him tonight. They were out there somewhere. The house was full. He searched the faces in the audience, and then he caught sight of his mother there as the lights began to dim. She was alone.

CHAPTER 13
TALLAHASSEE

IT WAS AN early summer morning in 1956 when groups of young Negro students began to line up on Duval Street. By mid-morning, the ranks had swelled from a few to fifty or more. White store-owners peered out anxiously to watch the gathering momentum. Then as a bus rounded the corner, the students formed a human chain, blocking the path of the oncoming bus, which screeched to a halt. Within minutes all street traffic had been halted. Horns blared, angry drivers shouted insults and slurs, but the human chain stood fast. It was the beginning of the storm that Billy Sloat had anticipated and that had now arrived.

GOVERNOR MARVIN RUDGE stared at the television in his office. Several senators sat in stony silence as images of the protests flashed across the screen. Sloat could feel the tension intensifying as the crisis unfolded before them. This was the moment that would demand a decisive response to the violence he had warned them about.

The new governor searched the face of each senator for some trace of reassurance, finally settling on Sloat's expressionless stare. They had come to urge him to call a special session of the legislature now recessed for the summer. He sighed, exhaling a deep breath, which signaled his acceptance of the gravity of the events escalating throughout the state. Sloat waited for the Governor's long overdue response.

"Very well, gentlemen," he nodded his approval. "I'll call a special session. We do have a crisis. But let's remain calm. We must. Can't let this get out of hand."

Sloat maintained his own calm, rigid pose, which concealed his inward satisfaction about the events now playing out.

ONCE THE SPECIAL session was underway, Sloat lost no time in advancing his strategy. In the weeks ahead, he recruited two senior senators from rural districts to draft the Pupil Assignment Statute, a brilliant move to nullify the court's recent rulings on segregation.

"No one can accuse us of trying to circumvent the court. After all," Sloat boasted, "we got to serve the best interest of the child, don't we?"

"But how does this statute accomplish that in view of the court's ruling against separate but equal?" his colleague asked.

"Very straightforward. A child is assigned to a school more qualified to serve the child's best interest, taking into consideration special situations that might endanger the child's safety and welfare. Of course, race, per se, would have nothing to do with this assignment, would it?" he said with a slight smugness.

"But the governor," his colleague asked, "would the governor go along with this? You know his liberal bent."

"He'll accept this proposal because it will avoid a direct attack on the court. What he is not going to like is the *Interposition Resolution*, but that is another matter," Sloat said.

And Sloat was right again. Governor Marvin Rudge expressed outrage over the *Interposition Resolution* already drafted by other Southern states condemning the court's decision as unconstitutional and undermining a state's right to govern its own affairs. He was especially taken aback by the provision providing unprecedented authority to a governor for mobilizing militia to counter violence from unlawful assemblies.

He called the special session to address the crisis and made a personal appearance before a packed and hostile chamber to emphasize his opposition to the *Interposition Resolution*.

"Not only will I not condone *Interposition*, I decry it as an evil thing, whipped up by demagogues, and carried on the hot and erratic winds of passion, prejudice and hysteria." The chamber exploded in catcalls, drowning out the governor's denouncement of the resolution. But he was determined. "If history judges me right this day," he thundered,

"I want it known that I did my best to avert this blot. If I am judged wrong, then here in my own handwriting, and over my signature, is the proof of guilt to support my conviction," he said as he inscribed his veto of the document.

In the confused chaos that ensued, Sloat quietly drafted his own Senate Bill Number 38. It would investigate organizations or individuals threatening the safety and well being of the state's citizens. The Legislative Investigative Committee would allow the committee its own discretion in determining which individuals or organizations would be targeted.

Sloat moved quickly to introduce the proposal and not lose the momentum created by the unsettling events gripping the state. In the senate sub-committee, he began his arm-twisting agenda.

"The NAACP is a communist front masquerading as a civil rights group," he said. "It's the root cause of the violence sweeping this state. We got to stop 'em and Senate Bill 38 will do just that."

The senator from Escambia County, was not convinced. "I don't know, Billy, some of the language seems a bit extreme. Maybe we tone it down a bit?"

Sloat jumped on the objection. "What don't you git?" he demanded. "Don't you watch the news, read the papers? It's going to take extreme to fight extreme." He glared at the senator who dared challenge his bill.

Resistance to the bill developed swiftly in the senate chambers. The senator from Palm Beach County was the first to denounce it. The elderly statesman was known for his liberal bent, and his objection was no surprise to Billy Sloat. "The liberties this bill takes far outweigh the liberties we seek to preserve. Do we want to destroy particular liberties to preserve others?" he said, questioning the bill's unchecked authority.

In the House of Representatives, a member of the Judiciary Committee added his opposition. "We're not going to harm the NAACP, we're going to hurt ourselves, hurt churches, hurt schools, create witch hunts and a reign of terror."

But once debate ended, the House overwhelmingly voted for the bill, and in the senate the measure passed twenty-eight to seven. When it was clear to everyone where the measure was headed, six of the seven senators who had opposed it changed their vote in support. The one remaining senator to cast the lone vote of opposition was Johnson Taylor, Sloat's nemesis from St. Petersburg. Sloat was elated. After so many years and against so many obstacles, he had finally struck his target. The Legislative Investigation Committee was one step away from its birth and he would be its anointed leader.

—⁓—

GOVERNOR MARVIN RUDGE stared outside his window at a squirrel gnawing on an acorn, but his concentration was on Senate Bill 38. He weighed his options carefully. If he signed this bill, he would be endorsing the irrational hysteria of a mob. If he vetoed this bill in defiance of the overwhelming majority of support from both the Senate and the House, he would undermine his own influence in the turbulent times he knew were ahead. His own personal views aside, would this be wise?

Finally, after troubled and uncomfortable deliberation, he had to trust that this committee would not abuse the broad power it would be given. Yes, his own personal views aside, he would allow the bill to become law without his signature. The Legislative Investigative Committee, or the Sloat Committee as it would come to be known, was born.

SLOAT SETTLED ON the first order of business. He had carefully chosen the seven other members whose loyalty was beyond question. Except for the initial subpoenas, which had to be public, closed-door meetings were essential to avoid the press' disruptive scrutiny, which would lead to criticism and interfere with what had to be a methodical and orderly process of investigation.

"This committee must have total control over the information to be released to the public," Sloat explained, "and only the Chairman will engage with the press. Only the Chairman," he repeated with a raised voice.

One of the senators appeared confused, taken aback at Sloat's explanation. He shifted restlessly, his over-weighted thighs barely contained by the delicate chairs of the conference room, his squirming heightened by an itch he tried to mask. "I'm not sure, Billy, I understand this precondition. Why the secrecy? What would we have to hide?" The itch persisted. He looked around before relieving it with his finger.

"Not hide," Sloat countered. "The last thing you want is to cause some harm to a person being investigated before the investigation is completed. There must be no public statements from any member about our activities. Contrary to what some of our colleagues have claimed, this ain't going to be a *witch hunt*. Of course we will make every effort to *protect* anyone under investigation," he insisted. "Therefore, only the chairman is allowed to engage the press or any other source. Is that understood?" He waited for some indication of opposition. There was none.

The seven senators nodded in agreement. The secret progression of their inquiry was essential. There was no need to challenge the chairman. They waited for the next order of business.

"Now, as to other matters," he said, "I want you to meet our legal counsel," and peering into the waiting room, he summoned the young attorney. "Gentlemen, may I introduce Borland Mayes."

The committee members eyed the attorney. He could not be more than thirty-five, but actually looked much younger. Just under six feet, his slight frame and pale skin gave the appearance of an unassuming, even innocent demeanor, of weakness even. But this was an illusion. Underneath the reserved and carefully controlled expression, there was a sinister quality concealed from any observer. As an assistant state attorney, his success in prosecuting dissidents involved in the Tallahassee boycotts was well known. What was not known was his unbridled ruthlessness in pursuing his prey.

Acknowledging Sloat, he offered his agreement about the need for secrecy. "Given the organization you are dealing with, gentlemen, the Chairman is entirely correct" he nodded toward Sloat. "The surprise element is critical. With the subpoenas, we'll obtain the membership lists of the NAACP. Once we have names, we'll begin closed-door interrogations. We already know the connection with communist infiltrators. What we need is proof. Therefore, gentlemen, the first order of business is to obtain the membership lists."

Sloat grinned his approval. His selection of Mayes as legal counsel was perfect. It was 1957 and they were ready to issue the first subpoenas to members of the NAACP.

CHAPTER 14
RETURN VISITOR

ANNABELLE SHAW SLOAT sorted through the morning mail, abruptly stopping at the return address with the name *Shaw, 2856 N. W. 26th Street, Washington, D.C.* The postmark was dated four days earlier. She hesitated for a moment, sensing that the note inside was not good news.

Dear Mrs. Annabelle Sloat,

I am writing to let you know that my mother, Ida Shaw, had a peaceful death two weeks ago. She was ninety-two. It has been a long time since we left Monroe, but your kindness and generosity were never forgotten. Because of you, we were able to begin a new life. Without your encouragement, my education would never have been possible, and for that I am eternally grateful. It was a long, slow progression. I spent early years making up for lost time, but with your support and my mother's insistence, I made it, albeit when I reached my early 40s.

After completing law school, I secured a position as a legal aide for the National Association for the Advancement of Colored People, where I have served up to the present time. Ironically, my current assignment will bring me back to Florida as an assistant to the legal counsel assigned to represent the state organization as it responds to the subpoena from the Legislative Investigative Committee, which your son, Senator Billy Sloat, currently chairs. Needless to say, I accept this charge with more than a degree of ambivalence.

I hope this letter finds you well and in good spirits. My mother talked of you constantly. Someday, perhaps there will be an opportunity to meet you again under different circumstances. Until then, please accept my appreciation for your good will and support.

Sincerely,
Owen Shaw

She folded the letter and placed it on the desk alongside the other mail. Her fingers twitched from the Parkinson's disease that had begun advancing more rapidly over the past year. She thought about Ida. She had been her companion, her confidante. She had been tough, had endured bad times and, against overwhelming odds, had lived to see her child amount to something.

Annabelle had watched her own son's passage to adulthood with disappointment at his contempt for anyone challenging his preconceived notions of propriety. And those dark secrets she relegated to memory— the turning point with the Klan and the shameful confrontations that followed. Disappointment. And yet it might have been she who had failed him. How else could she account for what he had become. She had provided him a home and material security, had sheltered him from the hard times she had known, and now he was the proud warrior ready to take on the NAACP, and nothing would stop him. But somewhere there was a lapse, something she had missed. Alone, with advancing tremors, she was wary of her approaching seventieth birthday. Money had provided comfort and satisfaction. Now both were elusive. Her life had been uneventful. She had accomplished nothing of significance. She had been a mere provider, with nothing to show for it except disappointment in her own son, whose ambition was politics and power. Would it not be good to go quietly as Ida had done? Instead, she held on with passive resignation. Yes, in many respects, Ida was better off.

On the desk was the photograph of Billy in his Sears Roebuck outfit that she had ordered through the mail, and next to him Owen. She studied the photograph of the boys, noting—not for the first time—the curious resemblance. Some things best left alone, she thought, best left where they are.

In the anteroom, next to the hearing room where the first session was set to begin, Billy Sloat waited with anticipation for the perfunctory introductions of the opposing participants. Hayward Renfroe would be a substantial opponent as chief counsel for the NAACP. He had already established his reputation in other legal encounters on civil rights issues. But This occasion was the most significant, pitting the NAACP against the state of Florida. The hearing room was already teeming with reporters and various state and local officials awaiting the imminent confrontation.

The senator rose from his chair as Renfroe entered, but halted at the presence of Owen Shaw, who followed his mentor into the room. He studied the face, the skin, the eyes, unmistakable features—Owen. He glared at the Negro, a year his junior but appearing years younger than his actual age.

"Hello, Senator," he said, extending his hand, "Owen Shaw," but Sloat ignored the gesture. Caught by surprise and disbelief, he was transfixed by Owen's presence.

Moments later, in the jammed hearing room, Sloat opened the committee's first public hearing before the overflowing crowd. Addressing Renfroe directly, he said, "Mr. Renfroe, are you prepared to comply with this committee's directive regarding membership records of the state-wide branches of the NAACP?" He emphasized the word *directive*.

"No, Senator, the NAACP does not recognize the validity of your *request*, and we regard the committee's *request* as a breach of constitutional rights," Renfroe responded.

"Mr. Renfroe, this is not a request. Let me repeat again, not a request. Your refusal to comply with this directive will place you in contempt of this committee, which is a lawful arm of the state of Florida. Will you comply with this directive?"

"No, sir." He cocked his head in defiance. "We will not be so coerced. We do not recognize the legitimacy of your request."

Sloat's eyes narrowed, and his mouth twitched. He glared at his adversary, the uppity nigger. "We have evidence that communist party members have infiltrated the NAACP. It is disgraceful that persons who claim to have a noble purpose in organizations such as yours won't help us get the facts."

Renfroe refused to comment.

Owen sat transfixed at the exchange between his mentor and an angry Billy Sloat, who was not accustomed to such defiance.

Now it was Borland Mayes's turn. He called the secretary of the Miami branch of the NAACP to the stand. She looked straight at him, her eyes steady and focused. He glared back, his voice rising. "Why do you refuse to cooperate with this committee? Why do you refuse to provide this committee with your membership list? What do you have to hide?" he demanded. She remained silent.

Renfroe jumped to his feet. "Because, Mr. Mayes, on constitutional grounds, Miss Davis is not required to provide that information."

Mayes fired back, "Any witness refusing to cooperate with this committee is not fit to be a citizen of this state."

"As you wish, Mr. Mayes. We will see you in court."

In the commotion that followed, Renfroe left the room, followed by Owen Shaw and the witnesses.

The next morning, Sloat sat pensively in the ante-chamber, fingers leafing through the transcribed procedure from the initial session. It had not gone well. He glanced at the stacks of newspapers and the headlines announcing the hearings and the disruptions that ensued. There on the front page was the photograph of Hayward Renfroe and next to him Owen Shaw—Owen either a pawn of the organization or, more likely than not, a communist infiltrator himself. So much, he mused, for his mother. She was responsible for this uppity bastard. He would never forgive her for this.

He glanced at his watch. Committee briefings would begin again within the hour. It was humiliating that he had to suffer defiance from such as Owen Shaw and his nigger mentor. He waited for the personal confrontation with Owen, who had asked to see him.

"He's here, Senator," the aide announced.

When Owen entered the room, Sloat remained seated. He leaned back in the chair, eyeing the Negro cautiously, a slight half-smile, half-sneer from his mouth. There was a momentary silence as the two men observed each other.

"Well, Owen," Sloat said, "you and your boss gave quite a performance in there yesterday. A fine performance indeed. Maybe you should have considered a career in acting rather than law, which you so clearly disrespect, if I may say, with contempt."

"It is precisely because of my respect for law that I chose this profession, Senator," said Owen.

Sloat's eyes narrowed. "In spite of what you think, I am a tolerant man. I bear no hard feelings against your kind, but as hell is my witness, I have no patience for the likes of you and your allegiance to that rabble flaunting the rule of law."

"Senator," said Owen, "we're not after tolerance. Tolerance is something offered, permission granted, if you will. For too long you have tolerated my kind, as you put it, with your contempt. That's over now. We don't want tolerance. We want respect. We want equality under the law. Separate is not equal."

"You can say that to me?" Sloat jumped from the chair and pounded the desk with his fist. "Without me and my mother, you would not be standing here today making a mockery of laws of this state. If not for my mother, you might just still be in Monroe shining somebody's shoes or riding a garbage truck in Tallahassee."

"Left to you, senator," he said almost in a whisper, "that is exactly what I would be doing, but for your mother." He walked toward the door, stopped, and not looking back, said, "Good luck securing the membership lists. You're going to need them, because without them, your committee is grounded. Hayward Renfroe will see to that." He turned one last time to catch a glimpse of Billy Sloat's rage.

—⁂—

SLOAT'S ATTEMPTS TO link the NAACP with communist organizations stalled on all fronts. In the months that followed, the committee failed to expose any links between the organization and any subversive group operating legally or illegally. If anything, the momentum of sit-ins and other protests increased.

A month before the legislature was to convene, Borland Mayes barged into Sloat's office. He had a document in his hand. His face was grim.

"What is it, Borland?" Sloat asked. He could tell from the wild look in Borland's eyes that the news was not good.

"The State Supreme Court has temporarily halted further investigations of the NAACP," he said, handing the summary to Sloat.

...The organization's objectives and activities are shown to be legitimate and there appears no compelling public need to warrant encroachment on the organization's rights granted by the constitution.

Sloat read the last sentence again, then crumbling the paper within his fists, hurled it across the room. Unless the court reversed itself, within the month, the legislature would scrutinize the committee's progress and, given the court's preliminary ruling, reconsider continued support. He looked at Mayes for some sign of direction but got only an empty expression. "Well, Borland," Sloat asked, "what now?"

"Uh...this is bad, Billy, really bad," Borland said, moving toward the window. Outside, the maple trees were showing their first signs of color, announcing an early fall, an unexpected change in the season. Sloat waited for him to continue.

"I hate to say, but this ruling is most likely the first step to a hearing before the U. S. Supreme Court, and you know what that would mean."

Sloat exploded. "God damn it. Are we the only ones in this state who understands what this is all about? The communists have infiltrated labor unions, the NAACP, the courts, even our schools, and we are made to look like fools. Look at this," he blurted out, pointing to a stack of books on his desk. "This is the trash they use to brainwash students," he said, picking up a copy of Lillian Smith's *Strange Fruit*, and flipping through the pages, "a white man carrying on with a black woman. And this one," he said, waving a copy of Steinbeck's *Grapes of Wrath*, "about our rotten capitalist system, and this—the most outrageous—advocating drugs, free sex, and a mockery of religion," he bellowed, holding a copy of Huxley's *Brave New World*. "This is the filth seeping into the universities like a sewer, indoctrinating our young, and no one gives a shit, while the communists feed their poison." He slammed the book on the desk. "And I'm made to look like the devil himself. Well, Goddamn it, I'll be the devil if that's what it takes to expose this."

"You are exactly right, Billy. I understand your rage. I share your anger," Mayes reassured him, "But I'm also a pragmatist. Time is against us, and we've been moving in the wrong direction."

"What in hell are you talking about," Sloat shouted. "You telling me that the NAACP ain't a communist front?"

"I'm saying we've been distracted by the NAACP. Of course they're complicit in all this, but they've got the protection of the courts, and the courts are going to legislate their agenda. Like I said, we've aimed at the wrong target."

"Wrong target?" Sloat asked incredulously, "Not the NAACP?" he repeated, "Then what?"

Mayes picked up another book from the stack on the desk. "This," he said, offering it to Sloat. "We have to get to the root of the problem—in the universities, where the communists peddle their propaganda under the guise of academic freedom, undermining the very principles this country was built upon. That's the wall blocking us, Billy, the evidence is right there. Those books on your desk."

CHAPTER 15
LIAISON

ON A COOL February day in 1958, Norton Brell resumed his regular visits to the courthouse men's room, where he often recruited subjects for photo shoots in a room he rented at the Midtown Motel. There the student could maintain anonymity and detachment from any reoccurring and unwanted contacts. He chose subjects from a wide range of body types, some muscular, others thin or corpulent, and every social type—from blue-collar workers to students and professionals, the full range of the male figure.

His obsession with the male body filled him with conflicting responses, at once desire and repulsion. He could accept neither his own nature nor that of the men he encountered. His photography was the outlet for his frustration and also an expression of self-loathing. But it wasn't just the photographs that held his interest.

—⁂—

B. J. HENSON was the perfect pick as chief investigator for the committee. His years in the Tallahassee Police Department as vice squad chief had given him connections throughout the state with other law enforcement units, and he was a master of interrogation techniques. Working directly under Mayes, he began undercover activities to identify communists, socialists, civil rights agitators, peace groups—any organization or anyone in the university engaged in recruiting America's youth to their ideology.

But his assignment to investigate radical faculty at the university led to an unexpected and major discovery that would entirely change the direction of the committee's inquiry, and its impact on the university and beyond.

Henson had completed his initial survey of records at the courthouse and came up with nothing of particular importance that connected two Jewish professors said to be associated with socialist movements. Leaving the records section, he stopped at the men's room. As he entered, a weasel-like individual followed him in, glanced his way, nodded, made eye contact. Henson stood in front of the basin, rinsing his hands as the student approached him.

Norton Brell looked around, making sure they were alone. "Haven't seen you here before. New in town?"

Henson knew instantly that this was an invitation. "Yeah," he responded, "just passing through."

Brell asked, "What do you do?"

"I'm a salesman,"

Brell looked away as he made his next move. "I'm into photography. Wonder if you might be interested in a little diversion," he said.

"What do you have in mind?"

"I'm set up in a room at the Midtown Motel. It's not far from here. Aside from a few bucks for your time, you might find the shoot interesting."

Henson dried his hands and said casually, "I've got an appointment right now. How 'bout we meet tomorrow this time?"

"Tomorrow then," Brell responded as Henson left the men's room.

THE NEXT DAY, Henson met Brell as agreed. But instead of going directly to Brell's rented room at the Midtown Motel, Henson insisted that they discuss the arrangements in advance of the photo shoot. Brell seemed annoyed by Henson's questions. How long had he been doing this? Who, besides the men he encountered in the men's room, were his subjects?

"Actually," Brell said smugly, "you might be surprised. They're not just pickups. I'm interested in a wide range of subjects. Some of them who offer their services are students, even two faculty members. But they all come from the same cut. It doesn't take much to appeal to their vanity."

Henson presented a smile that was virtually a sneer. "You mean, like me?"

"Well, that's universal. The handsome ones respond, the fat ones, even the butch ones like you. Are you interested or not?" Brell asked with growing impatience.

"Honestly," he said, "I'm interested in a little more than what you may be prepared to offer."

Brell felt a sudden arousal. "Like..."

Henson interrupted his response, "Like maybe I'm interested in more than just your photo shoot."

"All right, then. Whatever turns you on, it's O.K. by me. Let's move."

"No, I have to finish some business this afternoon. Give me your room number. I'll see you tonight."

As Henson walked away, Brell felt a wave of excitement. He could hardly wait for this latest encounter and the possibilities that awaited him in the room at the Midtown Motel.

—⁜—

HENSON KNEW HE was on to something, but he would need assistance in this unexpected development. He had known Clyde Munjay for several years, having met him at a law enforcement conference while Henson was still vice squad chief with the Tallahassee police department. The two had maintained contact ever since. Munjay was also extremely competent as a law enforcement officer, shrewd and efficient beyond what his youthful good looks suggested. On the surface he appeared unassuming, naïve even, and he used this to his advantage, but like Henson, he was ruthless once he was in pursuit of his subject. Munjay was now assistant campus police chief, and Henson had chosen him to help in this encounter.

Munjay was waiting for Henson in the lobby of the Rosemont Hotel. He saw him cross the lobby and move toward him.

"What's so urgent I had to drop everything and meet you here instead of on campus?" he asked, his voice betraying his annoyance.

"Because this has got to be kept quiet. You aware of the senate's investigating committee?" Henson asked, looking around the lobby to see if anyone was listening.

"You mean Senator Sloat's committee, the NAACP hearings?" Munjay answered. "Well who isn't. The hearings were a fiasco. Hell,

Sloat must be stupid taking on the NAACP. No way he would come out of that without a bludgeoning."

Henson looked around the room as he lowered his voice. "I think we may be on to something much bigger here than a few missteps with the NAACP." He leaned in close to Munjay and said with a whisper, "something that will blow the roof off this university."

Munjay persisted, "That's a bit melodramatic isn't it? Why the cloak and dagger secrecy?"

"Because the committee is empowered to investigate communist infiltration in the university," he said, "not homosexual recruitment."

Henson's remark caught him off guard.

"Homosexuals?" he blurted.

"No, homosexuals and communists," he said. "I'll need your help tonight."

—⁂—

THERE WAS A tap on the door. Brell glanced nervously at the clock on the bedside table. Seven o'clock. Opening the door, he invited the burly man in. A single lighting stand was set up in the corner of the dimly lit room along with the tripod and Leica M3.

Brell eyed his subject. Henson looked around the room. He seemed nervous.

"Do you have anything to drink?"

Brell turned to retrieve a Coke from the bedside table on the opposite side of the bed. Henson quickly unlatched the door, leaving an unnoticed crack.

"Thanks," he said as Brell handed him the Coke.

He took a sip, placed the Coke on the bedside table and stepped back to allow Brell a full view. Brell reached out to touch, but Henson gestured with his hand in a stop position.

"No, let me see you first."

Brell carefully, slowly removed his shirt, then his pants and began to slide the jockey shorts down when Clyde Munjay burst into the room and flashed the camera.

At first, the shock of what had just happened did not register, and then Brell became aware that this was a trap. He reached for his pants.

"No," Henson shouted, "just sit down, we're not finished yet," as Munjay took additional shots of Brell on the edge of the bed.

"Boy, you are in deep trouble," Henson said.

"Who are you? Why are you doing this?" Brell asked frantically, his voice cracking.

"I'm B. J. Henson, assistant chief investigator of the Senate Investigation Committee. This is Clyde Munjay, assistant chief of the campus police. Like I said, you are in deep trouble unless you cooperate with us."

"What do you want from me?" he pleaded.

"Your contacts, names," Henson said. "And details to help us in our investigation."

"And why should I do that? You've got no right to subject me to this. I want a lawyer."

"Listen here, you piece of shit. You'll cooperate or your ass will be out of the university by the end of the week and your name spread all over the *University Times Daily*," he snarled, teeth showing as he shoved his face close toward Brell's.

Brell shook convulsively, his eyes tearing, blurring the two adversaries looming over him. "Please don't do this, please."

"Then give us your cooperation and we may just forget this entire encounter," Henson assured him. Brell nodded in agreement. He just wanted to be out of here. Munjay produced a small pocket recorder, and the revelations began.

—⚏—

SLOAT AND MAYES were poring over Henson's latest reports on his investigation when Sloat's aide interrupted them. "There's a phone call for you, senator, Mr. Henson, says it's important."

Sloat took the call. "We're just reviewing your latest written report, Henson, and I'm disappointed. There ain't much here of any significance to the investigation," he growled.

"Forget the written report," Henson said. "What I've got is going to blow your mind." His voice resonated with excitement as he described the events of the preceding night.

HENSON'S ENCOUNTER OPENED a new set of opportunities. Mayes had been right about the futility of targeting the NAACP. Not that they were innocent of any communist activities, but it was too difficult to break them, given the protection of the pro-active courts. Now Sloat could see clearly what he had missed all along. Communists were using homosexual professors as tools for recruitment. Fuckin' fags.

Joseph McCarthy had recognized that tactic in his own investigations of communist influence, and J. Edgar Hoover, head of the FBI, saw how communist infiltrators used blackmail against homosexuals to enlist them as agents. Why had Sloat not seen this before? It was the ultimate way to infiltrate the universities, brainwash young minds, and convert the next generation to communism. Sloat was satisfied. *Let's see the courts react to this.*

Sloat arranged a strategy meeting in his senate office with Mayes, Henson, and Munjay. The two imperatives would be secrecy and surprise. Some of the procedures might be interpreted by others as underhanded, even unscrupulous, but they were dealing with a dangerous group, and it was necessary to use the same tactics that would be used against them.

To prevent scrutiny from the press and ensure that legislators would not interrupt proceedings prematurely, they would interrogate suspects secretly in private locations rather than in government venues. As a fact-finding body, the committee would be immune to the usual oversight of other government activities, and the strategy would prevent anyone from challenging the efficacy of the committee.

As chief counsel to the committee, Mayes would relay instructions to Henson and to Munjay. Henson would have an expense account to cover the off-site locations and to hire informants at his discretion. Once testimony was gathered, sorted, and evaluated by Sloat and Mayes, then and only then would it be open to the full committee and public scrutiny, and then to criminal prosecution.

Henson had his own strategy for surprise. Suspects would be summoned unexpectedly. A late night phone call or direct summons from a uniformed campus police officer would provide the element of surprise and intimidation to elicit cooperation.

Subjects would be seated at a table in the center of a room. A single light fixture dangling from overhead would illuminate the subject, intensifying anxiety. Interrogation would commence once the subject was warned of the consequences for not cooperating.

But Munjay had reservations about the procedures.

"Why the intimidation, the secrecy?" he asked. "What if the informants challenge us publicly for violating their rights?"

"They won't," Henson asserted. "Homosexuality is a felony in the state. Anyone going public would be guilty by association. Who'd want to risk that?"

"Still, the secret interrogations..." but Henson broke in before Munjay could finish.

"You're not dealing with the NAACP under protection from the courts. We'll offer special treatment to anyone cooperating, but perjury will be a criminal offense. Resistance?" he added, "public exposure! Any other objections?" Henson asked. Munjay had no further objections.

Acting on the initial confession of Brell, who had implicated several students and two faculty members, the committee was ready to pursue its investigations with relentless vigor.

CHAPTER 16
ACCEPTANCE

TWO YEARS AT the university had passed quickly. It was September of 1957, and David, now in his junior year, was closer toward a degree in veterinary medicine. William Lee and the humanities courses had been a welcome detour from the necessary but often tedious details of foundation courses required in his major. David became a voracious reader of the ancient classics, each encounter triggering unexpected associations, raising questions of purpose and direction in his life. For the first time, he was attempting to connect with something beyond practical goals in his career.

Among the Greek playwrights, Aeschylus in particular inspired him with his insight that out of suffering could come wisdom. He was far from wisdom and most likely would never achieve it. But the great thinkers of the past gave meaning to adversity, that out of it, character is nurtured, and this had sustained him whenever he thought of Stephen and what they had lost—until now. What character had he nurtured from adversity?

There was the estrangement from his mother, who had refused to accept his marriage to Barbara, his mother who had forbidden any contact between him and his father, and from a father who, for the past thirteen years, had made no attempt to connect with him aside from the gifts and the tuition, meant, somehow, to atone for his absence. What family was he left with, now that Greta and his mother had moved back to St. Louis?

There was Barbara. But had he done the right thing by her? Would an abortion have been preferable to her raising a child alone? It was, after all, a marriage of convenience, never consummated, an arrangement between two friends, attempting to address an unexpected problem. Now *he* was the absent husband and father, not unlike his own absent father. He had wanted to help Barbara through her unwanted pregnancy, but at eighteen, he had not considered the consequences beyond that—serving as a surrogate father and husband. What could he offer her beyond what he had already given? And what of Barbara's options, which would be limited at best? How—when—would she meet other men? Divorce was an option, but not without its own complications. The scattered weekends when he was home, when the child would run to him, and call out to him, made his entrapment even worse. He loved the child, and yet each encounter smothered him. There seemed no way out. He was overcome by guilt—that he was betraying the friend he had attempted to save. And adding to his confusion, other feelings—Zack.

He had become uncomfortably aware of Zack's presence, found himself wanting to touch him, to feel him, to know that there was something there beyond the separation he felt, and this intensified his isolation and his awakening desire. It had been three years without any intimate contact with anyone. He had had many opportunities, but between his confusion about himself and his feelings of guilt, he was emotionally impotent, and denied himself any external release with another person. No—no way out.

David wandered the campus in the darkness, maneuvering his way to the Hungry Gator. He found a seat at the end of the bar, ordered a beer, sipped it, and looked ahead into the mirror, noticing at once the figure entering at the other end of the room. Norton Brell.

"What a surprise, I've missed seeing you since the semester in Lee's class. How are things?" Brell asked casually.

David attempted a smile, but his depression forced him to search for some noncommittal response that would not be interpreted as rudeness. He tried to sound upbeat. "Actually, very good, considering. Next year I'll get an early jump on the vet program. And you? How's the photo business going?" he asked, feigning interest.

"Oh, I'm my own worst critic. Maybe I can snare you into a critique sometime."

"Sure, I'd like to see your work. Just say when," he said without commitment, taking a deep swallow of beer.

"Any more contact with Lee's classes?" Brell asked.

"I've taken two others as electives. Actually, we've become friends. You were right about him," he offered.

Brell said archly, "How so?"

"Remember that first week in his class, you told me that I wouldn't be bored. You were so right. Sometimes I've wondered if I made the right decision for veterinary school, I mean, there's so much out there to experience. Sometimes I wonder if I should've gone bohemian, seen the world before taking on college. William Lee has made a big difference in my outlook," he said, "in a good way."

Brell glanced around the room in a gesture of casual indifference. "Well, Lee knows how to turn on the charm, sounds like he's made another unsuspecting male conquest," he said with a trace of sarcasm as he turned back to David.

David felt a sudden flush of anger. "What's that supposed to mean?"

"Oh, look. He has a reputation of, how to say it, intellectually seducing his male students, especially the hunks, and I mean that as a compliment," he said raising an eyebrow.

"In that case," David countered, "I'm grateful for that intellectual *seduction*." He slammed the money on the counter, his anger like a knife slicing a path as he left the bar. "Enjoy your drink on me"

Brell made no response. He had fucked up again.

OUTSIDE, DAVID STOPPED at the phone booth on the corner. What was the number? He couldn't remember the number. He hesitated for a moment, then thumbed through the directory until he got to the L's. *Lee. William Lee.* He started to dial the number but quickly placed the receiver back onto the cradle. Another hesitation, but this time his fingers dialed the number before he would reconsider and hang up again. Several rings, then the familiar voice on the other end. "Hello, Lee here."

Fifteen minutes later, David was sitting in the room, awkwardly attempting an apology for the intrusion. "I'm sorry, I...didn't know anyplace else to...I shouldn't have..."

"Don't be silly, dear boy. Join me in a brandy," he said, pouring the liquor and offering it to his unexpected visitor. But he sensed David's anxiety. He had noticed the change in David's moods over the past several months, his withdrawal from conversation whenever Zack and David joined him for a weekend supper. Now there was something more troubling about this visit, a tension that was unmistakable.

"What is it? David," he barely whispered. David looked away, then back again, focusing on the professor, his eyes betraying his despondency, and then, suddenly, he placed both hands on Lee's face as if an indication of—what? Admiration? An offering? Lee smiled, placing his own hands on David's, gently withdrawing the offer.

"You're a good man and a fine student," Lee said. "So rare to encounter such sensitivity and intellectual depth at once."

David looked away to conceal his awkwardness at Lee's remark.

"Years ago, David, I cultivated a close friendship with one of the dons at Oxford. Oxford was a long way from Pine Bluff, Arkansas, and different in every way. It was my first time away from home, not to mention out of the country, and the experience was unsettling. But the don understood my uncertainty. He came to have an extraordinary influence on my life. I admired him and would have given anything to show my gratitude, but he knew better than I that it was only fascination, my offer, my own way of trying to show appreciation for who he was, what he had given me intellectually. His rejection came to mean more to me than any single experience until then. We remained close friends until his death, years after I discovered my calling as a teacher."

David did not cry aloud but could not suppress the tears. Lee understood for the first time the depth of his depression, which was alarming. He waited for some signal from him, but David sat motionless, unable to respond except for an empty stare.

After a long deep silence, he said to Lee, "I don't know how to handle all of this—these feelings—Zack. With Stephen, everything seemed natural. He was the only person I ever felt about that way, not like the love you feel for a parent. And then there's the thing with Barbara, and my problems with my parents—I feel like I'm losing control of my life. How did things get so screwed up?" he asked, with his voice on the verge of breaking.

When he had finished, Lee said, "Tell you what—stay here tonight. The sofa is yours. Tomorrow is Saturday. We'll talk about this then.

I think, David, this is the next stage in our friendship—a good one, I might add."

In the dark, lying on the sofa, David felt, for the first time, a kind of release. He closed his eyes and slept.

—⚏—

THE VOICE OUTSIDE his door shouted, "Phone call."

"For me or my roommate?" Zack shouted back.

"For you, Zack," the voice said.

Zack hopped out of bed, threw on some shorts and sauntered down the hall to the dorm phone. He recognized instantly the voice on the other end.

"Zack, we need to talk. Can you stop by? It's about David."

Zack detected the concern in Lee's voice. His heart pounded. "Is he O.K.?"

"Just come over," he repeated with some urgency. "I'll explain when you get here."

LEE TOLD ZACK about David's unusual behavior the night before, and his concern with David's apparent depression.

"I don't get it," Zack said. "Why this all of a sudden?"

"On the contrary, Zack, this has been building for a long time. I'm going to break a confidence here, something you need to know and that David has not shared with anyone here except with me just after we became friends."

"I already know about the relationship with Stephen," Zack said impatiently.

"It's not just about Stephen," he said, "It's also about his wife."

Zack's jaw dropped. *His wife!*

As Lee finished the account of David's marriage to Barbara, Zack Conner shook his head in disbelief. Why had David not told him? What did Lee expect him to do?

"Obviously," Zack said, "David doesn't trust me or else he would have told me about this himself. Looks as if I'm nothing more than just a distraction."

"David needs more than a distraction, Zack. Your loyalty and your personal feelings aside, David needs you more than he is aware."

"I know what you're suggesting, but he's not ready to let go of Stephen, let alone face himself. And now, a wife! Christ, if I made any move, I would lose him entirely."

"If you don't, we'll lose him anyway," Lee insisted. "You and I, Zack, well we're not exactly Vestal virgins. But, except for Stephen, David is new to all of this, and very confused. Listen, I have a friend who keeps a cottage over on the Suwannee River. Take David with you, spend some quiet time, let him open to you on his own terms. He's desperate, and he does trust you. And he needs you. Believe me," he insisted, "You're the one person who has the best chance of dealing with his denial and self-recrimination. Otherwise, I'm terribly afraid that he's reaching a breaking point with his depression."

"But he's had your trust. Why do you think I could make any difference?"

"Because it's not just a matter of trust, Zack. David needs more than distraction. He has to come to terms with himself. He needs acceptance."

―∾―

THE CABIN ON the Suwannee River offered perfect seclusion. The main road was almost a mile away, and the three-room cabin was nestled among scrub-oaks and palmettos with a clear view of the river from the porch with its tin roof. The path down the sloping ground led to a small, wooden dock where Zack and David sat, backs propped against the dock's posts, catching the last light from the sun, which had disappeared beneath the horizon. It was during the third weekend after their first visit that David opened up to Zack.

"I've been pretty lousy company lately," David said tentatively. Zack offered a smile but said nothing, allowing David to proceed on his own terms. David focused on the distant side of the river. "Reminds me of the Okefenokee, and that night Stephen and I spent in a cabin much like the one here." He looked at Zack, trying to read some response, but Zack remained quiet, the only sound the beginning murmur of the night creatures from the woods.

After a long silence, David said, "There's something I want you to know. It's complicated, and I'm sure you'll think I'm stupid." He paused again, this time looking directly at Zack, waiting for some response for him to continue, but Zack remained silent. "I'm married," he told him, this time anticipating surprise or shock at the revelation. But Zack just nodded.

"So?" Zack said, now looking directly at his friend.

"That doesn't surprise you?"

"Should it?"

"Well, in a word—yes. We've both traded confidences. Why would I keep something like that from you?"

"I don't know, why would you?

"As I said, it's a long, complicated story." And he proceeded to fill in the details about Barbara's pregnancy, his naïve attempt to help her, the loss of connection with his mother, and his father's abandonment of him. When David had finished, he reached over, taking Zack's hand. It was dark now, the only light the lone light from the cabin, steady, like a beacon. He could barely distinguish Zack's features, but he held fast to his hand. It was the first intimate physical contact with anyone since the night, in the Okefenokee, with Stephen, who had rejected him. He tightened his grip on Zack's hand, and Zack gave a firm response.

David said, "I'm not sure I'm ready for a commitment, Zack." Zack edged beside him and then, without the slightest hesitation, he pulled him close, their lips tentative at first then deliberate. That night, for the first time, when they had sex, David had taken the initial step toward confronting his unresolved ambiguities. He was no longer alone in coming to terms with himself. He had Zack.

CHAPTER 17
COMING TO TERMS

THERE WAS STILL the preoccupation with his father. It had been thirteen years since the night David's father had abandoned him. Why would he abandon him but continue the gifts each birthday? His mother had insisted that it was his attempt to assuage his guilt, but it was his mother who had forbidden the contacts, and it was she who had rejected David for marrying Barbara. And now there was the awkward arrangement with Barbara and her child.

Zack's support marked a turning point. David knew that the issues had to be settled, one way or another. He would begin by finding his father, and confronting him. He dismissed Zack's offer to come with him in the search. This was a journey for him alone, his next rite of passage, whatever the outcome.

On an early Friday morning, he drove the sixty-five miles to Jacksonville, and entered the marbled lobby of Seaboard Shipyards, stopping momentarily before the directory. It was just after his twelfth birthday that he had been in this place, and his father had refused to see him.

He took the stairs to the third floor, and entered the executive offices, where a middle-aged receptionist cocked her head and asked, "May I help you?"

David offered a slight smile. "I'm trying to locate someone—Walter Ashton. He worked here, years ago?" he said, his voice trailing into a question.

She looked at him curiously, vaguely aware of a familiar face, and said, "That was a very long time ago. Who are you?"

"He was my father. Can you tell me how to find him?"

She studied David's features now, unmistakable features of her former boss. "I'm sorry, we're not allowed to give out private information," she explained. "But Mr. Ashton was transferred to the corporate offices in Philadelphia years ago. You might contact the Philadelphia offices," she told him.

Moments later, David turned the car onto Main Street, and headed out on U. S. 301 toward Philadelphia. He got as far as Charlotte, pulled off the road and slept for several hours before setting out again. It was past midnight Saturday morning when he reached the outskirts of Philadelphia. He found a cheap motel, checked in and though exhausted from the drive, slept fitfully.

The next morning, he thumbed through the telephone directory. There were a dozen Ashtons listed. He skipped the obvious ones: Donna, Duncan, Edward, Frank, narrowing the search to the W's, and then the name grabbed him:

ASHTON, WALTER, 413 DRISCOLL STREET

He concentrated on the name, repeated it aloud, felt his heart race, looked at the bedside clock—8:30. He weighed his options, decided against contact by phone. Too risky. Besides, how could he be sure this was *the* Walter Ashton he was seeking? Too awkward. Instead, he would go directly to the house.

An hour later, he found the tree-lined street of what was an assortment of expensive row houses, and parked the car several doors down from 413. An attractive woman, walking a dog, passed on the opposite side of the street. Soon, a young jogger, eighteen or so, ran past. David focused his eyes on the house, mulling his strategy, considering various approaches, when suddenly the front door opened, and two men in running shorts and loose tee-shirts stepped out. He watched them intently as they descended the steps. The younger one, probably in his early forties, had the physique of a runner, his six-foot frame without a trace of fat. The other man was, David judged, in his mid to late forties, his body bulkier, but firm, obviously someone who took care of himself. There was no other sign of activity from the house.

This has to be it, David thought. But which one was Walter Ashton? Perhaps neither was the Walter Ashton he was searching for. The two men began jogging toward the parked car, and David slid down, not to be noticed as they ran past him.

A half-hour later, David saw in the rear-view mirror the two runners now walking briskly toward the house, not noticing him as they passed. He watched them enter, and close the door, and he waited, summoning his courage. Approaching the house, he rehearsed what he would say, then standing at the door, he hesitated before pressing the bell.

The door opened, and the younger runner, in a sweat-soaked tee-shirt, gave a curt nod and asked, "Yes?"

"I'm looking for Walter Ashton," he said directly.

The young runner frowned slightly and asked, "Who are you?"

David caught a deep breath, and said, "I'm David Ashton."

The young runner expressed surprise, processing what he had just heard, then turned slightly, and called out over his shoulder into the house, "Walt, come down here. Now."

The voice from inside called back. "What is it?"

"Just come," the runner replied, looking back at David.

The other runner was standing now, shirtless, just inside the door, beads of sweat wetting small mats of hair on his chest, and David felt a rush of blood, as his heart raced from the sight of the man standing before him. "I'm David," was all he could say.

Walter Ashton froze, the name resonating like an echo, and then spontaneously, he threw sweaty arms around the youth, and wept.

INSIDE THE LIVING room, Walter Ashton was still trying to comprehend his son's appearance, when he realized that David and Thomas had not been introduced. "David, this is Thomas," he said.

"Your roommate?" David asked curiously.

Walter hesitated, trying to find an appropriate response, then said, "More than that, David."

David let the words sink in. "Gay?" he asked finally.

Walter nodded. As much as he did not want to lose this opportunity with his son, he would not lie to him. The three men remained quiet, allowing the moment to take its course. Then David said to his father, "Can I ask you something?" He paused. "Why did you abandon me?"

The word *abandon* jolted Walter. "Not abandoned, David. I was exiled. When your mother pressed me about my being gay, she threatened to expose me if I ever tried to see you again—made me sign a statement to that effect. I didn't have another option. It was either that, or the end of my career, and that would have left all of us financially ruined. Do you remember that day when you were—what? twelve?—and came to the office, and I wouldn't see you?"

"Yeah, I remember," he said, his voice on the verge of breaking.

"It broke my heart. That's when I knew I had to leave. So I left, moved to the home offices here, and just eight years ago, I met Thomas," he said, casting a glance at him, "and he's been in my life ever since."

David tightened his lips into a frown. "How could she do that to you—to me?" In that instant, David hated her. "I never want to see her again—ever."

Walter placed his hands on David's shoulders, felt his hurt, then drew him close. "No, David. Don't. It's as much my fault. She felt used. I never meant to hurt her, never meant to hurt you. I love you, son."

David was crying now. Walter brushed David's wet face with his hands. The resentment David had borne for thirteen years was gone. There was so much to tell his father—Barbara and the marriage, his own acceptance of who he was, and now Zack.

The three men huddled close in silence until Walter asked in a whisper, "And you, David?" he asked. "What about you. Anyone special?"

David smiled. "Yeah—you."

———※———

THE GOLD HUE overtaking the trees announced that the North Carolina summer was over. Stephen marked the calendar. Two months until graduation. Then what? He wasn't ready for New York. He wasn't prepared to return home. And he hadn't a clue about what he would do after graduation if he avoided graduate school. But going home was definitely not a choice—in spite of his father's condition. The night of the performance, his first semester at Ridley College, convinced him of that. Was he that stupid to think that his father

would drive five hundred miles—for what? To see his fag son per-
form? No. Returning home was not possible. Even now.

Reluctantly he sorted through the correspondence about graduate fellowships. Penn State looked good, but the offer from North
Carolina was generous, even if the program lacked the draw of Penn
State. But he wasn't ready for New York, that was for sure, in spite
of Professor Durell's insistence that he would waste time pursuing
additional theater studies. Durell's enthusiasm for him aside, he had
to consider the fact that the intimate relationship, the casual sex
with his professor accounted for much of that. Still, he had another
month to decide. He could make up his mind after Thanksgiving,
couldn't he?

That was another matter. Should he go home even for Thanksgiving? David would of course be there with Barbara. What good would
come of it? David had a different life now. Wouldn't it just complicate
things? Then again, he could avoid them, couldn't he? All right, then.
He would go home for Thanksgiving, for his mother—he owed her
that for what she was going through with his father. But there would
be no contact with David.

CHAPTER 18
NEW GROUND

PROGRESS REPORT, WEEK OF SEPTEMBER 29, 1958,
CHIEF INVESTIGATOR, B. J. HENSON.

Questioning of several subjects, mainly students at State
University, has revealed considerable homosexual activities as
follows:

R. Landers, second year student, very uncooperative at beginning of deposition, later admitted his participation in homosexual activity at said university and gave disposition about
same along with three contacts.

D. Brown, third-year student, not a homosexual, is very helpful, continuing to work in close cooperation with this investigator and will act as informant to the committee.

It was learned that three subjects formerly employed at the
Ale House as part-time bartenders and also students at the university might have information. The subjects are J. Schmidt,
J. Williams, and one other whom we were only able to identify by his first name, which is Sam. Upon contacting them,
these subjects provided several names of individuals suspected
of being homosexual and one professor said to be "that way."
The informants indicate willingness to cooperate with this
investigation. One informant indicates that the professor, one
Edmund Dority, employed at the university infirmary as Chief
Pharmacist and Head of Student Health, is highly suspected
since on numerous occasions he has been observed with boys.

*One of the student informants also provided information on suspects
living in a house on Cross Creek, and those suspects are under surveillance at this time. Another suspect residing at 9907 3rd Avenue, for-*

merly of Balding, Utah, driving a 1954 Pontiac Convertible bearing 1958 Florida license plate 12W-98761, was observed in attendance and having dinner with two other males. Extent of this perversion is widespread. Surveillance will continue.

Sloat smiled with satisfaction. Finally, they were getting somewhere.

———

AT THE END of class, Nelson Bosnick collected the English compositions, dropped them off at his office cubicle and walked the five blocks to the courthouse, rounded the corner of the building and entered the men's room through the outside door. Immediately he caught sight of the young man standing inside. Bosnick glanced around the room, then at the young man, who in turn made eye contact and maintained his stance.

Bosnick approached the man. He glanced down. When the man offered a slight smile, the professor responded with an offer of his own. At that moment, Clyde Munjay flashed his badge and escorted the professor to the campus police office.

———

NELSON BOSNICK SAT at the opposite end of the table. He was frightened. His hands trembled as his fingers drummed on the table. Clyde Munjay waited for the man to calm down, then asked, "How long has this been going on, Professor?"

"A long time."

"How long?"

"A very long time. Since I was five years old."

Munjay maintained his calm approach, an impression of reassurance, and Professor Bosnick began to relax.

"Since you were five?" Munjay repeated the professor's response.

Since he was five, when he had watched with fascination the two young men wrestling in the pool, their taut muscles glistening from the wetness. Over the years he had tried to suppress his feelings, and the more he tried, the more intense was the desire.

At twenty-two, he started seeing a psychiatrist, who explained that his feelings were the result of a fixation on his mother. Subsequent meetings with the psychiatrist didn't help, and out of desperation he began dating a woman whom he eventually married.

During the first two years, reassured by the relationship with his wife, he felt for the first time that he had overcome his fixation. Then the following year, when they were vacationing in Italy, his desire was reignited by a young Italian, his brooding dark eyes and animal movements controlled, confident, inviting.

"And then what?" Munjay asked dispassionately.

"He fucked me."

"He fucked you?" he repeated with the same dispassionate tone.

"He fucked me," he whimpered.

"Did you enjoy it?"

"Yes—no—I mean at the time yes, then afterward it felt loathsome to me and I vomited. You cannot know...you cannot."

Munjay sat back again, indicating no judgmental response. He was patient and studied the professor without any sign of concern, waiting for him to regain his composure.

Bosnick felt a surge of relief and at the same time gratitude that now someone understood the hell he had struggled with for all these years.

"Well, we can help you. What we need is your cooperation. You can help us get to the bottom of this, and your cooperation will not go unnoticed. You do want to help us in this, don't you?"

Professor Bosnick wanted to cooperate

"We need contacts. Names."

—m—

PROFESSOR BOSNICK WAITED in the lobby of the Midtown Motel. He wanted to cooperate. It was time to confront his shame, his chance to expunge the loathsome secrets hidden for fifty-two years. This encounter in the courthouse men's room was a godsend. Here was someone who understood what he had fought most of his life, someone now whom he could trust. But in exchange, he had to cooperate. This was the opportunity for absolution. He would cooperate.

CLYDE MUNJAY OFFERED a reassuring smile and asked Bosnick if he was ready to give his sworn deposition. Professor Bosnick was ready.

Room 202 of the Midtown Motel was bare except for the folding table in the center and the lone light fixture, which dangled from the ceiling and over the center of the table.

Bosnick thought, as he sat on the opposite side of the table from Henson and Munjay, that it was reminiscent of some scene from Orwell's *1984*. The room was dark except for the lone light, which cast a glare on the individuals seated around the table.

Henson began. "You understand you are providing a sworn statement."

Bosnick nodded, saying he understood.

"Would you please state your name and occupation?" Henson said.

"I am Nelson Bosnick, Professor of English at State University."

"How long have you been associated with the university, Professor?"

"Since 1937."

Henson leaned toward him. "Professor, I would like to ask you some questions regarding other personnel at the university. Let's begin with Ellis Cohen. What can you tell me about Professor Cohen?"

"He is also in the English Department. He is rather pushy."

"Pushy in what way, Professor?"

"He's one of those liberal Jews, loud, opinionated. A troublemaker actually, always stirring up some kind of controversy. There are many complaints."

"What kind of complaints, Professor?"

"The books he assigns, the way he agitates students, even in department meetings, harping about segregation, discrimination, corruption, politics, issues that have absolutely no connection with the teaching of English literature. And of course the rumors"

"What kind of rumors?" Henson asked.

"That he is or was a communist sympathizer."

Henson leaned forward. "Interesting," he said, "very interesting. What is your association with him outside the university?"

"None," he replied.

"Have you ever seen this subject at the courthouse or in any of the university's men's rooms?" Henson asked.

"Perhaps five years ago, late one evening, standing outside on the sidewalk. He seemed embarrassed, I thought, but not in the men's restroom. As soon as he recognized me, he left."

"What do you think his motives were, Professor?"

"I wouldn't," he paused, "want to say, curiosity maybe."

"In your opinion, would you say this man is either a homosexual or has homosexual tendencies? Have you heard any rumors about this individual?"

"One time"

"Would you state the rumor, please, sir?"

"Someone—I'm not sure who—it was a person who had homosexual tendencies and he made this one statement, that Cohen knows how to have a good party."

"What else can you tell us about this man, particularly his opinions about politics? You mentioned his communist sympathies."

"He once said in a department meeting that we had no right to talk about communist repression when our own government represses people for things that are personal. And he once said how unspeakable it was that Wilde was railroaded because of repressive Victorian hypocrisy."

"Wilde? Who is Wilde?"

"Oscar Wilde, *the* Oscar Wilde, that notorious homosexual."

The remark piqued Henson's interest. "Who is this Oscar Wilde? Is he also in the English department? Where does he live?"

"No, not *lives*. Dead. Died last century. A literary figure."

Henson shifted in his chair, looked down at the list of names Bosnick had provided.

"Professor Bosnick, among the other names you gave to Mr. Munjay, you mentioned one Simon Prevatt, a professor of music. Was there a homosexual encounter between you and Mr. Prevatt?"

"I saw him at the courthouse once. There is a hole in the stall."

"Tell me about the hole in the stall."

Bosnick did not respond.

"Sir, did you put your male organ through the hole while Mr. Prevatt was in the next stall?"

"I...he refused."

"Professor, you did put it through, but he refused?"

"It was a long time ago. It's hard to recall what happened."

Henson shuffled some papers on the table, then continued his interrogation. "Among the names you provided Mr. Munjay yesterday was a John Collier, a professor of biology. You indicated that Professor Collier is a homosexual. What do you know about his homosexual activities?"

"He is a very troubled man. He told me that his wife has no suspicion of his inclination. He has tried to control his desires. He has seen a psychiatrist, but it hasn't helped. You can't know how difficult it is to live with something like this."

"What of his involvement with students, Professor?"

"Oh, nothing with students as far as I know, only fellows he meets at the Ale House and sometimes the courthouse."

"Nothing with students," Henson repeated. "And what of your activities with students, Professor?"

"Only on a few occasions. It's much too dangerous."

Henson paused momentarily, studying the list of names. "Sir, in regards to Dr. Edmund Dority, chief pharmacist and head of student health, would you relate to me what has happened between you and him?"

"I saw him in the restroom at the courthouse. Nothing has happened between us."

"Would you explain, please?"

"I saw him enter the stall and..."

"The stall with the hole in the side?"

"Yes, that one, and I followed in the other stall. I looked through the hole, but his penis was not erect. Then suddenly he got up and left abruptly."

"Have you seen the subject on other occasions?"

"Yes, I saw him in the men's room another time several years ago."

"In your opinion, would you say he is either homosexual or has homosexual tendencies?"

"I've heard a rumor or two. I don't know whether he would be the active or the passive member. I think it would depend on the person."

"It would depend on the person as to whether he would be the active or passive partner?"

"Yes."

"Then you would say he's homosexual," Henson stated with finality.

"Yes, I would guess so."

"Sir, you mentioned to Mr. Munjay a humanities professor, a Professor William Lee. Have you had any homosexual relations with Professor Lee?"

"No, sir. I've only heard rumors."

"What rumors, Professor?"

"Remarks, suspicions as to why he surrounds himself with young students, handsome students. Dinner parties at his house on occasions."

"In your opinion, would you say that Professor Lee is a homosexual?"

"I would say so, yes. Why else would he surround himself with male students? I've not seen the man more than five minutes outside the university, but his behavior—the students frequenting his house, the way he dotes on them—it's disgusting."

"What can you tell us about his teaching? How does he conduct himself with his students?"

"How do you mean?"

"His political views, his social outlook. Would you describe him as conservative in his views or a radical liberal?"

"Definitely the liberal side. There is quite a bit of nudity, I understand, in his presentations, slides of naked statues, especially male statues, which he claims are shown only as art, but nudes nonetheless. I am told by a colleague that he is critical of certain politicians."

"Can you be specific?"

"McCarthy for one, especially McCarthy. He has referred to him as a demagogue."

"And what is your opinion of the Senator."

"I don't have one."

"What else can you tell us about the man's homosexual lifestyle?"

"He shared his house with another man; it was at least five or six years. They were seen together at music and theater events on campus; they traveled together. There were all kinds of rumors. I thought it unbecoming they should be so close, two unmarried males shacking up together, as they say."

"Shacking up?" Henson asked.

"Why else would they flaunt their relationship like that?"

Another long pause. Henson lowered his voice. "Tell me how you feel about your own situation now, Professor," he said in a neutral tone of voice.

Nelson Bosnick squirmed, his body twitching from side to side. He had waited for this moment of absolution. "Well, I must confess, since I have talked to you and Mr. Munjay, I feel as if a tremendous burden has been lifted. I've told my wife, but she already suspected when we were in Italy." His voice quickened, his words more urgent now. "I tried. I prayed in St. Peter's Cathedral, knelt right at the place where St. Peter was buried, and begged forgiveness at the flagrancy of it. It's just about like I told you," he rambled on, "I have never smoked a cigarette, never taken a drag, this other thing, how it became a habit I don't know, but it's disastrous. I can see how something must be done about it." His face was a mix of agitation and relief.

"In other words, Professor, you feel this investigation should have been done a long time ago?"

"Yes, indeed, a long time ago."

"Professor Bosnick, at this time is there anything you would like to put on the record in your behalf?"

Now he was animated, and his words raced without stopping.

"It is really a relief to talk to someone who is aware and sympathetic and knows the problem, and I do want to try to overcome this and grow old gracefully and with honor and not lose everything I have because my estate is my profession and this could easily wreck everything."

Henson studied the subject, waiting for him to calm down. He nodded and said, "If that is all, we will conclude this for now. Thank you for your time," he said, "and your cooperation."

"One thing more, Mr. Henson," he pleaded, "Will there be any repercussions from my being found out?" He glanced apprehensively at Munjay and back to Henson.

Henson sighed, gave a bored yawn. "My job, Professor, is to find out the facts and give the facts to the committee. This is now out of my hands. Thank you, and good evening." Then he added, "Oh, and good luck by the way," dismissing the stunned professor.

—⁂—

PROGRESS REPORT, WEEK OF OCTOBER 6, 1958,
B. J. HENSON, CHIEF INVESTIGATOR.

Progress continues to be made concerning our investigation. Sworn deposition given the night of October 4 by Professor Nelson Bosnick implicates additional individuals on the faculty of the university. They are Ellis Cohen, Department of English, Simon Prevatt, Department of Music, Edmund Dority, Chief Pharmacist and Head of Student Health, John Collier, Professor of Biology, and William Lee, Professor of Humanities. Based upon evidence given in the attached deposition, said individuals will be summoned for sworn testimony. There appears to be widespread homosexual activity and definitely communist infiltration of the university.

Borland Mayes and Billy Sloat were pleased with the progress that Henson was making. Bosnick's deposition confirmed what they had suspected all along. The communists were using homosexuals to infiltrate the university. It was time now for Mayes to involve himself directly in the interrogations. Sloat would arrange a visit with the university's president and apprise him of their initial findings and the need to proceed with all diligence in the ongoing investigations.

CHAPTER 19
NEW FRIENDS

CHRIS CHADWICK'S FIRST contact with Zack and David was at the gym one Saturday morning a week prior to the fall term. A freshman at the university, the nineteen year old had already undergone a family trauma about his sexual orientation and took care not to establish close contacts with other students, particularly male students. He lived off campus, drove his car to the student parking lot, met his classes and left afterwards, avoiding unnecessary encounters. His only diversions from studies were the workouts at the local off-campus gym. It was there on subsequent visits that he noticed the two workout partners who were always together. It seemed to Chris that there was something more between them, a bond of sorts, an impression he could not shake.

He liked the easy interaction he observed between them, their frequent laughter, the unassuming smiles, a playfulness almost. He was mesmerized by their presence. He pictured their two perfect bodies fused together. In his mind, he imagined them as two lovers, confident, secure, devoted, unafraid of any rebuke that a family could hurl at them. He longed to know them, but the ordeal with his father before he arrived at the university was too fresh in his memory, so he maintained his distance.

It was David who broke the ice. The presence of the young student had made an impression the first time he saw him in the gym. He was not as tall as David, well under six feet. He had a body like a swimmer's, long, smooth muscles and a crew cut that rounded out the picture. *Damn, he's appealing.*

"What is your name?" David asked, with a forceful confidence.

The young student was taken aback by David's directness. "Chris. Chris Chadwick," he said with a trace of uncertainty.

"Well, Chris, I'm David and this is my good friend Zack, and we're glad to meet you. Why don't you join us?" It was more of a command than a question. Without the slightest hesitation, Chris accepted the offer.

"First year?" David asked. Chris nodded. "What's your major?" David asked.

"My dad wants me to major in business," he offered.

"And what do you want?" David asked.

"I'd like to study literature."

"Then why don't you?"

"My dad says it's not practical."

"Do you always take your dad's advice?"

"I've learned to," Chris replied. "Even though, most times, it bores me," he added.

"Well, I have some advice too. Ever heard about a professor named William Lee? You won't find him boring," David said with a broad smile.

—⁂—

NOT ONLY DID Chris Chadwick not find Lee boring, one week into the class and Chris was hooked. Well into the term, he abandoned the notion of pursuing a major in business administration. Whether his father liked it or not, he had made up his mind. He was going to major in literature. He even began composing free verse, which he showed Lee for his critical response, but most of all for his approval.

"Not bad," Lee would tell him. "A little surgery here and there, and you've got some lovely poetry." Chris thrived with Lee's encouragement. He had never felt so energized. By the time the semester had ended, he had become the newest addition to the extended family. His isolation was over. And yet, there was still the uneasiness, just when he felt liberated from what he knew waited back home with his father.

Zack and David perceived the boy's tentative acceptance of the friendship, but also a lingering fragility. Lee's involvement had boosted the boy's self-respect, but he still maintained an air of caution, like a young wild animal that had been wounded and was not yet fully trusting. They were determined to protect him and to earn his trust. Over the ensuing weeks, Chris became more relaxed when he was with them, gradually welcoming their friendship without reservations. On weekends in the fall, the three would make the trek up to the refuge on the Suwannee. There, with Zack and David, Chris could be himself, could accept David's and Zack's protectiveness and in return give them his absolute loyalty.

It was during one of the frequent retreats that he related his first and only aborted attempt at coming out. The three had made plans for the long weekend, but Zack had a makeup exam and would drive up early Friday evening in David's car. David and Chris loaded the weekend essentials in Chris's car, and forty-five minutes later they opened the cabin, popped beers and settled down by the river on the dock. The early afternoon sun sparkled on the water. The two, leaning against the dock pilings, were quiet, just taking in the diminishing autumn heat. Then Chris began for the first time the account of his coming out.

—✕—

HIS NAME WAS John. Throughout high school, the two were inseparable. John was his best friend and confidant. Their respective families were close, committed through their unquestionable religious faith and their support of the fundamentalist church that the two boys had been raised in since childhood. Chris's father was a strict disciplinarian and allowed no deviation from the religious values and traditions that he had instilled in his son.

He was a good provider, having been financially successful in the trucking company that he founded and brought to success over the twenty years since he started the business. He attributed his success to God's grace and never failed to give God ten percent of everything he earned. God had blessed him with prosperity, a wholesome family, and a prominent place not only in the church, but also in the community. He was especially proud of his son's academic accomplishments and his achievements on the high school swimming team. His was the perfect family.

The night of graduation from high school warranted a special celebration. At a local convenience store and with a five-dollar bribe, John bought an illegal six-pack, and the two were off to the dark, isolated athletic field of Denson High. Chris was at once both exuberant and apprehensive. Clearly he was into new territory. He had never in his life had so much as a cigarette, let alone beer. John was more confident, reckless even.

John had popped open the can and thrust the beer into Chris's hand. "Drink up, man," he had commanded. After the second beer, Chris could feel the euphoria as the alcohol numbed his senses, and then the sudden exhilaration as John began groping him. Chris shook with excitement as John unzipped his trousers. "Turn around," he said. Chris had stifled his initial cry from the sudden pain, and then, gradually, the pain gave way to a curious pleasure.

And then the flashlight cut through the dark, illuminating them.

That was the last time he saw John, whose father sent him to a special clinic down state. Chris's father arranged for therapy through the church counselor who assured him that his son's illness could be cured. And as abhorrent as it was to him, he believed it was a sickness; the boy would need his support, but with faith and persistence, he would be cured.

For the next month, the alternation of shock treatment followed by immersion in ice-cold water while photographs of male bodies were held in front of his face had its effect, and Chris confessed that he was *cured*, told his father how grateful he was that he had *stood by him* during those difficult weeks, had not *abandoned* him but had brought him back to *health*, to *normalcy*, to *sanity*.

His first Sunday back at home, the family attended church together, and at the end of the service, with the choir singing *Just as I am*, the preacher, his voice resonating with compassion, invited any sinner to come forward. Jesus wants you to come. To come. *Just as I am...come come...I come*, the congregation was singing. Chris raised his arms high over his head and proclaimed that God had saved him at last and he had answered Jesus's plea to come.

WHEN HE HAD finished, David looked at him and said quietly, "Time for a swim." He stepped out of his cutoff shorts and dove from the dock with Chris following. The two swam to the other side and back and pulled themselves up onto the dock. They rested there, the warmth of the sun eventually drying their bodies.

Chris edged close in toward David, resting his face, eyes closed, against David's chest. David studied the boy's features, the full mouth, the thick, blond, brush-cut hair; except for the brush-cut, Chris bore a remarkable resemblance to Stephen, particularly in his vulnerability, which now had given way to total trust.

In silence, David watched the boy. It was a moment from his past that he was once again experiencing. He was conscious of his arousal as he took in the smell of the boy's hair, touched the firm brown tan of his skin.

Chris opened his eyes and saw David's erection. Abruptly, David got up, trying to conceal his embarrassment, and heading toward the cabin said, "I'm going to jump in the shower."

Moments later, he turned the shower on full blast to the cold position, but his erection was stubborn. *Damn.* Finally the sensation eased, he turned off the water, grabbed the towel, and saw Chris watching from the open door. The boy approached slowly, placed his arms around David's waist, held him tightly for a moment, and then lowered himself.

In the bedroom, with his eyes closed, David saw not Chris but the face of another fragile youth, felt the heat of another body, recaptured in that moment sleeping memories, felt Stephen's presence.

AFTERWARD, THEY LAY quietly side by side, Chris, eyes closed, David staring at the ceiling. A wave of sadness and regret flooded his mind. He looked down at the boy now sleeping, his hand in David's hand. The boy had given him his total trust, and what had he given in return? The boy was vulnerable. They were both vulnerable, but he had exploited Chris's vulnerability. *Fuck!*

Carefully, quietly, David gently released the boy's hand and edged out of the bed. Outside on the cabin's porch, he fixed his gaze on the diminishing light as early evening gave way to darkness. In the distance was the sound of a car, and moments later Zack was trudging up the path to the cabin. He saw David sitting alone on the steps. David gave no indication that Zack had arrived, just sat there gazing out at the deepening night.

What's wrong here?

Zack sat down and waited. David looked at him. "I screwed up," he said and related the afternoon's events, starting with Chris' account of his aborted coming out and then the encounter that followed.

"He's just a kid. He trusted me. He didn't deserve this," David said, looking at Zack, "and neither did you."

Zack rested his arm on David's shoulder, moved in close, looking directly at him and said, "You don't owe any apologies. I'd be lying if I said that you weren't the most important person in my life. But you've been straightforward about us, no commitment, no expectations. Wish there was more than just the sex, much as I love it, but I know you aren't ready to give up what you had with Stephen. Maybe someday you can. Maybe someday you and I could have something like a real commitment. Until then, I'll accept you just as you are. And as for Chris, he's damn lucky you were there for him to begin his own healing. Now what's for dinner?"

THE THREE OF them finished supper in silence. Zack glanced first at David then at Chris, waiting for someone to end the awkward silence, but the only sounds that intruded on the silence were from the night creatures outside in the darkness that hid the cabin.

"Well, fellas," Zack offered finally, "I think the two of you have some settling to do. I'm going to bed. See you in the morning." He smiled first at Chris, then at David, got up from the table and left them to contemplate the future.

David settled on the steps to the cabin, and moments later Chris was beside him. David avoided eye contact with him, staring into the darkness, trying to find the right words, but all he could bring himself to say was "I'm so sorry, Chris," and now he was looking directly at him, waiting for some response, any response.

"Please listen, David. I was the one who approached you. You don't owe an apology. That night with John—it was the worst night of my life, and afterwards, when they were through with me, I never thought I could accept myself for who I was—who I am. I love you, I love Zack, and I love Lee. You are my family, and I want to thank you for making me feel good again about myself."

David turned to him, overwhelmed by the boy's attempt to reassure him. "Want to see a grown man cry?" He was searching for an appropriate response to this gift of absolution, but the only words that came were expressions of relief and gratitude.

"Thank you, Chris. Thank you," was all he could say.

They sat for a moment longer, then David got up, went inside to the bedroom and quietly eased into bed beside Zack, careful not to wake him.

CHAPTER 20
LATE AUTUMN, ROOM 202

SIMON PREVATT HAD already begun his lecture in his music appreciation class when B. J. Henson barged into the room, took a chair in the back and began taking notes. The students glanced quizzically at one another, reacting to the appearance of the stranger and the professor's obvious surprise. "Excuse me, Mr...." He paused, waiting for some reply from the stranger.

Henson said, without looking up, "Don't mind me, I'm here on official business. Please continue, Professor. We'll talk later."

Prevatt wanted to ask what official business was the cause of this unexpected and uninvited intrusion, but instead resumed his presentation with more than a slight trace of anxiety. He tried to concentrate on the lecture but sensed that something terrible was happening. *Who is this man? Why me? Why now?*

And then, just as Henson had barged uninvited into the class, he got up abruptly and left. Prevatt stood motionless as the students gaped in astonishment.

—⁂—

THE PHONE WOKE Edmond Dority from a sound sleep. He switched on the bedside lamp, squinted at the clock. Who would be calling him at five past midnight? "Hello," he growled.

"Dr. Dority?" an unfamiliar voice asked.

"Who is this?" he asked, irritated by the call.

"Dr. Dority, your homosexual liaisons are catching up with you," the voice on the other end whispered dispassionately.

Edmond Dority suddenly bolted from the bed, heart pounding. *Blackmail?* "Who the hell are you? What do you want?"

"I want you to get dressed, now, and come to the Midtown Motel, Room 202. If you are not here in the next half-hour, you will be in crap up to your eyebrows," the voice said, and then the connection was ended.

Dority's hands shook as he fumbled with the shoelaces. *Blackmail. Jesus Christ. Blackmail. Who?* Thirty minutes later he was standing outside the door to Room 202 of the Midtown Motel, his body shaking with anticipation.

Inside, Room 202 was bare except for several straight-back wooden chairs on either side of the table centered beneath the overhead light fixture. A recorder was placed opposite the side where Dority was seated. Henson began the interrogation. "I am B. J. Henson, assistant investigator for the Senate Investigation Committee, and this is Mr. Clyde Munjay, with the university police department. We have reliable information about your homosexual activity. It is in your best interest to cooperate with us in our investigation. Those people who do not cooperate, and we have had a few, may find themselves faced with criminal prosecution. Homosexual acts are a felony in this state, as I am sure you know."

"And just who provided you with this *reliable* information," Dority asked.

"That is privileged information," Henson said.

"In other words," Dority said, "I am not privileged to know my accuser. I think it is in my best interest to have a lawyer."

"Dr. Dority, our informant has provided particular details about your activities. You can seek legal counsel, but the fact remains that you are a practicing homosexual, and it would take one hell of a lawyer to keep you out of prison. And supposing you did not end up in prison, a public trial as to your innocence or guilt would be sufficient to ruin you professionally. People who cooperate might avoid criminal proceedings. Do you understand that?"

"What do you want from me?"

"We want to know the extent of this condition around the university and determine the measures to correct the situation. Now for the record, I would like to ask you some questions. What is your present position with the university?" His tone was cold, formal.

"I'm chief pharmacist and also head of student health."

"What are your duties as chief pharmacist?"

"To purchase all drugs for the university, fill all prescriptions at the infirmary and the orders for the clinic ward."

"Do you maintain the pharmacy shop?"

"Yes, for the students."

"At the university. Is that correct?"

"Yes, for the students."

"Are there others on your staff, or what is your setup there?"

"I'm the only registered pharmacist. We have four students who work in the pharmacy, four pharmacy students."

"Is that part of their training?"

"Yes."

"What homosexual activity do you engage in with your students, Dr. Dority?" Henson interjected.

With that question, Dority stood up, his voice calm and accusing now. "You summoned me to a motel at midnight on the pretext that an unnamed informant has accused me of homosexual acts, and you are coercing me to cooperate in your investigation or run the risk of public exposure. That sounds like blackmail to me. You can damn well put your questions to my attorney. Otherwise, fuck off," and he bolted from the room.

Henson tapped his fingers on the table. "Well," he remarked to Munjay, "he's managed to elude us for now. But we'll nail him yet."

Simon Prevatt would not be so fortunate.

—⁂—

PRESIDENT DWIGHT THURGIS looked again at his watch. The meeting with the senator was scheduled for nine, and Sloat was already fifteen minutes late. He studied the list of professors, college employees and students that Henson had provided. This was fast becoming a messy investigation. Astonishing. Even his long-time friend Elmore Simmons on the list. Who could have imagined the dean with a twenty-year tenure on such a list? There had to be some mistake. Not Elmore. And there was the math professor who had come to him for support, insisting that the committee, without any substantiated evidence and based solely on hearsay, was attempting to coerce and intimidate him with threats against his reputation and public exposure unless he provided names. *Where in hell is Sloat?* He glanced again at his watch. Moments later, Sloat arrived.

"Sorry to hold you up, Dr. Thurgis, but as I'm sure you know by now, we have a large mess on our hands at this university. Here," he said, thrusting an additional list before the nervous president. "Just got these—more names. So far, forty suspects and growing, and we're just in the first weeks of this investigation. What's so alarming is the students being infected. Now I know you want to help us weed this out, and I want you to know you will not regret helping us along with this."

"Well, of course, senator, but I must tell you I do not appreciate the heavy-handed tactics of Mr. Henson. I would just as soon not have anything to do with the man."

"Do you mean to sit there, Dr. Thurgis, and tell me we should go soft on these deviates? Well, let me tell you, we will use any tactic to get to the bottom of this—whatever it takes to flush out this infectious subversion. This is more than just a bunch of fags on your staff. They are tools of communist infiltrators, and nothing you or anybody else does is going to interfere with this investigation and the methods we have to use to fight fire with fire."

"No, no, I didn't mean we wouldn't cooperate. Of course, I'm concerned about this situation, but the university's reputation is on the line here, that's all I meant. It's just that there are rumors surfacing that this is turning into some kind of witch hunt."

The words *witch hunt* elicited an even stronger outburst from Sloat. "Listen here, Thurgis, this ain't no witch hunt. We got no intention of causing harm to any innocent individual. But if we can save even one student from this corruption, it will be worth it. Now as to our so-called 'heavy handed tactics,' as you put it, we will use every means to ferret out these people. If they are innocent, they got no need to fear this committee. I must warn you, doctor, our procedures will require the university's unquestioned support. I wish this could go in a more civil manner, but with what we're dealing with here—these civil rights agitators, the homosexuals, those so-called *peace-groups*—well, let's just say I hope you don't try to stand in our way."

No, Thurgis assured him, neither he nor the university would interfere with the investigation, and he was prepared to take any direct action that was required as a result of the committee's reports. After all, the reputation of the university was at stake.

———⚉———

Simon Prevatt was halfway into his music lecture when Henson barged into the classroom, accompanied by the department chair and Munjay in his campus police uniform. "Professor Prevatt, please come with us," Henson demanded.

The department chair turned to face the astonished students. "Your class is dismissed for today." The three intruders left the room with the suspect in tow.

Inside Room 202 of the Midtown Motel, Simon Prevatt sat across the table directly in front of Borland Mayes. Henson sat to his right, Munjay to his left, and at the far end of the table Billy Sloat sat quietly, observing the fidgeting witness. When Mayes had finished the preliminary introductions, he turned to Prevatt.

"We have been informed, Professor, of your association with certain peace-groups, and your homosexual activity. You are aware that homosexual behavior is subject to years in prison upon conviction." He paused momentarily, staring directly into Prevatt's eyes, and waited for a response. Prevatt's mouth twitched. Beads of sweat covered his forehead. He nodded his understanding. "Now, Professor," Mayes continued, "I want you to know that people who cooperate with us may avoid criminal prosecution or any criminal procedures for that matter. Will you give us your cooperation?"

Prevatt nodded his willingness, and Mayes started the recorder.

"Sir, would you state your name and association with the university?"

"I am Simon Prevatt, professor of music at State University."

"And, Professor Prevatt, you are voluntarily offering this testimony without any coercion from this committee, is that correct?"

"That is correct," he answered.

"Without any coercion," Mayes repeated.

"Without any coercion," Prevatt responded.

"Then Professor, please tell us what you know about one Professor William Lee. How long have you known him? What contacts of a personal nature have you had with him?"

"It was right after I came here, two years ago. He's on the humanities faculty, and I was just appointed to the music position. He told me that he was an opera buff and very much into music and asked if I would like to come over to his house and check out his record collection."

"And what occurred when you visited his house?"

"Well," he paused, "well, just listening."

"Professor, you *are* aware of the man's reputation as being a flagrant homosexual!"

"I have overheard some talk, wondered if it was true, but I have never engaged in any discussions with him concerning that."

"Don't you know he has the reputation of being perhaps one of the worst homosexuals out there as far as students are concerned?"

"No, nothing definite about such talk."

"I'm not asking you for anything definite. I mean his reputation. What is said and rumored out there."

"I hear rumors, but..."

"What do you know about his illicit living accommodations with a man known to have been his previous lover? Did you meet the man's lover?"

"No, they were no longer together when I arrived here."

Mayes stopped the recorder and leaned forward, his face inches from Prevatt. "Now, listen, and listen closely. We know about Lee's homosexual activity, and we know about your activity. What we need from you is an acknowledgement of the man's behavior."

"I...we...there was never any overt contact," Prevatt answered.

"I think you're lying."

"No, he protested, "that is not so."

"Sir, you indicated you would cooperate in exchange for our not turning you over to the state attorney for possible prosecution. You understand your own reputation and position at the university are in jeopardy here."

He started the recorder again. "Professor Prevatt, I would like to ask you again what occurred when you arrived at Professor Lee's house," his voice once again steady, controlled, professional.

"He...after talking for a few minutes...he..."

"He WHAT, Professor Prevatt, what happened next?" Mayes insisted.

"He approached me for an...immoral act."

"A homosexual act?"

"Yes, a homosexual act."

"Did he commit a homosexual act?"

"Yes," he mumbled.

"Would you repeat that?" Mayes urged.

"Yes, a homosexual act."

"In his house?"

"Yes, in his house," he answered, his voice breaking.

Mayes continued. "Now, Professor, I realize this is probably embarrassing to you, and it is to us, but I want to know the extent of the act he committed and the act that you committed on him."

"I didn't commit an act on him," he protested.

"Then it was he who performed the act on you," he said. "Did he give you what is commonly referred to as a *blow job*?"

"I..."

"Did he, Professor?" he demanded.

Reluctantly, he answered, "Yes."

"What homosexual acts have you had with any students that you know of?"

"I have had no acts with students that I know of."

"That you know of?"

"That is," he hesitated, "that is correct."

Mayes arched an eyebrow, gave a slight smile and said, "As you are under oath, is there anything you would like to add or change in what you've said before us today?"

Wiping the sweat from his brow he said, "No, nothing."

"Thank you, that is all professor," he said, "for now."

When he had left, Sloat merely nodded his approval at Mayes's close up interrogation technique and the cooperation they were getting from President Thurgis. He couldn't wait to give a report to the full committee.

—ᴡᴡ—

IT WAS EARLY November, 1958. Clyde Munjay's desk was cluttered with random pieces of paper—traffic citations, complaints of noise from late night parties in the dorm rooms, dull minutes of routine campus security meetings, all boring pieces of trivia. He held the burger in one hand, mustard dripping from the corner of his mouth as he again read the recent list of names that Henson had passed along. Now, finally, he was part of something really big, something turning out to be not just the most significant event in the university's history but one with far-reaching consequences beyond the university itself. And *he* had been selected to coordinate this end of the investigation, to be a part of this history-making event.

With his free hand, he wiped the trace of mustard from his mouth, finished the burger, and tossed the paper wrapper in the trashcan beside the desk. His one o'clock appointment had arrived. He motioned for the student to be seated.

"I appreciate you taking time to see me," the student said.

Munjay ran his tongue over his teeth, clearing the last remnants of food, swallowed, and said, "What brings you here?"

"I've heard talk," the student said.

Talk. Suddenly Munjay was interested. "What kind of talk?"

"That there's some kind of investigation going on."

"Investigation," Munjay repeated, propping his elbows on the desk and leaning forward.

"About queers on the faculty," the student said casually. "If that's true, I thought you might like to check out the humanities professor I had."

"Who would that be?" Munjay asked.

"William Lee," the student replied.

"O.K., I'm listening," he said, touching the record button on the recording device at the edge of the desk.

"I really worked hard in that course. Never missed classes—O.K., maybe a class or two now and then, a few on some special occasions, but I always made up any tests I missed and at the end of the course, when I went to see him about my final grade, he said he would consider raising the C with what he called some extra credit activities."

The student had Munjay's undivided attention. "What kind of extra credit activity?"

"An A in exchange for a blow job. Of course I refused. And he told me if I wanted to contest the C, I could take it up with the dean."

"And did you take this up with the dean?"

"I did go see Dean Simmons, told him about this, and he said that he would pursue it, but first he wanted me to put all this in writing. Only if I would put it in writing."

"And did you give Dean Simmons a written statement about the incident?

"Well of course not. Would you? Who's going to win in a situation like that, me or him? And besides, far as I know, Dean Simmons might be queer himself, defending someone like that."

Munjay sat quietly for a moment and then in a very solemn voice said, "This is a very serious allegation, and Professor Lee could lose his job over it. Are you willing to give a sworn statement about this allegation?"

The student's face betrayed a hidden satisfaction as he replied, "I will."

CHAPTER 21
ELMORE SIMMONS

THE STUDENT'S REMARK to Munjay was not the Committee's first suspicion of a homosexual link to Dean Simmons. Other informants had suggested some possible connection. Unfortunately, they could offer nothing substantive or else were unwilling to.

"Get Bosnick again," Henson said. "Find out what he knows about Simmons. Tell him we might be able to offer some special consideration if he can help with this."

Dismissing class early, Bosnick arrived at Munjay's office exactly at 11:30 PM...

Munjay offered his hand, asked Bosnick to be seated, gave a reassuring smile and asked him if he would like coffee or something else to drink, and then got to the point.

"You have been very helpful to us in this investigation, Professor, I want you to know that," Munjay said.

"I want to help in any way I can. Can you tell me if there will be any repercussions with my helping you?"

"I think we can make this easy for you, but we need to be sure you're sincere in helping us, that you've told us everything you know, or just the things you want us to know."

"Could I...could I please have some water?" Munjay handed him the glass. "I've told you what I know, that is the truth," he said, spilling the water on his shirt.

"But is it the WHOLE truth?" Munjay asked, maintaining his calm and reassuring tone, while adding a suggestive warning. "How long did you say you have been with the university? Twenty years or more?" he asked, already knowing the answer to the question. "You told us that this thing had been going on since your childhood. What are you prepared to tell us about your early experiences at the university from the time you joined the faculty?"

Bosnick was slow to react to Munjay's question. "There were things, occurrences, that happened, but that was a long time ago. What does that have to do with what you are looking into now?"

Munjay gave a quick glance of disapproval, looked at his watch, and said, "I'm afraid I am wasting your time, Professor. Good day," he barked, as if dismissing a reluctant child seated opposite him.

"No, wait, I do want to help you, as I have said already. I do want to put all this behind me, to clean the slate, so to speak, and get on with my life," he said, his voice cracked with desperation.

"Then tell me what you know about..." he paused, "...Dean Simmons."

Bosnick's face went white. *Simmons!* His mind raced back.

It had been only the one encounter, twenty years ago. Both were young then, and Elmore Simmons was still single. Neither of them had particularly enjoyed it, especially Bosnick. Just a passing thing, nothing more. But it had provided the emotional support that Bosnick needed. Simmons was the one person whom he could trust—the one person who empathized with him, who never passed judgment. Simmons was a bisexual and had had relations with both men and women. He understood the stigma one carried as a result of one's sexual nature. Simmons had been quick to remind Bosnick of the difference between an encounter and a commitment, whether male or female.

Then there was the abrupt disconnect when Simmons announced his engagement to a woman named Ruth. The isolation that had followed left Bosnick alone to cope with his sexuality and his guilt. After the marriage, the only remaining contacts between Simmons and him were strictly professional. But Simmons never once made an unkind remark about him, or about the disgusting sickness Bosnick concealed, not even after he became dean.

When he finished, Bosnick wondered if he had done the right thing telling the young officer about this encounter that happened over twenty years ago. But Munjay assured him that he had. Now it would be Simmons's turn to tell all that he knew.

—◊—

"YOU WANTED TO see me, Dwight?" Elmore Simmons asked as he entered the university president's office.

"You had better sit down, Elmore," Dwight Thurgis said solemnly. "I have some unpleasant news."

Simmons sat himself in the dark-brown leather chair opposite the president's desk. At other times when he would visit the president's office, Thurgis would sit in the adjacent chair, creating an air of casual informality. This time, he remained behind the formidable executive desk, which served as a barrier between the two men. "It's about the committee, about you and Bosnick."

Bosnick.

Simmons said nothing, waited for Thurgis to continue. Then Thurgis said, "What else should I know about you and Bosnick?" as if passing sentence on a convicted suspect.

"There was one encounter. Twenty years ago. And I have had no other encounter with anyone since I married Ruth, no one."

"Well, be that as it may, I am not in a position to defend you. The committee has brought this to my attention. They're preparing a summons for your interrogation, and they expect me to act on this. I think it is in everyone's best interest if you just quietly resign and leave before they can summon you."

"You mean in your best interest, so that you can avoid taking a stand against this witch hunt."

"No, to spare everyone, you, me, the university, the embarrassment."

"It's all quite simple. I unexpectedly and, as you say, quietly resign midway through the semester and vanish—just like that," he said, snapping his fingers. "And then what? What do I do then, Dwight?"

"Look, this is nothing personal. Personally, I could care less about your extra-curricular activities, whatever they might be. You have to understand the reputation of the university is at stake here. Sloat, with not so much as a phone call, can slash support for this university if he chooses. He can make things very difficult. If you become associated with his investigation, your own reputation will be compromised. Leave quietly, claim to have health issues, wait this out and then start over someplace else. You have had a sterling record up to now, take your winnings, leave while you're ahead," he pleaded.

"What are you running here, Dwight? A university or a gambling casino? I thought this was a place for the exchange of ideas. Instead, it's become a venue for the exchange of compromises. You compromise your principles in exchange for Sloat's political favors. The university is cleansed of the riffraff, and Sloat is assured of victory in a second run for governor while everyone applauds the success of his witch hunt crusade, a real win for everybody. You're right, Dwight, it isn't anything personal. You have to have a commitment to people for it to be personal."

Thurgis shoved the letter of resignation across the desk. "For your own good, sign this," he demanded.

As he was leaving the president's office, the secretary offered a broad smile. "Isn't it a lovely day?" she remarked cheerily. "Such beautiful fall weather we're having, Dean Simmons, don't you agree?" Simmons did not hear the greeting. He just stared ahead and quietly walked through the door and down the long hallway alone with Dwight Thurgis' pathetic voice still ringing in his ears.

—∞—

LATE AFTERNOON. THE car pulled up next to the curb in front of Ruth Simmons's house. The weekly bridge gathering had run later than usual, and it was dusk now as Ruth got out of the car.

"Thanks for the lift, Louise."

"Next week?" her bridge partner asked. Ruth nodded.

Approaching the house, she noticed their own car parked outside the garage in the driveway. *Why is the car in the driveway?*

The front door was locked. She fumbled for her house key and entered the darkened hallway. "Elmore?" she called, switching on the small table lamp just inside the door. "Elly?" she called again.

No response. She dropped her purse on the living room sofa, removed her hat and the delicate white gloves and continued toward the kitchen and the doorway to the garage.

"Elly?" she called again.

Slowly she turned the knob of the door and peered tentatively into the darkened garage. And then she saw him, the faint outside light barely revealing his motionless body dangling from the rope fixed to the rafters.

IT WAS SEVERAL days after the funeral that the letter arrived in the mail, the envelope, with no return address, addressed to her. She recognized instantly Elmore's handwriting.

> Dearest Ruth,
>
> I know this has been hard for you but I want you to know, no matter what you may hear to the contrary, that I love you and have never broken my commitment to you since our marriage. The eighteen years we have had together have been the happiest years of my life.
>
> I wish there had been an alternative to this, but there was no other way that I could find. My good friend William Lee can explain the circumstances, and I know that he will help you through this. Ask him about Nelson Bosnick.
>
> The retirement proceeds should provide you comfortably as you get on with your life as you must, and as I pray you will. Please find it in your heart to forgive me. I love you.
>
> > Elly.

She read the letter a second time. *what you hear...no other way...Lee... circumstances...love you.* She reached for the phone, dialed the number, and after several rings, the voice on the other end said, "Hello, this is William Lee."

—⁂—

IN LEE'S STUDY, books—floor to ceiling, Oriental rug, smell of leather, scent of books, cat perched on sill, on the fireplace mantel a picture of former lover, mismatched furniture, character, warmth, aroma of green tea.

"Ruth?" William Lee repeated, "Ruth?" his voice interrupting her random thoughts. So much of the room reminded her of Elly's study except for the cat. They had no pets. Pets could tie you down. What would you do with pets when you traveled? Better not to be tied down during those long summer breaks when you were roaming the world, just the two of you.

"Sorry, William. My brain is so scattered." She held the tea, taking in the aroma, her fingers encircling the cup as if she had received an offering. "Elly never cared for coffee, but he loved morning tea. He had other aversions, too, like mushrooms, couldn't abide mushrooms, joked about how they'd give you warts, and, of course, you should never sleep with an open window without screens, crows could fly in, land on your face, give you crow's feet. Silly the things that come to mind at a time like this."

For a moment they were quiet. The only sound came from an old ship's clock mounted on the wall near the mantel.

"How much do you know about Elly's life before you met him?" Lee asked.

Without any hesitation, she said, "Do you mean his bisexuality?" Her response took him by surprise. "Well, Elly had his own imperfections, but pretense was not one of them. He was very clear about that. I asked him once about those encounters, but he insisted that what mattered was moving forward, not dwelling on the past. The only thing that mattered was our commitment to each other." She placed the cup on the table and, folding her hands, said, "I never regretted one moment of my life with him. I only regret that I was unable to give him children, but that just made things stronger between us."

This was a difficult moment. Lee wanted to offer support, reassure her, but he also had to tread lightly, not entirely sure what doubts, if any, she might consciously or unconsciously harbor.

"May I ask what you know of a bisexual lifestyle?" he asked her.

"Lifestyle?" she responded with surprise. "What is a lifestyle?" she demanded. "Is it a *lifestyle*, any more than being heterosexual is a lifestyle? My God, William, you of anyone should know that."

He was momentarily taken aback by her response. Had he touched a raw nerve, offended her by his question?

She realized she had overreacted. "I'm sorry, William, forgive me."

"No, go on, I'm listening."

"I used to think being gay was a lifestyle, but it isn't. A lifestyle is a *choice*, like monogamy, for instance. Gay or straight, we're free to make choices—to lie or tell the truth, to be generous or cheap, to support a family or abandon a family, as my father left my mother for another woman." She paused, looking away from him. Then she studied his expression. Was she going too far with this?

He waited for her to continue.

"Now, I know our sexuality is not a choice, but what we are given," she said, "what we're born with. But commitment is something else—not a gay choice or a straight choice. Elly taught me that. Commitment is a choice based on *trust*, William, like religion, something you take on faith, not like a fact, not like *knowing* we'll all die someday. You can never know for sure, and so you trust someone as I always trusted Elly. And he was right, William, look forward not backward."

The room was quiet now. He had meant to offer her reassurance, and instead it was she who offered it to him. Yes, of all people, he should know this. Funny how he had always considered his own sexual orientation a *lifestyle*, a *choice*, but which, as Ruth had said, was not a choice at all, but something inborn.

"I'm sorry," she said, "I didn't mean to pontificate. It's a difficult time for everyone, what with the committee and all. I know Elly's death is tied somehow to the committee, but how? I know that Elly would never betray me or anyone else for that matter."

"What did he tell you about the committee?" Lee asked

"That they were investigating people for un-American activities and for homosexuality. He never mentioned any specifics, but I knew this preyed on his mind."

"I only know from rumors what is going on," Lee said. "It's a witch hunt, for sure. They summon people secretly. It's like the Inquisition, hearsay evidence or entrapment, guilt by association, intimidation with threat, blackmail."

"But how was Elly connected with any of this? Why would he be driven to hang himself?"

Lee hesitated. Was this the time to retreat or forge ahead? What good would come from his revealing something that had happened so long ago, before Ruth was part of Elmore Simmons' life? Whatever he revealed would only be conjecture, and yet it was the only possible connection that linked Elly with the committee. She had shared Elly's letter with him.

...good friend...explain...circumstances...help you through this...

"Before this, before you met him, how much did he tell you about Nelson Bosnick? Anything specific?" he asked.

"No," she said, "nothing," waiting for him to continue.

"It was something before Elly met you. A last encounter before he met you," he said with a sense of certainty, and proceeded to give her the details.

NELSON BOSNICK. SHE repeated the name silently in her mind. *Nelson Bosnick.* She would spend the next several weeks finding out exactly who Nelson Bosnick was and what connection he had with her husband's death. She would observe his every action, chart his involvement with the committee, and then lay out her plan.

CHAPTER 22
SURVEILLANCE

NORTON BRELL WAS summoned a second time. Who else could be implicated? What contacts had he had with other students? Did he understand that without his full cooperation, they would submit his name along with the photographs to the state attorney for criminal procedures? Yes. One other name came to mind. *Zack Conner*.

—⁊⁊—

DAVID READ BARBARA'S letter again. She had met Gerard Singleton at the law firm where she and her mother worked. He was the newest junior partner, smart, ambitious, enthusiastic, a real asset to the firm. No assignment was too small or too inconsequential. They had met at a reception, and the two hit it off instantly. And, she confessed, she felt awkward, given the circumstances. Yet, there was a sense of connection between them, something more in their meeting than just another casual encounter. She was eager for David and Gerard to know each other. Gerard was working on a case in Miami but would be back at Thanksgiving.

David couldn't wait for Thanksgiving. This was an unexpected turn in his relationship with Barbara. He headed home for the weekend, eager to reassure Barbara of his support whatever she decided to do, to learn more about Gerard Singleton, and to tell her about Zack.

—⁊⁊—

BARBARA'S MOTHER EMBRACED David. "Come in, darling," she greeted him. "Barbara is upstairs getting dressed. She'll be right down. Here," she said, taking his overnight duffle bag, "I'll just put this in your room. Oh, it's so good that you're here. We've been so worried."

"Worried? Why?" he asked.

"We've heard rumors, some kind of investigation at the university."

—⁓—

THAT SAME WEEKEND, after David left, Zack stood in the Ale House, having beers with a group of casual acquaintances, several of whom were gay. At one point, one of them nudged him, directing his attention to a man sitting at the bar, his face accented with dark, piercing eyes, void of expression, staring intently at Zack, watching his every move.

"Watch out for that one," his acquaintance said. "He's some sort of government investigator. He's been watching you for a long time all evening. I've heard that there's some sort of gay investigation going on around campus."

Zack felt his blood run cold. Unable to move, he tried to ignore the man's stare and to continue the idle chatter at the jukebox as if nothing unusual was going on. Then, finishing his beer, he made excuses and quickly left the bar, walking down the street toward his dorm room in Collins Hall. He didn't dare look back to see if the man had followed him.

The next day, in the cafeteria, Zack sat with several students he had been with the previous night when the companion who had warned him about the stranger came into the room and, pulling up a chair, sat at their table, flush with excitement.

"They've been interrogating me most of the day," he exclaimed. "They got me to admit I'm gay, and they've been pressing me to give them names of all my gay friends. I think they're going to kick me out of school. If that happens, I swear I'm going to take a lot of others with me. Isn't it exciting?"

Suddenly Zack was aware that his world was about to crack wide open. *Must warn David. Must get hold of Lee and Chris.*

—⁓—

ZACK'S ENCOUNTER AT the Ale House with the frantic student alarmed Professor Ellis Cohen. His usual calm, confident nature was marked now by an uneasiness with this turn of events. Elmore Simmons' death and the widespread rumors created a growing paranoia about the committee and the enlarging web of entrapment that was spreading throughout the university.

Cohen was not a man easily intimidated by bullies of any kind. He had never been reluctant to speak out against any form of repression, and this would be no exception. The committee would at least face an adversary in him. Still—as he told David, Zack, and Chris huddled on the sofa in Lee's study, they had to be prepared. Looking for some indication of assurance from Cohen, Lee watched pensively, waiting for him to continue.

"Expect the worst," Cohen cautioned them. "Assume you'll be summoned and that they'll use every means to intimidate you. Whatever their strategy, remain calm, admit nothing. And in the meantime, keep a low profile, all three of you," he said, glancing over at David, Zack and Chris.

Turning to Lee, he said, "It's just a question of time before they attempt to snag you, William. When they do, you'll need to keep your wits. I know how you welcome a vigorous intellectual scuffle, but this is not the time to be clever or heroic. However they try to bait you, and they will, keep your distance."

William Lee offered his old colleague a faint smile as he scanned the faces of the three students who had become his friends. They were entering unknown territory. And for all of them, this was only the beginning.

—∿—

THE DAY HAD turned chilly, and a light, steady drizzle added to Simon Prevatt's depression. Half of the students in the music appreciation class were routinely skipping. He had lost not only enthusiasm but also control over the class. And now he was being summoned a second time. How long must this go on? What else did they want from him beyond the outrageous perjury he had already committed?

The committee had shifted the interrogations to the Rosemont Hotel, a strategy intended to keep reporters or other interested parties off guard. But the room was like the one at the Midtown—sparse, cold, bare, reeking of intimidation.

Simon Prevatt's face betrayed his weariness as he sat across from Borland Mayes. The second interrogation had begun.

"There are things you did not tell us the last time you were brought here, Professor. Now I want you to think clearly and carefully and testify fully of your own mind, do you understand?"

"What do you want to know now?" Prevatt asked, his voice strained with fatigue.

"You know that you have had homosexual contact with students out there. We know there are things you did not tell us about. Do you still deny you have had homosexual contact with people you knew to be students?"

"At the time," he said, "I was not aware they were students. Yes, there are some that I now know to be students. Yes," he answered.

"Who are they? Give me their names," he insisted.

"I can't think clearly," he said evasively. "I don't know, I don't recall. I know you think I am absolutely stupid, but..."

Mayes interrupted with a snarl in his voice. "No, I don't think you're stupid. I think you think we're stupid. You came in here, under oath, purportedly telling us all you knew about this thing, and you didn't tell us all you knew, and I know you didn't. Now I want names."

Prevatt was near a breaking point, and Mayes could sense it and pressed on. "Give me the names!" he demanded.

"I realize I have made some pretty bad mistakes. I know I was wrong. I just got into it and kept going. It's hard to resist, it's taken me off the track. But I know this now, so tell me," he pleaded, "does this mean an end to my job?"

Mayes's reply was cold, indifferent. "None of us is in a position to tell you what the outcome of this is going to be," he said, turning off the recorder. "But if I were you, I would start looking for another job." He paused, then said, "If you can find one."

—〰—

PACING BACK AND forth in the lobby of the Rosemont Hotel, Nelson Bosnick strained to control the intense anxiety that had kept him awake at night. He intended to confront Borland Mayes about the breach of confidence. It had to be some kind of mistake. He had given them his total cooperation in return for their assurance that he would not be compromised. *Must be calm. Stay calm.* They kept him waiting for an hour before the investigator's aide announced that Mayes would see him.

Mayes sat at the table, gave a swift glance at the agitated professor, shuffled through papers, but remained seated. "What is it now, Bosnick?" he said with some irritation at the intrusion.

"Before, when I talked to Mr. Munjay, he assured me this could be kept quiet if I cooperated in the investigation, but it has come out in my job."

"What do you mean, it has come out in your job?" Mayes asked with growing irritation.

"I was called in and told that there was an investigation going on, and that I was involved in it, and that I had a choice of leaving or staying."

Mayes leaped from his chair and said almost in a shout, "Who called you in?" he demanded. "What do you mean, a choice of leaving or staying?"

"My immediate supervisor. She told me that information had been passed to her that if I voluntarily left the university and terminated my employment by January, the investigations would be dropped. But if I stayed, the proceedings would continue."

"Well I can tell you, Bosnick, your immediate supervisor, whoever she is, has no control over this investigation at all, and nobody can stop it except the committee itself. I don't give a damn who it is, including President Thurgis himself. Do you understand? Nobody out there has any control over this or can stop the proceedings. Now get the hell out. I have important things to finish here."

It was not the response he had anticipated. He wandered slowly back toward the campus, more distraught and uncertain about his future than ever.

Munjay and Henson took in the full fury of Mayes's rebuke. Confronting Munjay directly, Mayes barked, "Someone is either leaking information or has a loose tongue. I want to know where that woman got information about Bosnick, about these proceedings, and how much she knows."

Henson said, "Well, there are bound to be rumors, talk, about what's going on here."

"I'm not talking about rumors, I'm talking about specifics. Who in hell leaked that faggot's name to his supervisor? If the informants are compromised, that source of information is lost and we're dead in the water. Now find out where that bitch got her information on Bosnick."

—⁓—

UNLOCKING THE DOOR to his office cubicle, Bosnick saw the envelope that someone had slid under the door. It was addressed simply BOSNICK. He tore the envelope open and read the terse statement inside:

> Your position is in jeopardy, but I can help you. Meet me at the commons tonight at seven, by the pond.
> A concerned acquaintance.

—w—

EXCEPT FOR BOSNICK, the commons was deserted. The warmth of the early November day had given way to an evening chill. Fog began to blanket the pond and the bench where he sat waiting for the visitor who had left the note offering help. He welcomed the fog. It enclosed him, concealed him, shielded him from the turmoil of his abominable sin. There was something comforting about the fog. Just as it muffled the distant roar of cars to a faint murmur, it hushed momentarily the unrelenting, accusing tongues that resonated in his head.

Down the path there was the faint trace of a figure moving in his direction. Ever closer, the figure approached, slowly, deliberately, each step carefully measured, it seemed to him. In the fog, awash in the dim reflected light from the distant street-lamps, the approaching figure appeared as a ghostly apparition, and for a moment his imagination conjured up the image of Elmore Simmons. Then at once the figure was standing directly in front of him. The face was familiar, but in the diminished light he had difficulty discerning her features. He had seen her before, but where? And then the woman confronted him.

"Nelson?" The woman's voice had an icy edge.

Now he recognized the face. Ruth! Elmore's wife. His pulse raced. He struggled for a response but could only gape at the woman whose husband he had helped to kill. Frantically, he searched for something to say, but the only words that came were "Ruth, I'm sorry..."

She held up her hand to silence him. "Regrets not expected, not accepted," she said.

"I honestly didn't know it would come to this, I was only..."

She interrupted him, "Betraying a confidence? Ruining a career? Destroying a life? What other lives have you helped them destroy?"

His eyes fluttered. He looked away to avoid the accusation in her eyes.

She reached inside the brown leather bag strapped around her shoulder and removed the small pistol. Bosnick's eyes widened, the cold, steel barrel of the gun aimed directly between his eyes.

"Elmore gave this to me, for protection, a long time ago. I never found a use for it, until now." She hesitated, studying the frantic expression on his face. "There is one cartridge in the chamber, Professor Bosnick," she said. "I had every intention of using it tonight, but I see now how wasted you are." She thrust the gun into his hand. "Perhaps you can find a use for this," she said. Turning from him, she vanished like a ghost in the thickening fog.

CHAPTER 23
ZACK

IT WAS HIS math class. A campus policeman in full blue uniform barged into the classroom and called out his name. Zack raised his hand. With a curt toss of his head, the man shouted, "Come with me!" The instructor stood speechless. Zack was ordered outside to a waiting patrol car and taken to a room somewhere in one of the administration buildings. It was a small room with one window that had been completely covered. In the center of the room, there was a table and several wooden straight-back chairs. It was here that Zack would receive his first grilling from Munjay and Henson.

The session lasted an hour. Henson insisted that Zack confess to being gay. When he refused, they began to pound him with demands to give them names. Again he refused.

"Listen, you faggot, we have sworn testimony about you. We can easily have you kicked out of school for not cooperating. We have the names and phone numbers of your parents and can tell them what a disgusting son they have. Is that what you want?" Henson growled.

Name, rank, serial number. Zack said nothing, his face expressionless, his body steady and poised in spite of the relentless drilling. Finally, Henson said with some exasperation, "You can go...for now."

Outside, Zack felt his entire body go limp. He had remained calm and composed during the interrogation, but the grueling session had left him drained and anxious. Who would be next? He had to tell David, Chris, and Lee about the interrogation but also keep his distance from them, the isolation from them their only protection.

SOON AFTER THE confrontation with Munjay and Henson, Zack noticed that his mail seemed very slow in arriving. A letter that would normally take two or three days to reach him would show up in his mailbox at University Station a week after being posted. Clearly, they were intercepting his mail. Some of the letters had been steamed open, then resealed. In the past, he had written for some gay catalogs and gay-oriented articles. Now he was terrified that they might intercept them. Back in his dorm room, he scoured every drawer, looking for any sort of incriminating evidence, tearing letters and notes into tiny shreds and flushing them down the toilet.

He was summoned twice again, each time during class, by a uniformed policeman, each time the same setting, the same set of questions. At each interrogation, they intensified the coercion tactics. Unlike other students who—summoned and pounded relentlessly with threats of exposure—ultimately became informants, he continued to refuse to cooperate, and that refusal to cooperate became an obsession and a challenge to them.

They were determined to break him. But he would not be easily broken, and this heightened their resolve. It also heightened his resolve to resist them. He would sit facing them without the slightest trace of fear. What they could not see, what he would not allow them to see, was the internal terror he hid from them. *Name, rank, serial number.* It was a discipline he had acquired in the Marines in counter-interrogation techniques that now reinforced his determination to withhold the information they so desperately wanted.

The more they harangued him with their interrogation, the more he understood who they really were: an illiterate bunch of rednecks, clumsily wielding power over others, trying to break them. He would not be broken.

Worse than the confrontation with the committee was the isolation from David, Chris, and Lee. He did not dare to contact them using the dorm's hall phone where others might overhear his conversation. Instead, he walked several blocks to the public phone, making sure that he was not followed.

While Chris and David had cars, it was much too risky to park outside Lee's house. The rendezvous had to be carefully coordinated in the event that the house was under surveillance. They would establish prearranged pick-up locations, and Lee, making sure that he was not followed, would fetch David, Zack, and Chris. Once in the garage, the four could enter the house unnoticed. It was these infrequent, clandestine reunions that sustained them as the Thanksgiving break approached.

—⁂—

IT WAS A siege. Zack could not recall anything like this during his time in the Marines. There he was trained to focus on the external enemy. Here the enemy was the informant within, unseen, unnamed.

"I just don't get it," he said, having related the grilling he had undergone. "No one outside the three of you knows anything about me. I've had no personal contacts with anyone else in the university. No one knows anything about my relationship with you. Who gave them my name? Why would someone want to implicate me? What motive would they have?"

The only response came from the crackling fire and the regular cadence of the ship's clock on the wall near the mantel. Then Lee, looking directly at David, ended the silence.

"Brell!"

Brell. David was connecting the dots. Brell, the only logical connection. Brell, whom he had met that first semester in Lee's class. Brell, who had been overly interested in David's activities outside of class. Bell, who resented David and Zack's close relationship. Brell, the only casual acquaintance he had made until they had met Chris at the gym. Lee was right. It had to be Brell.

"Norton Brell is a pathetic young man," Lee said. "Four years ago he was in my humanities class. He's a precocious fellow, extremely bright, talented, and very disturbed. He tried on many occasions to edge himself into my weekend music encounters with some of my best students, but he just didn't fit. There was something about him that I couldn't quite place. Very much a loner. Others in the class ignored him. Pretty obvious that first time, David, when you had signed up for my class, that Brell was obsessed with you. I could see that clearly enough. The question now is whom else will he attempt to implicate?" There was an uneasy silence.

"Well, boys," Lee said, ending the silence, "I'm starved. Let's have a glass of wine and some dinner. Happy Thanksgiving."

However tentative, however fragile, this narrow space of safety offered protection from events beyond their control. Why wouldn't it? Here was their refuge, the center of their family. Their rock.

Lee concealed his apprehension. He knew the committee would zero in on him. He was, after all, the prime catch, wasn't he? And the anticipation of what was coming unnerved him in spite of his outward appearance of calm. Must remain calm. With Thanksgiving break at hand, the boys would head for home, leaving him alone to contemplate his strategy once the assault came.

—⁂—

SLOAT'S IRRITATION WITH Henson's unsuccessful interrogations of Zack Conner was unmistakable. The ultimate goal was to use Lee's contacts for an even broader encirclement, and Conner was the wedge they needed. They had convinced themselves that Lee was the center of a homosexual recruitment ring. They had noted his flagrant disregard of public opinion, how Lee flaunted his reckless lifestyle with another man with whom he had shared his house, on many occasions traveled with, and openly attended public functions with. No, this man was high priority. The others had been hapless subjects easily broken, with the exception of the dean. That was another irritant for Sloat. The last thing the committee needed was a spectacular suicide to draw attention to their activities. He had to agree with President Thurgis about Henson's heavy hand.

Sensing Sloat's impatience, Henson outlined his next move. "The depositions from the three witnesses are enough to nail the son-of-a-bitch. I say we go after him before the Christmas break."

"No," Sloat objected. "You know and I know that what we got is perjury. It's too risky."

"We have the sworn affidavit of the student who went to Dean Simmons about Lee," Henson reminded him.

"Yes, and the dean is dead. It's the student's word against Lee's. No," he said. "We need something substantial. We'll just bide our time. But those students—Conner and Ashton—they're the key to Lee. Break them."

—⁂—

DWIGHT THURGIS GOT up, stood behind the barrier that was his desk and motioned for Cohen to take a chair at the far side of the office, one adjacent to windows that provided a view of the commons outside. He settled in the chair beside him, his way of creating a sense of informality, a gesture of casual civility for his guests. With a forced smile, he greeted his visitor. "Well, to what do I owe this pleasant surprise, Ellis?" He knew already why Ellis Cohen had insisted on a meeting just prior to the Thanksgiving break.

Cohen ignored the superficial gesture, coming directly to the point. "Dwight, why are you aiding them?"

Thurgis gave a quick, disapproving look. "Aiding whom?"

"This inquisition."

Thurgis squinted, brushed his eyelid as though some bug had invaded its space, an attempt to avoid Cohen's scowl. "Pretty harsh jargon, Ellis."

"Pretty sorry state of affairs," Cohen said. "Sloat and his ilk don't surprise me, but, you, Dwight, I would not have expected this from you."

Now all traces of civility were gone. "Let me tell you something, and you listen carefully," Thurgis said. "The laws of this state are very clear about moral turpitude. Under the law, as president of this university, I am requested, no not requested—obliged—to cooperate with this committee which, as a matter of fact, is legally authorized by the state to take whatever corrective action is necessary."

Cohen glared his disapproval. "And holding secret proceedings in motel rooms, dragging teachers and students from classes, is that your idea of corrective action? Good God, man, they're smearing people with hearsay evidence, with guilt by association, by innuendo, even blackmail."

"I don't know," Thurgis countered. "I am not trained in such legal matters. I only know that if we refused to cooperate, they would claim we had something to hide. If we refused to take action against accused faculty and students, they would claim we were protecting, aiding, and abetting deviants of all stripes."

"Including political *deviants*?" Cohen asked pointedly.

"Including people with a past record of participation in the Communist Party," he said archly. "You might do well to consider that possibility, Ellis."

Ellis Cohen had considered that possibility. It was during the Depression in the thirties that he had become disillusioned with the system. Thousands of jobless and homeless people living in tin or cardboard lean-tos—Hoovervilles as they came to be called—fathers who out of desperation had abandoned family, children begging food from strangers on the streets while the government did nothing. Yes. Disillusionment with the system, which led him into the Party, and then disillusionment with the Party as yet another problem with the system. And now the system was at work again, this time to cleanse itself of what it regarded as un-American.

"Oh, for Christ's sake, man, put yourself in my shoes." Thurgis protested. "The question is not who or how to stop this investigation, but who would want to challenge it? Who is to challenge a former governor and now the most powerful lawmaker in Tallahassee in what you call this inquisition? With the slightest nod, Billy Sloat can punish this university, can cut appropriations, and where would that leave us?" Thurgis moved next to the window, avoiding eye contact with Cohen. "No, in an ideal world, Ellis, there would be no room for such as this, but practically speaking, there is no alternative."

Cohen got up from the chair to leave. He stopped at the door, his back to Thurgis. "Well, Dwight, you're dead wrong there. There is an alternative."

Outside in the reception lobby, the cheerful young secretary called out as he passed, "Happy Thanksgiving, Dr. Cohen."

Yes, he thought. Much to be thankful for, isn't there?

CHAPTER 24
CONNECTIONS

ANDREW WILSON ALMOST took a side road to skip the scene ahead. Two cop cars, an ambulance, a fire truck—probably someone the city desk would want him to explore. He eased close and checked to see that his notebook was in his pocket. He might need his beat-up Yashica Mat camera and flash.

When he arrived at the scene, he saw that two survivors were being rushed to the hospital. He lifted his camera to take a picture of the one teenager in the car who was alive barely, but he eased the camera down to his side. The *Times Sentinel* wouldn't run gory shots. It also wouldn't print a picture of the other three who had been crushed beyond recognition. Wilson backed up and snapped several medium shots of the wreck: nice mangled vehicles, but no mangled bodies.

The driver of the truck had a blood alcohol level three times over the limit. Except for severe facial lacerations, he was intact. The surviving teenager, however, was a different story. She had to be cut from the twisted wreckage, her right arm completely crushed from the impact, bone from the left arm protruding through flesh. Incredible that anyone could have survived such a crash. One witness described how the driver of the truck had been racing miles over the speed limit on the narrow street when he lost control and crashed into the car full of teenagers, hitting them head-on.

Andrew Wilson remembered another wreck seven years earlier when he had had lost control of his car, crashing into a tree. His own blood alcohol level had been several times over the limit. It had been the seminal moment when he acknowledged his drinking problem, that he was an alcoholic, a danger to himself and to others. As the wreckers cleared the debris from the street, he thought how this could have been his car, these teenagers his target and not the tree.

Andrew Wilson had won several state-wide awards for investigative journalism with the *Tampa Times Sentinel*, and during the past four years had covered the capitol in Tallahassee. He was now at an all-time high in his career. His success was all the more remarkable, given the earlier obstacles he had overcome as an alcoholic. His abuse of alcohol was already a problem while he was still in high school and completely out of control with binge drinking and orgies by the time he was in college, ultimately landing him in a detox facility, and afterwards getting him kicked out of the university. That was behind him now, but he had not forgotten what it was like when you bottomed out with no place to go.

He had taken pride in his success in avoiding alcohol one day at a time and had become an active member of Alcoholics Anonymous, sponsoring others who were trying to stay sober. It had been the darkest time in his life, and he emerged from the ordeal confident and determined to make a difference, not just for himself but for anyone struggling as he had struggled. From his weakness came a strength and a resolve to reach out to others who had lost self-respect and any hope for a productive future.

Every week, no matter what other opportunities might surface, and no matter where he was, he seldom missed the meetings of Alcoholics Anonymous. That remained his highest priority of personal activities.

It was almost midnight when he stopped by his office to retrieve the draft of an article he was preparing for the Sentinel. There was a message on his desk marked *confidential and urgent*. He opened the envelope and read the brief message inside.

Dear Mr. Wilson,
  Perhaps you have heard recurring rumors of an investigation at State University. There is more to this than rumor. Perhaps you have heard about the recent suicide of Elmore Simmons, former Dean of Liberal Arts. This was not a random suicide

but directly linked to secret hearings. If you are interested in details, contact me.

Ellis Cohen,

Professor of English

In fact, Andrew Wilson had heard scattered rumors about some kind of hush-hush investigation over at State University. Another reporter had mentioned that Senator Sloat had been questioned about B. J. Henson's activities at the campus but routinely refused to comment on an investigation which, he claimed, was merely in its preliminary stage. Other reporters had questioned the senator about his association with the committee, and his response was always the same. He just couldn't say anything at this time without jeopardizing the probe, and he was adamant in reassuring curious reporters that he would provide an appropriate response in due time.

Cohen's *confidential and urgent* correspondence piqued Wilson's curiosity. He had covered Florida politics long enough to know that inside the capital circle, there was almost always some activity that a politician was not eager to share with the press. He would make the four and a half-hour drive over to the university and meet this English professor who was offering to provide details about secret hearings and a related suicide.

—⁂—

THE CAMPUS WAS virtually deserted for the Thanksgiving break. The brisk November chill and the absence of activity provided an atmosphere of unsettling calm. Wilson studied the professor, who had just finished relating a most incredible narrative of intrigue, intimidation, and ruthlessness, of students hired as informants, secret interrogations in area motels, suspects prohibited from confronting accusers, professors removed from classrooms, people branded as "queer" because of the clothes they wore or their mannerisms, a secret list being compiled for dismissal after the Christmas break—all activities that, if true, would constitute an outrageous abuse of power sanctioned by the state itself. And equally astonishing, the president of the university himself complicit in the committee's proceedings.

—⁂—

WILSON HAD BARELY two weeks before the Christmas break. He scanned the names that Cohen had given him. Edmond Dority was first on the list. He dialed the number.

"Pharmacy," the voice answered.

"I would like to speak with Edmond Dority, please," Wilson said.

"I'm afraid he can't talk at this time. May I tell him who is calling?" the student asked.

"Andrew Wilson with the *Tampa Times Sentinel*," he said. Seconds later, Edmond Dority was on the phone.

—⚭—

EACH TIME SIMON Prevatt answered the phone, he wondered if this was the call summoning him to the president's office. The deep circles under his eyes betrayed his lack of sleep. It was two weeks before the Christmas break, and all he could think about was wanting this all to be over.

Prevatt's phone was ringing again and he reluctantly picked it up. The voice on the other end asked, "Professor Prevatt?"

"Who is this?" he asked wearily.

"Andrew Wilson with the *Tampa Times Sentinel*. I'd like to meet with you."

—⚭—

NELSON BOSNICK HAD not returned his calls, so Andrew Wilson waited outside the office cubicle. He soon saw Bosnick shuffling aimlessly down the hallway, shoulders stooped, eyes diverted to his feet. He had not shaved and the gray stubble on his face was almost concealed by the chalk-white sagging skin.

"Who are you? What do you want from me?" he asked.

"I'm with the *Tampa Times Sentinel*. I'd like a few moments of your time."

—⚭—

WILSON TOOK NOTES as each individual recounted the ordeals of the interrogation, but it was Zack Conner's interrogation that riveted him: students unable to defend themselves against a state-sanctioned inquisition, the most vulnerable targets of what was clearly a political witch hunt.

Cohen was right. This was only the beginning of the vendetta. Already gaining momentum, it would spread beyond the university to become a major assault on civil liberties everywhere in the state. He determined to pursue his own investigation of an investigation. What he could not foresee was the cost.

—⁓—

BARBARA AND HER mother cleared the table from the last of the Thanksgiving feast, leaving David and Gerard Singleton alone in the living room. David listened as the young attorney told about his position at the law firm and talked about plans for Barbara and himself once they were married and settled in their own house. Gerard Singleton was exactly as Barbara had described him to David weeks earlier—bright, well-mannered, engaging—but David sensed uneasiness in Gerard's attempts to appear casual. Finally, growing tired of small talk, David said directly, "Does my being gay bother you?"

The question surprised Gerard. He had encountered homosexuals randomly—nothing overtly indicated, but homosexuals nevertheless. David was different. He didn't fit the stereotype at all—especially in his relationship with Barbara and the way he had protected her. Gerard had never really given much thought to the gay subculture. Homosexuals were outsiders, beyond the norm. Here in this room was a man who did not seem to him to fit the pattern at all.

"Truthfully? You're the first openly gay man I've actually met. And no, it doesn't bother me."

"Wouldn't matter if it did. Glad it doesn't. What did you expect?"

He studied David's face. Not the slightest trace of anything that he associated with gay people. Instead, a confident, relaxed human being whose sexual preference was merely different from his own.

"To tell the truth, I wasn't sure what to expect. Right now I'm trying to process all of this, you, your loyalty to Barbara, the whole thing. It just doesn't fit, I mean, you're so..."

"Normal?"

"Yes, normal," he added, "And impressive."

"How so?" David asked.

"What you did for Barbara. I'm not sure I would have done the same thing under the circumstances. Who would?"

"I would. I did. I would again in a heartbeat. I'd be lying if I told you I never had any doubts about the arrangement. But I love Barbara, and I'm just glad she's met someone who can love her in a different way."

"And what about you?" Gerard asked.

"What about me?"

"I know about Stephen. Do you keep up with him?"

"His mom tells me he's doing all right in New York. That's about it," David said.

"I'm sorry it didn't work out."

"Don't be. Things don't always work out the way you like. The investigation is the thing now, just trying to get beyond it."

"If there is anything I can do," he said, but David interrupted him.

"Can you change attitudes? That would help," he said.

Yes, this is one impressive son of a bitch. And very likeable.

—⁓—

THE BUS PULLED into the Greyhound's single-bay bus depot. The sign above the entrance said:

WELCOME TO HOMERVILLE, IDAHO,
POPULATION 11,250.

Zack got off, walked to the pay phone in the storefront lobby, and called home. "I'm here," he said and settled into the folding chair, waiting for his dad to pick him up. Not much had changed in Homerville since he had left years ago for the Marines and now college. The single movie house, which ran only on weekends, the local drug store on the corner, which also sold groceries, an auto repair shop of sorts, and the regional high school at the end of Jones Street were landmarks that looked much like a soundstage movie set. Now as he surveyed it, it looked unreal. It was ironic. He had lived a closeted life in Homerville and, joining the Marines, exchanged one closet for another. But it was home.

His dad's ten-year-old coupe rounded the corner. Zack threw his duffle bag in the back seat. "Good to see you, son" his dad said, and they were off.

Thanksgiving dinner was a big event for Zack's mother. She loved to cook and to show off her culinary skills. She had invited the Hugheses and of course Doris Hughes, whose place was next to

Zack's. Zack's dad said grace while hands were clasped around the table, but once amen was said, Doris continued to hold Zack's hand a moment too long. Zack's mom gave a hopeful glance toward them, smiled, and said, "How wonderful to be together again, everyone." *What a lovely couple they make.*

DORIS'S LITTLE BROTHER sat at the other end of the table. *How old was he now? Eight? Ten? How cute they all thought he was, dressed in his mother's cast-off dress at three. But wait 'til he's fourteen!*

Holding a glass of wine, Zack's dad said, "Welcome everyone, and welcome especially our son Zack. Welcome home, son."

Home. He was a fugitive who had escaped and had returned to his prison. What no one in Homerville could know was that he was an outsider, a self-proclaimed outcast in a town he had given away to memory.

"We're proud of you, son, this one's for you, God bless."

"God bless," the others repeated.

Zack gave a tentative smile. *Yeah. One closet for another. God bless.*

—⁂—

CHRIS SENSED HIS father's uneasiness. His mother's attempt at light conversation only heightened the tension. "Tell me about school," his father said.

"Like what?" he asked.

"Made any friends there?" his father said.

"Classes keep me busy. Not many. A few"

"Who?"

"Just a few."

"Anyone special? A girl?" his father asked archly.

Chris glanced at his mother, then at his father. "Like I said, school keeps me busy. Don't have time for that."

Silence. Chris' mother rose quickly from the easy chair. "Coffee? Anything?"

"Yes, coffee, dear," his father said. She scurried from the room. Then he asked pointedly, "How's your spiritual health, son? No old temptations, I hope."

Chris took a deep breath and said with confidence, "It could not be better. Matter of fact, outstanding."

"You'd tell us otherwise," he said. There was no reply. His mother returned with the coffee.

"Cream? Sugar?" she said, breaking the uneasy silence.

—∞—

WILLIAM LEE RATTLED around in the empty house, Charlie his only companion for Thanksgiving. He was an indoor cat. Without his front claws, he would be defenseless outside. But he didn't seem to mind his imprisonment. Closeted away from the world outside, here there was safety.

Yet, Lee could see the cat's random curiosity about the jungle out there. Once he had ventured out and the neighbor's cat had attacked. Charlie's ragged ear was the visible reminder of the danger outside for anyone bold enough to venture outside the closet.

Lee envied the cat's security. Charlie had no sense of past or future, nothing to contemplate, only the present, hidden away from the danger outside. With the slight touch to the cat's ragged ear, he gently rubbed the tip until the cat offered up a significant purr. "What do cats think, Charlie? Do you think at all? When you sleep, Charlie, what do you dream? Do you dream?" Lee thought, how good to come back as a cat when you had died. But inside or out? That is the question.

—∞—

STEPHEN TOOK THE stairs to the second floor of the nursing facility, located the room and tapped gently on the half-opened door. His mother was beside the bed. When he moved toward her, she nodded her gratitude that he had come. Scott Smith's eyes flashed in rapid movements and he squinted to see the visitor. "Stephen?" he barely whispered.

"It's me, Dad."

"Stephen?"

"Yes, I'm here, Dad," he repeated, and turning to his mother, he said, "why don't you go home now. I'll stay for awhile." She nodded again, moved toward the door, hesitated briefly and then left them there alone.

"Well, it was nice of you to come."

Nice of me to come? Is that all he can offer me now? That it was a nice thing for me to do? To come here to watch him die? But he was already dead to me, so how could I come to see him die?

"I wouldn't hold it against you—not to come, I mean. Why would you, after everything?"

But that's just the point. It wasn't about everything. It was about nothing. There was never anything there, was there?

"Can I ask you something, Dad?" He moved toward the bed. "What was there about me that you couldn't love me? Can you tell me?" He was standing now next to the bed. He bent so close that he could feel his father's forced breath against his cheek.

"Stephen, when you can't feel love for yourself, how can you show love for someone else?" He rolled his eyes, stared at the ceiling. "I wish it had been different. You're a good boy. I'm a lousy father." He coughed, attempted to clear his voice. "I don't think I was ever cut out to be a father. You were a casualty—collateral damage, as it were—of my own failing. In a weird way, I did love you—do love you. Regrets are pointless. What possible end would they serve now that I am where I am. I hope you'll get on with your life. Find someone. Do you have someone, Stephen?"

"No," was the quick response. *I almost did once. You're right. Regrets are useless.*

"Well, I'm sorry for that. I hope someday you will. It's hell to be trapped in your own spiritual impotence. What else can I say?"

Nothing more, Dad. You said it all.

"Well, I hope...you and your mother...well...anyway, have a nice Thanksgiving. Goodbye, Son."

—∞—

"Dwight," he paused then continued, "may I call you Dwight?" Sloat said.

Dwight Thurgis had dreaded this latest encounter with Sloat, which he had known was inevitable since the committee's arrival on campus. The weeks of interrogations had moved quickly and efficiently, thanks largely to his cooperation and his reluctance to impede the Senator's investigation. He looked over the list of names—more than sixty—of faculty, administrators, students, staff personnel. This was merely a list of names, not people, he had to remind himself. He had an obligation after all. It was nothing personal.

"Of course, Senator," Thurgis said.

"Please, it's Billy. I know this ain't been easy, you having to do all the dirty work at this here university. Believe me, I know how hard it is to put personal feelings aside and stand by your principles. It ain't easy, I know," Sloat said.

Obligation. Can't let this be personal.

"I cain't tell you how much I respect you for doing your job and for all your cooperation. It's painful, I know, having to call in all these people who we have exposed, people who you have known for years...and have to fire them."

A job to be done. Names. Nothing personal.

"Doctor...Dwight," he corrected himself, "let me congratulate you on your difficult job and say I am glad you did not shirk your responsibility."

Responsibility. Difficult decisions. Nothing personal.

"I have told many people that when the cards are down, Dr. Thurgis is not lacking," Sloat reassured him.

Not lacking. Thank you for the evidence. Most welcome. Dirty job. Has to be done. Nothing personal.

"Now comes the hard part. You got two weeks left before Christmas. How many of these people can you let go? We'll have more names for you in January. But we have to git this here started. And this is just the start, Dwight. This ain't just about your university. We got lots of work to do at the other two universities. We're talking 'bout deviants and communist infiltrators, like maggots eatin' away at unsuspectin' kids—an international conspiracy. Thank God for people like you. I knew we can count on you when the cards are down."

Dwight Thurgis stared off in the distance. Yes, this was the hard part. But it wasn't personal.

CHAPTER 25
PAYING THE PRICE

SEVERAL MAJOR NEWSPAPERS in the state ran the first installment of Andrew Wilson's report. Two unnamed witnesses had told of secret interrogations, intimidation, evidence attributed to unnamed informants about their guilt through association, and threats of public exposure unless suspects cooperated.

Three reporters waited in the foyer just outside Sloat's office, copies of the *Sentinel* in hand. When Sloat entered, the reporters surrounded him with a cacophony of questions. "There is absolutely no basis for these allegations," he shouted over their voices.

"Senator, what can you tell us about claims of secret hearings?"

"We are not conducting hearings, as you call them. We are in the middle of investigating certain activities," he insisted, "not hearings."

A reporter asked, "What kind of activities, Senator?"

"Communist fronts and homosexual activities, and there is no secrecy. We're trying to protect innocent witnesses till this investigation is complete—that's all—and when it's complete, we'll disclose the findings and take action, including criminal prosecution if that is called for. What I will tell you is that certain faculty are uncooperative, stirring up trouble, trying to impede our efforts. If resistance to this quiet investigation continues, we certainly will go ahead with public hearings. That is all, gentlemen." He slammed the door as he entered his office.

"Who the Hell is this reporter?" Sloat shouted at Mayes. "I will not tolerate this criticism. Get information on him. Dig up whatever you can find. We got to stop him before he does real damage," he barked.

—∿—

IT WAS A Tuesday in January 1959. Andrew Wilson took his usual seat as the meeting started and said, "My name is Andrew and I am an alcoholic."

After the usual introductions, the new woman who had just joined the small group said, "I am Deana, and I am an alcoholic."

When the meeting was over, Deana Inman approached Wilson. "You're Andrew Wilson, aren't you? I read your column on the investigations," she said. "What is this world coming to? Aren't there enough real things to worry about without intimidating people with tactics like that? Anyway, I thought your column was great."

"Thanks," he said.

"This was difficult for me tonight," she said.

"The first time always is," he said.

"I just didn't know where else to turn. God, I'd give anything for a drink just now," she said.

"There's a café in the next block. How about some coffee instead?" he offered.

—∿—

THEY TOOK A booth near the window. Deana Inman told him about her unhappy marriage, about her husband's drinking, about his abusive behavior and the boredom, which led to her own abuse of alcohol. He studied the woman's face as she continued the account of her marital problems. How old was she? Thirty maybe? Short cropped hair, no makeup, attractive nonetheless. Very attractive. No children to hold her back. Why would she stay in a relationship like that?

When she finished, she said, "And what about you?"

"What about me?" he repeated.

"Married?" she asked, looking down toward the table.

"Separated for now."

"Sorry," she said.

"Don't be. I'm not the easiest guy to live with."

"How so?"

"Bigamy," he said casually.

"Bigamy?" was her startled response. "You're a bigamist?"

"I'm married to my wife and married to my job. Unfortunately for my wife, the job has taken priority. Tallahassee is a long way from

Tampa. What is the cliché about absence making the heart grow fonder? Don't believe it," he said.

"Any kids?"

"One, a girl, thirteen, pretty like her mom."

She looked at her watch. "Well, it's late. I should be going. Thanks for coffee and for the company. And the support," she added. "I needed this." She said, getting up from the booth.

"Can I give you a lift?"

"No, thanks, I'll just get a cab."

He reached inside his wallet, retrieved a card and handing it to her said, "Here, call me if you need support."

She took the card and smiled. "How very kind. What a nice man you are," she whispered. "Yes, I'll be sure to call you."

—⁂—

"There's a reporter from the *Sentinel* who would like to see you," the secretary said. Dwight Thurgis made a grimace. "Tell him I can't see him now. Tell him to come back."

"I'm afraid he's persistent. He drove here from Tallahassee. Says he wants to clarify your role and the role of the Board of Control in the senator's ongoing investigation."

The mention of the Board of Control got his attention. Sloat had made the Board's chairman aware of the committee's activities, and their involvement had placed Thurgis in an uncomfortable position. He wanted to call Sloat, but knew the reporter would not be put off. "All right, tell him to come in, but tell him I only have a moment until my next appointment."

Wilson introduced himself. Thurgis remained seated behind his desk.

"I know your time is valuable, Dr. Thurgis, so let me get right to the point," Wilson said. "What is the extent of your involvement and the Board's complicity in the committee's investigation of communist infiltration and homosexual activity in the university?"

Thurgis was curt. "I think Senator Sloat has already made clear the intention of the committee in its investigation. Under state law, there are procedures for revoking a teacher's certificate on grounds of moral turpitude. When the committee issues its report, I am legally obliged to act in the best interest of the university, its faculty, and its students."

"Are you waiting for the report or acting on allegations now?" Wilson persisted.

Thurgis sputtered. "Mr. Wilson, the law in Florida is very clear about the penalties for homosexual activity, a felony if you will. I have every intention of complying with the law."

"And the committee's methods?"

"I don't know what methods you are referring to," he said with agitation. "Once I have their report, I am obliged to act upon it. Others can debate the legal or ethical issues."

"But from your personal perspective, Dr. Thurgis, what are the ethical issues?"

"There is nothing personal here. If I do nothing, they will think I have something to hide. If I refuse to cooperate, I would be accused of harboring sexual deviants. I don't make the rules, Mr. Wilson. The Board does. I just enforce them."

"In other words, Doctor, you're not responsible for any of this, just following orders, aren't you? Heard that before, haven't we? Merely the pastry cook in the kitchen minding the ovens?"

Thurgis exploded. "I resent that insinuation. This interview is over."

"Thank you for your time, Doctor, and for your insight," he said as he got up to leave.

Outside Thurgis' office, the cheerful secretary smiled. "Have a wonderful day, Mr. Wilson," she said as he walked down the hallway.

"Susan," Thurgis shouted, "Get Senator Sloat on the phone. Tell him it's urgent."

—ɷ—

SLOAT READ THE second installment of Wilson's investigative reporting. The negative publicity and the unrelenting criticism of the committee's activities had begun to spread throughout the state. Up to now, they had managed to contain the damage, with Sloat's denials of secret interrogations, and his assurances that they were attempting to protect innocent individuals in the early stages of the investigation. But Wilson's reporting was beginning to affect the committee's ability to deflect criticism. They had to act before this was out of control.

"What do we have on the bastard?" he asked Mayes.

"Well for starters, he's an alcoholic and he's separated from his wife. Spends most of his time in Tallahassee as the Capitol reporter for the *Tampa Times Sentinel*, has won state recognition and one national award for investigative reporting," Mayes said.

"Do we have a plan of action?" Sloat asked impatiently.

"We have a plan," Mayes said. "Her name is Deana Inman. Pretty too."

—⁂—

ANDREW WILSON WRESTLED with his insomnia, the unfolding events and his investigative installments on the committee contributing to his restlessness. After an hour of agitated movement, he had finally drifted into a light sleep when the intrusive ring of the phone jolted him back to consciousness. Squinting, he glanced at the clock. One AM.

"Hello," he answered, still groggy from the sudden awakening.

"Andrew," a woman's voice pleaded. "I need help."

"Who is this?" he said.

"It's Deana," she said.

"Who?" he asked, shaking sleep away.

"Deana Inman, from the AA meeting, remember? Oh God, I don't know where else to turn," she said, her voice breaking. "I had to get out of there."

"Out of where?" he asked, now fully awake. "What's happened? Where are you?"

"At a motel," she said on the verge of tears. "He was drunk. He threw me against the floor." She fought the tears but began to sob. "Had to get away from him."

"From whom?"

"Fritz. My husband. I think my foot is broken." She was crying hysterically.

"It's O.K. It's all right," he kept repeating. "Tell me where you are. I'll be right over."

He did not bother to shave or even brush his hair as he threw on a pair of tattered jeans, bolted down the stairs, jumped in the car and was speeding through the deserted streets toward the motel.

He tapped on the door to Room 105. There was an interval of a half-minute before the door opened, revealing the woman with dark circles under her eyes and what appeared to be bruises on her face. She wore only a loose bathrobe, nodded for him to enter, and limped toward the bed, obviously in considerable pain. She sat at the edge of the bed, head down, not looking at her visitor.

"Tell me what happened," he said, sitting next to her.

"He had been drinking. I poured the vodka down the sink and he began shouting, grabbed me by the wrist and threw me against the stove. I think my foot is broken from the fall."

He got up from the side of the bed, knelt in front of her.

"Let me have a look," he said, gently taking the foot in his hand.

All at once she flung the robe open revealing her nakedness, grasped the back of his head in her hands and shouted, "Eat it" and pulled his face into her exposed vagina.

Police rushed in from the adjoining room, cameras flashing.

"Mr. Wilson, you are charged with the abominable and detestable crime against nature," the officer announced as he was cuffed and taken to the waiting patrol car.

—⚙—

LIKE HIS INVESTIGATIVE reporting of the committee, Andrew Wilson's trial generated sensational coverage. Throughout the trial, the *Sentinel* kept him on, pending the outcome, but after refusing to plead guilty to a lesser charge and after one hung jury, forty-five-year-old Andrew Wilson was convicted of attempting to commit the crime and placed on five years' probation. And the *Sentinel* fired him.

—⚙—

"YOU HAVE TO believe me. I'm innocent," he pleaded.

Cathy Wilson believed him. After fifteen years of marriage, she knew his strength and she also knew his shortcomings, and cheap one-night stands with gutter sluts were not among them. No, she would accept his innocence and she would stand by him. But the marriage would never be the same. The unfolding allegations and finally his conviction would see to that.

The following year Andrew, Cathy, and their daughter, April, finished loading the U-Haul trailer with the last of their belongings. As they drove away, only April looked back. In Pensacola they would attempt to piece their lives back together. But Wilson's career was finished, and like a broken jar that had been glued back together, the fragments were unmistakable. As Mayes had once said to Nelson Bosnick, no one was going to stop the committee. No one.

CHAPTER 26
TIDY ENDINGS

ANDREW WILSON HAD been merely a detour around the first dismissals. Now President Thurgis was ready to act on the committee's first twenty names. But how to proceed in an orderly fashion? Alphabetically?

That would work.

And so the litany of names would bring the accused into the inner sanctum of his office for the long-awaited directives.

It took only five minutes for Bosnick's termination, but a bit longer for Edmund Dority. Yes, of course, the president assured him, he could indeed seek legal counsel, but merely the charges of impropriety, the suggestion of moral turpitude, would be sufficient to finish him, and wouldn't it be better to just resign and quietly move on?

John Collier was another matter. He had known John many years. How do you tell someone you have known so closely for so long that his career is finished? Thurgis explained his regret in having to exercise his responsibility, assured him that there was nothing personal in his decision, and then it was over. John Collier resigned his position as a professor in the biology department and then from the university.

Collier's case had begun the previous Monday. He had come home from classes dead tired and had fallen asleep. At 6:00 PM the phone woke him, an unfamiliar voice summoning him to appear before the committee's chief counsel. Then the ordeal began. His life had been scrutinized, examined, dissected and now would be discarded. An hour and a half later they were through with him, and his life was ruined. He had not been as involved as it appeared. But the innuendos and the allegations from informants were sufficient. The committee had pronounced his guilt. No matter that he had had no contacts with students. His nature, the secret he thought he had concealed so well, was enough. His termination was final.

January was off to a good start.

—∞—

NELSON BOSNICK RUMMAGED through the empty house. His wife had removed most of the furnishings, leaving a bed, the sofa, a couple of chairs, and his desk.

He unlocked the drawer and reached inside for the gun that Elmore's wife had offered him the night by the pond. He ran his fingers around the barrel, examined the chamber that held the lone cartridge, cocked the trigger, squinted his eyes, and pressed the barrel against his temples.

He felt the cold steel of the barrel against his chalk-white sagging skin. One slight squeeze and the single cartridge would obliterate his guilt. But he could not bring himself to press the trigger. How disgusting he was, how utterly useless his life, and yet he could not pull the trigger.

—∞—

DAVID SCURRIED UP the three flights of steps to his dorm room, opened the door, and to his astonishment encountered the stranger.

"Who the hell are you? What are you doing in here?" he demanded.

"Your new roomy," the short, dark-haired, macho-looking guy announced.

"Eric is my roommate," he countered.

"Was," the stranger said. "I'm Roger and you are...?" David said nothing. *Something wrong here. Don't trust him.* Roger took off his shirt and rummaged through the dresser-drawer for a tee shirt.

"Damn, they keep these rooms hot enough. Mind if I crack the window?" he said, and not waiting for a response, opened the window several inches, threw the tee on his bed and turned toward David. His body was tight, muscular, the abs the classic six-pack. "Hate warm rooms. Bad for the sinuses," he said, throwing himself across the bed, hands behind his head, one leg half raised in a provocative position.

—⁓—

DAVID'S PROTEST ABOUT the unannounced transfer made without his roommate's consent got nowhere. The housing office gave no explanation. All assignments had been made, and no changes were possible.

"The guy is a plant, David," Zack had warned him. "Don't trust him. Keep your distance." David had already reached that conclusion. He stayed away from the room as much as possible and studied in the library at night.

It was a Sunday afternoon, and David was lying on his bed reading when Roger came barging into the room, apparently drunk. He mumbled about the big after-the-game party, about the booze and the hot women, and stumbling around the room began pulling his clothes off.

"Damn this room is hot," he moaned, steadying himself against the dresser with one hand and pulling off his jockey shorts with the other, then flinging himself naked on his bed. He lay there, slowly fondling his penis until he had a full erection, all the while talking about the horny women who had gotten him drunk and then wouldn't put out.

"Jesus," he said, "I need to get my rocks off. What do you say, Davie boy? Ever done it with a guy, just for fun? Want to try?"

Get out of here. Now. He could almost feel Henson breathing down his neck as he bolted from the room.

—⁓—

A WEEK LATER, David walked through the passageway separating the two dorm buildings. When he rounded the corner, he almost bumped into Henson and Roger, who were engrossed in conversation. He hurried by, pretending he had not seen them, ran to his room, placed his books on the shelf and waited for Roger and the confrontation that was long overdue.

Roger stepped into the room, glanced at David and slowly closed the door. The two stared at each other. Finally, Roger said, "What?"

"You tell me," David said.

"Tell you what?" Roger said.

"Why you became an informant. Is it because you hate queers so much, or did they just make a special deal in return for your cooperation?"

Roger sat down on the edge of his bed. There was no response. He watched David. David continued to wait for a reaction. The two men studied each other, each waiting for the other to say something.

Then Roger offered a slight smile. "Nice Chevy you drive. From your folks? Hey, man, you got it nice."

David said nothing, allowing time for him to continue.

"Yeah, real fine, man. Me? Just a good ol' boy from Leesburg. That's orange country, but my folks, we grow peanuts. Ever drive through Leesburg? Summertime it's hot as hell in Leesburg. Not much going on either. Just work the fields, down a few brews on weekends, screw some girls. Then you get here. Whole different world, man. No wheels of course, but just the right time to earn some serious money. Not bad work either. Proud of it actually. Yeah, just one of them."

That contravention with Roger was the last. A week later, he moved out, leaving David the solitary occupant of the room.

—⁓—

IT WAS THE one April of his life that Zack would never forget. Once again he was called out of class. This time he was told to go directly to the dean's office. He walked across the campus toward the administration building, his feet as though set in concrete.

Was he now to join other students who had been expelled and without any recourse unless they wanted exposure?

He entered the dean's office, white-faced and trembling with anticipation. The dean watched him cautiously, then asked him to be seated, but Zack stood there.

"Mr. Conner, I am afraid I have some very bad news for you," he said, his voice deep and solemn.

Zack placed his hands inside his pockets, attempting to conceal his trembling.

"You had better sit down, son," he said.

Zack waited for the sentence.

"I think you should sit down," the dean repeated.

He continued to stand.

"I'm sorry to have to tell you that your father died this morning."

Your father died this morning. Your father died. Your father.

All at once, Zack broke down into uncontrollable sobs. Relief.

It was only that my father died this morning!

—〰—

By the end of the school year in June, they were barely halfway through the list of names. Twenty administrators, faculty, and staff, and twenty-five students had been terminated, and the interrogations still gained momentum. Except for William Lee. Sloat became obsessed with outing him, convinced that of all the fags, this one was the most despicable.

Mayes was relentless. But his interrogation of other suspects, the promise of leniency or the threat of exposure, produced no evidence against Lee. The only sworn testimony now was the student who had accused the professor, since Simon Prevatt had already been terminated.

"Find Prevatt," Sloat said to Mayes. "Tell him his dismissal was a mistake. Tell him we can help him if he is willing to cooperate. Tell him that Lee was responsible. One way or the other, I want to nail the son of a bitch."

Simon Prevatt had already left for destinations unknown, but Henson would locate him and bring him back as Sloat insisted. He still had contacts with law enforcement agencies, not just in the state but out of state as well. He knew the procedures. He would find Prevatt. It would just take a little time.

—〰—

The campus was deserted. Most of the students had left for the summer. A few remained for summer classes, but all in all the campus was quiet. David had already headed north to spend time with his dad, leaving Chris and Zack in the company of Lee.

The closest train stop was twelve miles away, the Seaboard line into Jacksonville, where Zack would catch the connection west to New Orleans and then a long bus route to Homerville. Chris opened the trunk of the car, and Zack threw his bag inside, climbed in the car, and they were off to the small one-track station in Waldo. As usual, the train was delayed. They bought Pepsis and found a shady bench out of the sun.

"Why so quiet?" Zack asked Chris. The boy gave no indication that he had heard the question. He sipped on the Pepsi and looked straight ahead. "Listen, kiddo. This hasn't been fun for any of us. But the last thing we need is to let the bastards wear us down."

Chris looked at Zack. "It isn't just that," he said.

"Then what?" Zack asked.

"David," he barely said the name.

"David?" Chris's response caught him by surprise. "I thought all that was settled."

"I'm sorry, Zack. David settled up long ago. It's me. When I'm with you guys, when I see you together, I keep asking why I can't have something like that. Why David couldn't have loved me instead of you, and then I feel so ashamed, because I love you both."

"So that's it." Zack edged close to him, placed his arm on Chris's shoulder. "Listen to me, Chris. David loves you, just as Lee loves you, just as I love you. He's just not *in love* with you. In fact, I'm not sure he's in love at all."

"Not with Stephen? Not with you?" he said, pouring out the remainder of the Pepsi.

"He can't let go of the memory. Stephen wasn't just a passing thing. There was something unique about that relationship, something that most people, myself included, would not completely comprehend. The first time is the hardest to let go of. You should know that. Sometimes it grows and grows, but most often, just passes. Don't be ashamed, Chris."

In the distance, they heard the train's whistle. They walked to the platform. The train crawled to a stop. Zack embraced the boy, held him for a moment, gave a large smile, then climbed aboard.

Chris stood there, watching as the train moved off until it was no longer in sight. Then he got in the car, sat for a moment weighing the heavy sadness that smothered him even more than the summer heat.

He dreaded the prospect of going home to his family. What is family anyway? Once he had been threatened with expulsion from family. You could only have membership in family much the way you had membership in a club, a church, a social group, so long as you adhered to the rules. Deviate from the rules, and you are out.

His father had defined the standard, set the boundaries and made the rules. Sometimes the rules must have seemed harsh, his father had told him. But which was preferable, a hard rule or no rule at all? Rules were the bedrock of society, what held family together.

Rules ensured order, propelled the species forward, provided security. Without rules the inherent degradation of the human species would prevail, and society would sink into anarchy.

It was like original sin, his father had reminded him. The garden was given for man to cultivate. There had been security for the man and the woman, the fruits of the garden abundant. There was but one rule, his father had noted. They could eat of any tree except for two. Which trees? The Tree of Life, and the Tree of Knowledge. Knowledge of what? Of good and evil, of course.

That was the rule.

All you had to do was abide by the rule. But was the rule fair? Without knowledge, there was only a perpetual state of ignorance.

Do good. Renounce evil. The rule was ignorance, a little price to pay for contentment and security. Break the rule, and you were out. His father had made that unmistakably clear. Chris had acquired the knowledge. But of what? Good or evil? Yes or no? Black or white? Which would he choose? He had already made his choice. He had quietly exchanged his blood family for an extended family. David, Zack, and Lee. In his extended family, there was no shame, regret, or expectation other than to be who you are. There was only one rule. *Know thyself. To thine own self be true.*

And so Chris delayed his journey to his family, who were now merely a surrogate family with their rules and expectations. Instead, he would take a short course, remain at the university for the summer and wait for the reunion with his extended family, with David, Zack and Lee.

Later that evening, having dropped Zack at the train stop, Chris wandered aimlessly toward the Ale House and, entering, sat at the end of the bar. Except for the bartender and a few stragglers, the place was empty. He ordered a soft drink and let his mind wander back to David and to the conversation with Zack before he got on the train, which took him away for the summer.

"Hello, young man deep in thought," a voice said. Chris turned to the stranger who had taken a place several feet away at the bar. "Buy you a drink?" he asked.

"Not legal till next year," Chris allowed, "but thanks."

"So, you're twenty. Must be a junior," he said, trying to engage in conversation.

"Actually sophomore. Got a late start of one year." Chris sensed that the guy was coming on to him. And he admitted to himself that he actually didn't object. The guy was handsome in an off sort of way. Strong facial features, but a slightly deformed nose, perhaps from a break. His short-cropped hair suggested a military connection. Chris had not seen him in the usual meeting spots on campus. Must be military.

"Good guess," the stranger smiled. "I finished my service in the Navy last month and decided to get an early start. I'm Rick, by the way," he said offering his hand. "Rick Warren."

When the two had finished introductions, Rick confessed that he was more than apprehensive about starting school. He had joined the Navy right after high school. It had been six years, and he wasn't sure about whether he would be up to it academically.

"And of course there is the age difference," he added. "A twenty-four-year-old freshman in a class of eighteen year olds is something of a challenge."

Chris could identify with Rick's apprehensiveness. His own arrival at the university had been stressful too, but for very different reasons.

"What did you do in the Navy?" Chris asked.

"Oh, nothing particularly exciting. Mostly office details, administration kind of things," he said.

"Like what kind of things?" Chris persisted.

"As I said, mostly just boring details," he said rather evasively.

"Oh, like you were an admiral," Chris teased him.

Rick laughed. "Just a J.G. Look, if you don't have any plans, would you have dinner with me? Hate eating alone."

Why not? Chris told himself. He seemed a nice enough guy, and he smiled at the handsome stranger to indicate his acceptance.

—◆—

RICK WARREN WAS the distraction Chris welcomed against the summer isolation from the others. The more they were together, the less he thought about his frustrated disconnect with David and Zack. It surprised him how easily he could open himself, could reveal fragments of himself that he had shared only with David, Zack, and Lee. They had been his reference point. Now someone else had reached out to him at the most unexpected time and in the most surprising way. He welcomed the encounter, accepted the deepening connection with Rick Warren, a connection that was evolving into something he could not have imagined possible.

At first, there was merely the growing acceptance of a new friendship, but soon Chris sensed that the encounters were beginning to move into something more intimate.

What he could not know was the unique intensity that his presence awakened in Rick. One Saturday late afternoon, they had met at the university indoor pool. Rick had watched Chris's smooth, hard body cut through the water, his eyes fixed on the graceful, effortless movement, aware for the first time of his attraction toward the boy.

Rick had always considered himself straight. Not once had he ever acted on a gay impulse. There had been times when he found some situations enticing, but he had never acted on them. And there were the details about his Navy experiences he did not share with Chris, would not share, could not reveal to this youth whom he found so desirable in this surprising and unwelcome way.

He had disclosed fragments of the truth to Chris. His assignment was indeed office-related. Upon receiving his commission, he was assigned to the Office of Naval Intelligence, or the ONI as the unit was commonly referred to. Those three letters were sufficient to incite fear and anxiety in anyone who became the objects of their investigations. Particularly homosexuals. Rick thought about the nights when he would lead his team into gay bars searching for Navy personnel, about the protests and denials as their targets were taken away and later summoned to the office's inquiry only to be dishonorably discharged for association with homosexuals in a gay bar. And he thought about the hearsay evidence provided by sailors who were actually exposed and were coerced into naming others of like persuasion, whether guilty or not. It was not an assignment he particularly enjoyed. In fact, it left him with an unpleasant feeling of guilt. But he didn't make the rules. The Navy did.

And now he was dealing with demons that his encounters with Chris had summoned, demons he somehow reluctantly was accepting, uncertain now about the unexpected direction his life was taking. It was his military experience that the university's guidance counselor had passed along to the committee, and which the committee now found useful in its investigations. Was it too late to back out?

—∞—

THEY HAD HAD an early supper, caught the last showing of *North by Northwest*, and afterward had gone to Chris's house off campus, not for a Pepsi but for a real drink. Rick kicked off his loafers, stretched out comfortably on the sofa, and relaxed totally. He took a swallow of the Scotch. "Well here I am contributing to the delinquency of a minor."

It was Chris who made the move. He set his glass on the coffee table and, moving in, ran his hand lightly over Rick's short-cropped hair. In the next moment, the two were encircling each other, Rick abandoning any remaining inhibition, the encounter intense, one he had never experienced, and he wanted it to go on without end. Afterward, the two lay spent, bodies of sweat fused together, and slept until dawn.

—∞—

"THE SENATOR IS not pleased with your progress, or should I say the lack thereof," Mayes said. "You've been with us over a month and so far not a single contact," Mayes complained.

"It's summer, for God's sake."

"You're moving too slowly."

"It's summer. I can't manufacture contacts," Rick Warren protested. "What does he expect?"

"He wants names. He wants the prize faggot."

"And who would that be?"

"That's what you're paid for, J. G. Warren. You know who it is. Get busy."

CHAPTER 27
APPEARANCES

THE SUMMER OF 1959 had drifted into fall. The change in September was subtle, the Florida summer heat persisting. But the change in Chris was obvious. David and Zack were astonished at his exuberance. This was not the quiet, brooding Chris but a reinvented extrovert, confident, sunny, obviously infatuated. It was Rick *this* and Rick *that* and the repetitive *we*. Clearly the boy was engaged in a serious relationship. And who exactly was this object of desire that Chris was inviting into their extended family? When would they meet him?

Soon.

—⬥—

CHRIS'S ATTENTION DRIFTED in and out of the lecture and the subsequent discussion of vampire folklore. The class had finished reading Bram Stoker's *Dracula*, and the professor had droned on about the way in which the bloodsucker attempted to gain the victim's soul. It was not the blood that the fiend desired but the soul. One assertion in vampire folklore described how the soul was linked to blood. Was it not the blood of Christ that was shed to save man's soul, the sacrifice to atone for original sin? Clearly the soul was linked to blood. Devour the victim's blood and gain the victim's soul, at least as in this particular bit of lore which the professor described. It was actually the *soul* the fiend desired.

And of course the victim was not merely an innocent. No, there was complicity between the unsuspecting victim and the soul thief. The vampire was not merely capable of deception; he was a master of deception. The victim was not merely the *unwilling partner* in the deception but a *participant*. The professor reminded them of the Devil's encounter with Faust, the paragon of intellect, who in spite of his intellect had unwittingly summoned the demon into his dwelling, the demon that had assumed another form.

Things were not always what they *appeared* to be. Even the devil could affect the disguise, could transform himself into another creature entirely, a seemingly benign and friendly dog whom the good Dr. Faust would invite unwittingly into his home. The demon had to be *invited*. And Faust like others in folklore became the unwitting participant in complicity, ignorant of the imminent looming loss, the loss of his soul.

Chris glanced repeatedly at the classroom clock as the professor went on about the bloodsucker, eagerly anticipating the new arrival to his extended family.

THE WEEKEND MARKED the family reunion. Lee had prepared the welcome feast and, along with Zack and David, eagerly anticipated Chris's arrival with his new friend. From Chris's rambling description of his new relationship, each had formed an image of the stranger who had been responsible for Chris's transformation.

When they arrived, David was surprised at what he sensed in Rick was an awkward uneasiness, not at all the image he had formed from Chris' descriptions. There was a reticence that somehow seemed out of place, as if Rick were not convinced of their acceptance of him. David couldn't quite define it, but there was something unsettling.

Lee also picked up on Rick's uneasiness. There was a lack of connection somehow, a deliberate space that Lee sensed Rick struggled to maintain. He was pleasant enough, easily talking about his experiences in the Navy, but there was yet the sense that he was holding back, unable or unwilling to fully bond with the three of them, as he had apparently bonded with Chris.

But Zack had a better sense of Rick's awkwardness. Like Rick, he too had come directly from the military, had found himself the older outsider in a much younger freshman class, wondering if he had it in him to compete with the crowd of students fresh out of high school. It was difficult adjusting again to civilian life. So to Zack, Rick's awkwardness seemed quite natural. Zack could empathize with Rick in a way that the others might not. They would just have to give him time. Time was all he needed.

—m—

"WE HAD HIGH expectations of you. You have been a disappointment."

"Explain yourself," Rick asserted.

Borland Mayes was taken aback by Rick Warren's impertinent response. He was not admonishing a younger informant of the committee. Warren's selection was based on his six years experience in the Navy, four of which were with the ONI. The other informants were amateurs: Warren was a professional. The others were part-timers. Warren was generously compensated, along with a housing provision. They expected results. He was, after all, employed by the committee, virtually a member.

"We're into September, and not one contact. Not one," Mayes said. "What's your excuse now?"

"So, what's the rush?" He reached into his pocket and retrieved a coin, smiled at Mayes and flipped the coin repeatedly. "Patience pays dividends. Haste makes waste."

"We're not buying patience. Sloat wants current activities concluded by the end of the year. Then we move to the other universities. After that, the secondary schools. God knows what we'll find there. This is just the beginning. That's why brought you on board. Understand?"

Rick understood more than he was ready to acknowledge with Mayes. Even before Chris, he had been unsure of his involvement with the committee. He was not homophobic. The Navy thing was just another assignment. He didn't write the laws. No one forced him to join the Navy, but once in, he had sworn to observe its regulations. Pure and simple. Now he had a choice.

After a rather long deliberative silence Rick said "You know, Mayes, I really came here to further my education. I guess I also had other expectations."

"Meaning?" Mayes asked suspiciously.

"I guess I didn't really grasp what you meant about subversion in the university, and your mission to uncover it. Seems to me like you want to hang a homosexual whenever and wherever you can find one." His response had an air of hostility now. *Cool it. Don't rush it.*

"You telling me you want out of this?"

"I'm telling you that I think you picked the wrong person for your slimy activity." Rick flipped the coin again. This time it hit the floor and ricocheted across the room.

Mayes threw a contemptuous look. "Was our compensation inadequate to augment your G.I. Bill, or have you just been too preoccupied with your young student friend?"

The remark caught Rick off-guard. "What does that have to do with this? "

"Well, let's see," Mayes said. "Your schooling is paid for in part with your G.I. benefits, and your present role as an officer in the Naval Reserves accounts for the rest. It would be most unfortunate to lose that, wouldn't it, not to mention your commission in the Reserves. Right? Do I make myself clear?"

Rick felt the trap spring. This was coercive blackmail. Now *he* was the one whose *cooperation* was demanded. A dishonorable discharge from the Reserves? His education terminated? His record smeared? Where was the way out?

"What do you want from me?" he finally managed.

Mayes was confident now. The lawyer in him paused just long enough to ram his point home. "William Lee and associated company."

Rick's astonishment was total. *Lee. The others. And Chris.*

"We overestimated your potential, Warren. You're a smart guy, but as I said, we had higher expectations of you. You've been paid well. Now it's time to deliver. No more stalling. We're into fall. Sloat wants this finished, and he wants Lee—now."

"Why Lee? Why this fixation on him?"

"It's Sloat's obsession more than anything else. The bastard epitomizes everything the senator loathes—the smugness, the defiance, the queerness. The others we broke easily, including that smart-ass reporter. Lee and Cohen are another matter. We'll handle Cohen, that little Jew. But you have until December to nail Lee." He paused. "And his harem."

Once outside, Rick could feel the sweat soaking his shirt, streaming down his face, not from the lingering summer heat but from his realization that there now seemed no escape from the trap he found himself in.

Confession time. Whose? Not Lee's. His own.

—⁂—

"JESUS CHRIST. THE ONI," Lee gasped. "And the committee. Christ almighty. What to tell Chris?"

"You have to tell him," Rick pleaded.

"No, you have to tell him. Tell him how you delivered him—delivered us to the executioners."

No, Rick thought. There must be another way. He would find a way to stop them.

—⁂—

HENSON HAD LOCATED Prevatt through his contacts with the Georgia Bureau of Investigation. It had not been difficult. The former music professor had taken a temporary part-time assignment as a substitute teacher in a secondary school in Atlanta. When questioned about his previous teaching experience, he claimed that he had left Florida to care for an aging relative who died after a prolonged illness. But the Georgia Bureau had already begun a routine background check and uncovered the real reason for his exit from State University. By the time Henson tracked him down, he was unemployed, desperate and depressed. It had been, after all, a mistake, Henson assured him—his dismissal from the university. He might yet clear his record. They simply needed more damaging evidence against Lee in exchange for Prevatt's exoneration.

"WE LOCATED PREVATT," Mayes told Sloat.

"Outstanding. What did you tell him?"

"Told him his dismissal was all a mistake. He's willing to cooperate."

"And Lee's former student?"

"Primed and ready."

"And Warren? I don't trust him."

"He's ready. He'll cooperate. He's not going to jeopardize anything for his little boyfriend. We just need his deposition."

"And the Jew? What about that arrogant Jew you interrogated? We need to call him back."

No, he was not homosexual, Cohen had answered, but for all he knew, Mayes could be. Had he ever had such tendencies? What truth did he want? President Thurgis had made himself an academic whore. If they wanted anything else, they could issue a subpoena.

"Well, Billy, additional confrontation with Ellis Cohen is not a viable option. We've not been able to connect him with anything. And he's dangerous. If we call him back, he'll likely challenge us with violating his civil rights. No, our target now is William Lee. He's our prime catch. Between Prevatt, the student, and Warren's deposition, we're ready to finish him."

"All right then," Sloat agreed. "Let's move."

—◊—

ANDREW CARNEGIE INSTITUTE was the university-supported high school, a laboratory for educational research advancing the quality of teaching and learning. Graduate assistants from the Education Department taught classes, counseled students, and prepared for careers in teaching. Only the most exceptional graduate students were invited as members of the elite faculty. Worden Stone was particularly exceptional. For one thing, he ranked third in his class standing. And he was a Negro.

He was also circumspect in keeping his private life apart from his professional activities. For three years, his students had set the norms for the English curriculum at the school, a mark of his success as a teacher. Now, in his final year as graduate assistant and respected member of the Institute's faculty, he was eager to pursue his career in education.

It had not been easy. As the one Negro participant in the program, he had gone the extra distance to prove himself. And he had been careful to conceal his sexual orientation. Several of his peers made no attempt to conceal their resentment at what they regarded as his "uppity" demeanor and subtle hint of effeminate mannerisms. No matter. He had survived and, with only weeks left, would be leaving the university with a doctorate in education and a waiting appointment at an all-Negro college in Central Florida.

He remained at his office late in the evening finishing the final exam for the senior English class. He was tired. It had been a long day without even a break for lunch. An early north Florida fall chill made him shiver, and he slumped inside the thin jacket to keep warm as he meandered toward his ten-year-old second-hand car. Once inside, he turned the ignition key, but the car only grunted without catching on. Several more tries and suddenly the engine started and he was moving along side streets of well-appointed houses, houses hidden behind tall ligustrum hedges that announced privacy.

When he turned a corner, the car gave several spasmodic lunges and then stopped cold. He turned the ignition switch but there was no response. He sat for a moment, contemplating his next move. He was nowhere near a pay phone. Should he try one of the houses?

Tentatively, he walked toward the large white house set back from the street, its lights cutting through the dark. He paused at the opening between the ligustrum hedge and the driveway. Then he took the few steps when a spotlight from the patrol car flashed on him and a menacing voice shouted, "You there. Halt." Moments later he was taken to the county jail and booked on a charge of prowling.

It was close to midnight when B. J. Henson arrived at the jail. Henson stared contemptuously at the Negro. He could tell by the way he was dressed and his manner that this educated, uppity nigger was queer. Did he know he was under oath? Was he aware of the penalties for perjury? What was he doing casing a white neighborhood in the middle of the night? Henson kept pressing him to admit to sexual crimes against nature, and when he refused, they assured him that he would never be awarded a teaching certificate.

One week later, Worden Stone was summoned to the president's office, and Dwight Thurgis announced his expulsion from the university.

It was an expulsion that would not go unchallenged.

—⁂—

OWEN SHAW RETRIEVED his bag from the claim area, walked over to the Hertz counter at the Jacksonville airport, and minutes later was on Highway 301 for the sixty-five-mile drive to the university to meet Worden Stone. It had been three years since the confrontation with Billy Sloat. Then he was present as an aide. This time he would be the plaintiff's legal counsel. And Sloat—how ironic, he thought, to have faced an adversary whose mother had been the means to his education, to his achievement, and without whom he would not be here at all. As Billy Sloat once told him, he might be riding a garbage truck or shining someone's shoes in Tallahassee.

Except this was not Tallahassee, and he was not riding a garbage truck.

He drove through the tree-shaded campus of the university. It was different from the urban university he had attended. Here was a sleepy oasis tucked away in a typical Southern town. From outward appearances, there was no trace of Sloat's assault on its tranquility. He found a spot near the university library, parked the car and went directly to the second-floor reference room, where a nervous Worden Stone waited.

His client's demeanor took him by surprise. What had he expected? Here was a young Negro who had been expelled from the university on the pretext that he was homosexual and whose other problem was being colored in an all-white university.

The student greeted him with a soft, limp hand and a subtle effeminate mannerism in his voice. They found a small private conference room at the back of the main reference area. Owen studied the young man's gestures as he recounted the events leading up to his expulsion. Yes, there was little doubt as to the man's orientation. When he finished, Owen moved the notepad aside, folded his hands, and looked directly at his client.

"Clearly their real intent is to get you out based on your race," Owen said. "The homosexual thing is merely a pretext. You will deny that you are gay."

"But I am gay, gay and colored, the way God made me. Why should I deny who I am?"

"Because they can't get rid of you for being a Negro. But there is no defense for being gay," he said. "Clearly they are discriminating based on your race. That is our position. Do you understand?"

"No, I don't understand. And you don't know the hell that's going on here. It isn't right," he protested.

"Well, life is not fair. If it were, we would not be having this conversation," Owen said.

"This isn't just about me, about you, about race. It's not a Negro issue, a white issue, a gay issue, it's about people. You can't cherry-pick who has rights and who doesn't."

"Well, Mr. Stone," he said, "you have a choice. You can get your life back or you can allow them to crucify you. Those are your options. We've come a long way in our fight for equality. Perhaps a time will come when gay people will demand their rights too. But unfortunately, that is not our fight right now. What would you like me to do?"

But Owen Shaw already had the answer to his question. There would be no crucifixion. Worden Stone would survive the ordeal, be reinstated, await graduation.

—⁂—

THE STONE AFFAIR was settled quickly. There was no contact this time between Owen Shaw and Senator Billy Sloat, and Owen was just as glad that it had been avoided. He drove the back rural roads that would take him back to Monroe to see Annabelle Shaw Sloat for the last time.

The nursing home was tucked away from the main road between Monroe and the next town. It was a small facility with no more than ten or so residents. Owen seated himself in the oversized wicker chair next to the window. Outside the trees shaded the manicured lawn and the last remnants of summer flowers just before the onset of winter. The all-white reception room offered a clean, airy appearance suggesting a private residence rather than a nursing facility.

Owen got up from his chair as the nurse pushed Annabelle Sloat's wheelchair into the room.

"Just let me know when you're ready to leave," the nurse said and left the room.

Owen leaned down and lightly brushed Annabelle's graying hair with his hand. Her eyes shifted left then right in confusion, trying to place the strange face before her.

"Do I know you?" she asked in her childlike voice.

"I'm Owen, Miss Annabelle. Remember me?" he asked in a low whisper.

"Owen?" she asked. "Owen?" she repeated.

"Owen Shaw, Miss Annabelle."

"Oh, Billy. Yes, Billy. I am so glad to see you. Did you come to get me?"

"I came to see you, Miss Annabelle, to tell you that I love you and to thank you for the difference you made in my life," he said.

"You have to get me out of here, Billy. I'm a prisoner here. Every night that man climbs through the window and into my bed. I know he's been drinking. I can smell it on him. He's a bad person, Billy. Ask Ida." Her eyes were wide with confusion. She grasped his hand tightly. "Get me out of here, please."

"It's all right, Miss Annabelle. I'll make sure that man doesn't bother you again," he said.

She frowned as if trying to place the face. It was someone familiar. But who?

Owen leaned down and placed his lips against her forehead. "Goodbye, Miss Annabelle."

"Oh, you are such a good boy. You will come to see me again, won't you?" she said, smiling now.

He called for the nurse. He looked one last time as she was wheeled from the room. "Goodbye, Annabelle," he said, and then he was gone.

CHAPTER 28
WILLIAM LEE

THE CLASSROOM WAS dark except for the projector's light illuminating the screen with the image of Michelangelo's *David*. William Lee continued his discussion of the famous sculpture as if nothing unusual was taking place.

Henson, Munjay, and the new dean stood at the rear of the room. Lee paused to change the next slide.

Henson barked, "Dr. Lee, we have a summons. You will come with us. Now!"

Confused students glanced at each other, at the intruders, at the professor.

Lee looked at his watch.

"This class ends at 9:15."

"Now!" was the command.

"No. In fifteen minutes."

The next image on the screen was the Sistine Chapel Ceiling. Lee continued as if nothing out of the ordinary had occurred.

— ⚕ —

LEE WALKED BRISKLY across the lobby of the Rosemont Hotel. He acknowledged Simon Prevatt, as the two exchanged knowing glances, but he was surprised to the see the student, whom he could not place. It was a familiar face. What was he doing here?

The student glanced at Lee, then looked away. He seemed nervous. Prevatt sat motionless. Nothing was said.

Lee had barely taken a seat when Munjay summoned him. Inside the room, the same arrangement—the table, the chairs, the lone bulb dangling from the ceiling.

Mayes, Henson, and Munjay occupied their usual places at the center. Sloat sat at the far left, and at the opposite end of the table sat Rick Warren.

Mayes started the recorder.

"State your name and profession," he demanded.

"William Lee, professor of humanities, State University."

"You realize you are under oath?"

"Yes."

"Do you realize what perjury is?"

"Yes."

"The giving of false statement under oath?"

"Certainly."

"Do you know the penalty for perjury in this state?"

"No, I do not."

"Up to twenty years."

"And is there a penalty for coercing others to commit perjury?" Lee asked.

Mayes stiffened.

"Is there?" Lee repeated.

Mayes shuffled papers that littered the desk, evading the question. The trap was set. Here was Sloat's prime catch. They would not screw this up.

"What do you teach out there?" Mayes asked with contempt.

"Humanities, C-5," he answered.

"In your class lectures, do you ever discuss matters of sex?"

"Of course. This is a university. We read many works where sex is an issue, as it is in many of the great works of literature."

"Then sex itself is a subject that comes up in your courses frequently," he said as a statement of fact.

It was Lee's turn to go on the offensive. "As it does in any course in literature," he insisted. "It's impossible to avoid discussing it. Sex is a primary motivation in many works of art—literature, painting, whatever it is. These are grown people engaged in study, not children."

"In the study of sex, professor? Is that what your class discussions are about?"

"This is not a grammar school. My conversations with students are open and frank."

"Do they include discussions of homosexuality?"

"They include any legitimate discussion on an academic level. That is my professional responsibility as a teacher," Lee said with pride.

"And what of your professional responsibility to instill appropriate moral standards in your students, Dr. Lee?"

"My job is to teach, not to indoctrinate."

"Well, as a teacher, it is your responsibility to set a decent moral example." Mayes pressed on.

"Enlighten me, Mr. Mayes. Tell me what you consider a *decent moral example* to be."

"Well, sir, I can tell you what it is not. It is not two men living a deviant lifestyle together in the same house, flaunting their homosexuality. It is common knowledge, sir," he said with his voice rising.

"No, you're wrong there, Mr. Mayes. It's just common talk."

"It is not, as you say, just common talk. We have sworn..." but Lee interrupted.

"Hearsay. What you have is sworn hearsay perhaps, but as far as I know, there is no crime in two people sharing a house together, nor in ten or fifteen cowboys sharing a bunk house."

Mayes looked at Sloat and knew from the grimace that he was not pleased. The interrogation had stalled. He settled again on Lee.

"Let me ask you directly, then. Have you ever had homosexual relations with a music professor by the name of Simon Prevatt?"

"No."

"Are you sure?"

"Yes, I am sure."

"Did you, shortly after he arrived at the university, invite him over to your house?"

"Yes, I did."

"And what was the occasion?"

"Well obviously he has already provided you that information, but it certainly had nothing to do with sex," Lee stated emphatically.

Mayes hurled his rejoinder with a snarl. "Let me warn you again, you are under oath. We have multiple witnesses who have..." he sputtered, then recovering said, "...who are prepared to confront you about your homosexual activity and your moral turpitude regarding students at this university."

"Then I would ask to face my accusers."

"And so you shall. Two are waiting outside this room, and one is seated at the end of this table," he said, looking directly at Rick Warren. "Mr. Henson, please escort the witnesses in."

The student approached the interrogation table, his head swiveling left and right at the people seated there. His visit to Munjay's office had been routine. This setting had a sinister quality. Lee's presence was unsettling. He had not anticipated a direct confrontation with his former teacher. Was it too late to back out?

Prevatt came behind him. He scanned the faces, and settled on Rick Warren, their eyes locking momentarily, knowingly, until Henson asked him to be seated.

"We will begin with you, Mr. Prevatt. Do you recognize the man seated with you at this table?" Mayes began.

"Yes, he is Dr. William Lee."

"Previously you gave sworn statements regarding your encounter with Dr. Lee in his home shortly after your arrival at the university, isn't that so?"

"Yes, I did." His voice a lifeless monotone.

"Now, Mr. Prevatt, I want you to tell us exactly what took place between you and Dr. Lee that afternoon in his house." He offered a confident smile this time in Sloat's direction.

Prevatt hesitated, his eyes connecting again with Rick, waiting for Mayes to repeat his command.

"Well?" Mayes growled impatiently. Another glance toward Rick, anticipating Rick's signal for him to continue. Rick nodded for Prevatt to finish.

"We listened to recordings. Dr. Lee offered me tea." He paused. Mayes waited, anticipating his response.

"And?" Mayes urged him on.

"And that was it."

Mayes shouted. "What do you mean, *that was it*?"

"I mean that's all there was to it," he said in the same monotone.

Mayes roared at the witness. "That is not what you told us previously in your sworn statement. You were under oath. Repeat what you told us under oath," he demanded, his voice cracking with rage.

"In my sworn statement, I committed perjury. You coerced me into making false statements, damaging statements about Dr. Lee. The truth is, I never had a sexual encounter with the man. Except for the one time in his house, I hardly knew him."

"What do you mean you were coerced? You committed perjury. You can be prosecuted for committing perjury. How dare you accuse this committee of coercion." His eyes darted back and forth like a wild animal that had been snared, first at Sloat, then at Warren.

Rick had waited for the right moment to move. He nodded at Prevatt. The procedure was becoming chaotic. Now he smelled blood. Mayes motioned for him to come forward.

"Mr. Warren, for the record, tell the committee about your contact with Dr. Lee and certain students that he has had in his house on repeated occasions."

"You want the account of my involvement in the record?"

"Yes. Tell everything you know."

"I do not know the man well. I was hired by you, by the committee, as an informant to provide damaging evidence, by whatever means, pertaining to his moral character."

Mayes's mouth dropped in astonishment. This unexpected turn caught him totally off guard. He glared at Rick, the veins in his neck engorged with blood. He had, Rick thought, the look of a man on the verge of a stroke. Sloat rose abruptly from his chair and stormed from the room. Mayes was frantic now. He fired back at Warren, then at Prevatt, his voice a threatening crescendo.

"You were warned about the criminal statutes concerning perjury," he shouted at Prevatt. Then he turned to Warren. "And the United States Navy may find your recent associations compelling."

"Well, Borland, the press might find your activities also compelling: intimidation, entrapment, blackmail, details I can provide as your paid informant. I can't stop your assault, and I can't undo what you destroyed, but I can do damage control, and I will." He turned to Prevatt and said quietly, "Thank you Mr. Prevatt, for coming back, for setting the record straight. You had more to lose than to gain. You've paid your debt. Leave now. For that matter," he said turning to Lee, "why don't *we* leave too?"

Rick, Prevatt, and Lee left the lone student to face the interrogators. Now it was just his word against the accused professor.

"Am I going to be prosecuted for perjury?" he whimpered.

Mayes dismissed him with a wave of the hand.

———

"WE HAVE TO find Chris. Let him know we're O.K." Lee's voice was urgent.

Just weeks from the end of the term, Chris had dropped out of classes. No one had seen him since Rick confessed his role in the investigation. David and Zack had made repeated attempts to make contact but without success.

Rick was persistent. Each day he would go to the house. He would pound fiercely on the door, calling Chris's name, then pleading with him to open the door, but there was no response.

CHRIS CLOSED HIS eyes, not sleeping, his mind replaying confused images. He was back at the deserted athletic field. It was dark. *The burning sensation of beer as he swallowed, hands caressing his body, ecstasy coursing through him, a light blinding him, recrimination, his father's voice, indistinct, eyes accusing, sickness and healing, images of naked men, electric shock, spasms, icy water, drowning, gasping for air, the sinner, the healing, just as I am, the sinner, I come.*

It had been the defining moment of his life, isolation, terror, humiliation. But nothing compared to this. He had betrayed a trust. His recklessness had severed the one vital connection he had in restoring self-respect, and he had wasted it on Rick Warren, on a stranger whose betrayal destroyed any self-confidence he still had.

Was Lee all right? How had he survived the interrogation? Had he? What was next? Who was next? David? Himself? He wished Lee could know his remorse, could offer him forgiveness, but in his heart he could not forgive himself. He was not merely a victim but a participant in the crime.

It was the soul the demon wanted. Devour the victim's blood and gain his soul. The soul thief was not just capable of deception but a master of deception, and the victim was not a mere innocent but a participant in the crime.

He was a participant. He had invited the executioner into the circle. He was equally to blame.

HE WAS NOT Catholic, yet he sought absolution from the priest. When he finished his confession, the priest turned away. He would find no absolution unless he renounced this self-destructive desire. His guilt was beyond complicity in the betrayal. His soul was in jeopardy. His lust would consume his soul and damn him for eternity. His sin was infinite. Only by renouncing its unspeakable nature could he save himself.

The priest watched him leave, watched him descend the steps and once on the walk ignore the car but walk away from the lighted street and into the wooded area shrouded in darkness. The priest came to the door. He hesitated. In a conflicted moment, he was pulled between his faith and his heart, between his dogma and his empathy. He hurried down the steps to follow the young man into the dark. He started to call out to him when he heard a muffled pop, as if a car had backfired, and saw the flash of light in the dark.

—⁂—

IT HAD BEEN three hours and except for the four of them, the waiting room was deserted. They huddled close, awaiting the inevitable pronouncement.

The surgeon scanned their weary faces. "He lost a lot of blood, and the trauma from the gunshot makes things precarious. Right now he's stable. That's all I can tell you. Go home. Come back tomorrow."

But they stayed.

The sofa in the waiting room was barely wide enough for two medium-size adults. Rick curled himself into a tight ball and closed his eyes, but not to sleep. If he believed in God, he would be pleading for the all powerful, omniscient, omnipotent being to grant a second chance and set things right. But he was no believer. Not even in himself. So he would not plead but would only wait for Chris to return, or continue alone into the deepening shadow. That's all he could do.

He felt a hand brush his face. He opened his eyes to see Lee kneeling beside him. He turned away, unable to accept the gesture of reassurance.

"It was a courageous thing you did, Rick. You said Prevatt had more to lose in coming back to clear the record. But his life, his career was already finished. You had more to lose by coming forward, by setting Mayes and Sloat up. If Chris had known—" but Rick would not let him finish.

"He didn't, he just didn't," he said. He sat up and placed his hands over his face as he bent forward. He wanted to cry, but he couldn't.

It was midnight when Chris Chadwick's parents arrived. Lee approached Chadwick, extending his hand, but before he could say anything, the man turned away. One glance at the four men in the waiting room told John Chadwick all he needed to know. His son had back-slid into depravity, and this was the price to pay for his sin. *The wages of sin is death.* Whether his son would live or die was all the same to him now. He would sooner see him dead than living a life like that.

A nurse led the couple to the intensive-care room. Lisa Chadwick approached her son tentatively. She touched his face and whispered something that she knew he could not hear. John Chadwick said nothing, just stood at the foot of the bed watching his son with a raw frigidity, and then quite suddenly said, "He's made his choices; he's in God's hands now. May God have mercy on him."

He tugged at the sleeve of her blouse. "Come," he said, but either she did not hear him, or did not want to hear him. Whatever choice Chris had made, whatever he was, he was her son, and she would not allow herself to think that God would abandon him.

"Let's go," he insisted. "Now."

"Let me stay," she pleaded.

"We'll come back in the morning. Come," he repeated, his voice cold, indifferent.

How peaceful he seems, the sweet, gentle face, her child, her son. She cannot give him life, but she can give him her unconditional love. At the door she looked again at the child, the boy lying peacefully but alone in the room.

CHAPTER 29
RANDOM THOUGHTS

THE SERVICE WAS brief. Chadwick decided against a church service and settled on the funeral home instead. Except for several close friends from the church, he had insisted on a private service. Nevertheless, David, Zack, Lee and Rick sat quietly at the rear of the chapel, and as soon as the service ended, they left as quietly as they had come.

The following Sunday, Pastor Snyder delivered his customary fiery sermon. He pranced back and forth behind the altar at the front of the church, the platform barely able to support his two-hundred-thirty-five pound-frame of fat. He bellowed, throwing his arms in a wild upward motion. "The spirit is willing but the flesh is weak," he thundered.

"Amen, praise Jesus," came the response from the congregation.

Willing for what? Lisa Chadwick asked herself as the words rolled off the preacher's tongue. *What* weakness was the flesh subject to?

"The wages of *sin* is *death*," he shouted, saliva escaping from the corner of his mouth as his voice reached a fever-pitched crescendo.

"Yes, Jesus, praise God," the congregation screamed back, the cacophony of their voices approaching hysteria.

"He is an angry God who *loves* the sinner but *hates* the sin," he moaned, his head shaking violently like a wild animal that had been entrapped. "Death is the wage of the sinner's blasphemy against God, a vengeful God, an angry God whose wrath is without pity for the unrepentant," came the final warning from the raspy, fatigue-ridden voice as the choir broke into *Onward Christian Soldiers*.

An angry God, Lisa Chadwick repeated as the congregation joined in the song. In her heart, Lisa Chadwick had committed the unforgivable sin. Blasphemy against the angry God that had taken her son. So when would she receive her wages? She had already lost the only treasure of any value. She was ready to collect on the debt.

—⁓—

LISA CHADWICK SAT in the rocker, the crochet needle and ball of string on her lap. She examined the unfinished scarf, the intricate designs of diamond patterns alternating with circles, subtle hues of color that Chris would have approved. She had lost interest in the project. What did it matter now? Her mind drifted to a hospital room and a boy alone, with tubes hanging from the bedside rack and the incessant beeping of a monitor announcing that life was still present.

The voice from the opposite end of the living room broke her trance.

"What's wrong?" Chadwick murmured. "You haven't said three words since supper, which you never finished."

She looked up and raised her brows to indicate a response.

"How long will this go on?" he demanded.

How long, she asked herself, could a marriage last? Children were supposed to outlive their parents. There was nothing left in this marriage that resembled a family. They were just two disconnected people occupying the space of a house. She wanted out, but there was no out to escape to.

"It's Chris still, isn't it?" he intoned. "When are you going to cut loose?" he demanded.

Sooner than you think, she wanted to tell him. Sooner than you think.

—⁓—

THEY WERE SORTING through Chris's personal items when Rick discovered the poems tied neatly in a bundle, and a note that was attached.

Random Thoughts by Chris Chadwick
For Rick
What is the thing most feared? Death?
Not Death? Some edge beyond?

A place where one must go in fear or valor,
To struggle, to protest
To become resolute with power?
I do not know except for this:
That each must seek the peace
Alone against the dark,
The course fixed by our own indifferent hand,
Which sets us constant toward the friendless land.
Yet think of this: that two familiar strangers
Touched gently in the night and for a narrow moment
Rested from the journey, pushed against the dark
Talked to stars, heard the sea, forgot despair;
In some quiet place where strangers meet
Their fingers tingled with Familiarity
And their bodies, fused with droplets of sweat
Slept until dawn.

He read the lines again and again, and the release he had sought finally came.

—◊—

THE SIGN ON the front lawn indicated *SOLD*. Lee had not expected the house would sell so quickly. He packed the last of the boxes and uncorked a bottle of chardonnay, passing glasses to Rick, David, and Zack.

"You don't have to do this, you know," Rick reminded him. "They won't hurt you now. You can put this behind you, resume your career."

"It's already behind me. There's nothing for me here. The campus is a tomb. Too many buried memories. The others had no choice. I do, thanks to you, and it's a relief to let go."

"And go where?" David asked him.

"New York. A friend is opening a bookstore down in the village, the first of its kind. Gay-friendly you might say, but along with the classics too. And Charlie goes with me," he said stroking the cat. "The only things I'll miss here are you guys."

He could see in their faces their regret and their apprehension, but also their acceptance that his decision was final. "Come now," he said.

"You'd think I was Socrates who had just swallowed the hemlock at his execution instead of this delicious chardonnay." He held the glass up and drank it in one gulp.

—◆—

SIMON PREVATT DROVE to a deserted area of the campus, pulled the car off the unpaved road and cut the engine. His breathing was heavy, his eyes bleary from the lack of sleep. He could make out random Christmas lights from the dorms in the hazy distance. Except for the muffled voices of carolers far away singing peace on earth, good will toward men, there was an oppressive silence.

Why had he come back? Once terminated from the university, there had been no reason to return. By leaving, he had escaped public exposure. Yet in returning, he might be forgiven. And so he had returned. But he had defied them this time. He had not provided them what they wanted, and there was a price to pay for that. After all, they had the power. He had only his soul, what was left of it.

For an instant, he came close to losing his nerve, thinking there might be another way, but something twisted in his brain. From the time of his first interrogation, he had weighed his options only to conclude that there were none. They had already pronounced his guilt. Guilt by insinuation, by implication, by complicity—real or imagined. Truth was what they defined as truth. It was all the same to them. There was no defense against the committee, whose goal was to purge the sins of others. Yet his own sin he could not expiate. He had sinned against his own conscience. In January they would take their revenge, reveal his name and prosecute him for the lie they had demanded of him. Nothing would stop them.

But there was one control Billy Sloat and his committee lacked in spite of their absolute, unchallenged authority. In the darkness, far away the dormitory lights blinked on and off—on and off, accented by the clear, brisk, north Florida chill.

He held the gun to his chest and fired.

—◆—

THE EXODUS ACCELERATED. The best professors migrated to other less hostile environments, and few came in to replace them. Cohen was among the deserters. He packed his few remaining books, sealed the boxes, and stacked them in the corner for the movers. Whatever was left could go into the trashcans outside in the hallway.

He was searching his desk one last time to make sure he had not left behind anything of significance when he heard a tap at the door. Standing in the doorway was Dwight Thurgis, who surveyed the empty shelves, the bare walls which once displayed framed diplomas, photographs, posters, and which now displayed mere outlines in contrast to the darker hues of the vacant walls.

Speechless, the two faced each other. Thurgis ended the awkward silence. "I wanted to protect the university. How could I know it would come to this? You must believe me, Ellis, I had no idea it would come to this."

"Why, Dwight? Why, when you sold yourself to them? What was to protect? The best are leaving in protest, and the scavengers you hire to fill the vacuum won't take any of this personally, they'll just be glad to have a job. Who else would want to teach in a place like this?"

"What else could I do? Those people have the power. Who can stop them?" he protested.

"There's your answer. No one when men like you do nothing,"

He reached inside his pocket fetching the office key. "Here," he said, placing it in Thurgis' hand. "I was going to turn this in to maintenance, but you can save me the trouble. Goodbye, Dwight," he said, leaving Dwight Thurgis standing in the musty room with stacks of boxes which the movers would soon retrieve.

—⁓—

EXCEPT FOR PERSONAL effects, Rick had nothing to move, and now there was nothing to hold him back. David and Zack placed the two boxes in the car's trunk, and Rick threw the rest of the things in the back seat.

"Thanks," he said, giving the two a faint smile.

"What now?" David asked.

Rick frowned. He wasn't sure actually what was next except time to sort things out. "After that, I'll transfer credits and finish someplace else. Right now, just drifting awhile. And you guys?"

"One more semester, then find another school out of state," he said looking at Zack. "And Zack is coming too."

There was an uneasy moment, each waiting for the other to offer some reassurance that their paths would cross again in a better time, a different space. But David knew somehow that was not likely.

On the front seat of the car was a manila folder. Retrieving it, Rick offered it to David. "Here," he said, these are for you, something Chris wanted us..." he paused, "wanted you to have. Read them later," he said as David accepted the folder.

"All right then," Rick said, embracing the two. "I'm gone. Keep in touch?" He hesitated for a moment. He hadn't the slightest idea where he was going. He would just start driving. And for a while, Chris would be there.

—◊—

NORTON BRELL WAS finishing the last of the prints in his darkroom at the far end of the house when the phone rang. Who would be calling him in the middle of the day? Who would call him at all? He seldom had any callers, the phone little more than a convenience.

"Yes, hello. What do you want," he asked, his voice a monotone of boredom.

"Norton Brell?" the voice on the other end asked.

"Who is this?" Brell asked, annoyed at the intrusion.

"It's Borland Mayes, Mr. Brell."

Suddenly Brell's boredom vanished. "Mr. Mayes, so nice to hear from you again. How's the investigation coming along?"

"Well, since your initial involvement, we've made excellent progress. In fact, we'll be wrapping up here and moving on to the other universities. As a gesture of appreciation for your help with Dority and the others, we have something special for you," Mayes said. "Meet us at the University Club in an hour. It's short notice, I know. We're buying lunch," he said, hanging up abruptly.

Something special—the photographs. Henson had promised they would return the negatives and the photographs from the night of his entrapment at the motel in return for his cooperation. Brell closed down the darkroom, hurriedly changed clothes, and headed for the University Club, not wanting to keep Borland Mayes waiting.

So, he thought, they're ready to move on. In spite of his initial encounter with them, he had to admit that they had been skillful in juggling their secret tactics against the issue of moral turpitude, appealing to the public's prurient interest in homosexual activity at the university.

In the lobby of the University Club, he had seated himself near the main entrance for a clear view of the door—and waited. He had been there for more than an hour. Where were they? His mind replayed that night in the motel and the photographs. All he could think of was the photographs. Just then, he saw Mayes and Henson entering from the side door of the lobby, Mayes carrying a legal-size envelope. *The negatives*. Brell sprang from the chair, relieved at their arrival, energized by the anticipation of the envelope's contents.

Except for the three of them, the club's dining room was empty, the lunch crowd gone now. Brell nibbled on the club sandwich, trying to make conversation while Mayes and Henson watched, neither having ordered anything from the menu.

"How's the club sandwich?" Mayes asked dryly.

"Good," Brell replied, his eyes darting left and right at the two sitting across from him, and then at the envelope positioned next to Mayes. Then, unable to maintain his composure any longer, Brell pushed the plate away, looking directly at Mayes. "You mentioned you had something for me," he said, attempting to conceal his impatience.

Mayes smiled and slid the envelope toward Brell. There was a brief pause, then Brell's fingers tore at the envelope, but inside, along with what appeared to be written copy, there were only the photographs. Brell's face was a mixture of panic and confusion.

"I don't understand," he said, "where are the negatives?" He turned to Henson. "You led me to believe you'd return the negatives if I cooperated."

Henson cocked an eyebrow. "No, I told you we might just forget that whole encounter in the motel in return for your cooperation, and we're keeping our word—and the negatives. You keep the photographs and the accompanying article."

Brell's hands shook uncontrollably as he scanned what was obviously a news release intended for the university's student newspaper.

"...The committee's investigation of homosexual activity among faculty and students at State University has been concluded,"

according to Borland Mayes, Chief Counsel for the Senate Investigation Committee, "and the committee expresses special
appreciation for the contribution of Norton Brell, a third-year
photography student, in identifying individuals early in the
investigation."

It took moments for Brell to comprehend what was happening. He
was merely more of the wreckage left behind.

CHAPTER 30
SELF-DESTRUCTION

MAYES HAD BEEN wrong. He had believed that nothing could stop the committee. The committee was on a collision course with itself. Nothing is forever. The committee was a virus that mutated and for which there seemed no immunity. It was itself immune to any resistance, as Mayes predicted. Even the new governor welcomed the purge of homosexuals not only in the educational system but throughout every government agency to clean things once and for all. A database would be developed to identify the location of every known homosexual as a potential sexual predator. But in their arrogance, they turned out to be wrong.

Governor E. Bradly Green was the new governor replacing Rudge once his term was over. Unlike Rudge, he had no intention of curtailing Sloat's progress to root out subversion. He signed a bill authorizing expanded inquiry and providing additional funding for the committee's ongoing activities.

Sloat was delighted. The committee was poised to launch its most ambitious project since its inception, its comprehensive and definitive publication: *Homosexuality and Citizenship in Florida.*

He leafed through the sixty-seven-page draft of the pamphlet. On the purple cover, there was the black-and-white image of two naked homosexual men in a lip-locked kiss, and underneath was the title:

A REPORT OF THE FLORIDA
LEGISLATIVE INVESTIGATION COMMITTEE

November, 1964   Tallahassee, Florida

"I like the cover. Gets attention. The rest is crap," Sloat protested.

The aide was defensive. "Senator, it is an official document. We use special language for official documents. It's protocol."

"Screw protocol. I want arousal. What good is it if it don't arouse people to action. We spent years getting to this point. I want results."

"What changes do you want, senator?" the aide asked.

He read again the preface to the pamphlet. It was weak, too tame, almost apologetic. With pen in hand, he struck through particular lines, substituting other verbiage.

> The Legislative Investigation Committee was a <u>mandate</u> to investigate the extent of <u>infiltration</u> into state agencies <u>by practicing homosexuals</u>. To understand and deal with the <u>growing problem</u>, an understanding of its nature and manifestation is essential. This report can be a value to all citizens. Every parent, every individual concerned with the <u>moral climate</u> should be aware of the <u>rise in homosexual activity</u> noted here and <u>possessed of the basic knowledge set forth</u>.

He turned to the aide. "These changes," he insisted. "I want details, and I want more pictures. You know what they say about pictures."

Six hours later, the aide returned with illustrations and accompanying details. "Do you want to make any other corrections?" the aide asked.

He scanned the revisions.

> Front cover (illustration); Fetish (illustrations); Who and how many are homosexuals? Why be concerned? What to do about homosexuality; Florida laws on sex offenses; Glossary of homosexual terms and deviate acts; fixation on youth (illustrations); child molester crimes; unnatural sex crimes; (illustrations); crimes against nature law; public sex (illustrations)

The brief description of Crimes Against Nature Law (800.01) still too general, he insisted. More details. Spell it out.

Another hour and explicit details from actual state statutes followed.

1. CRIMES COMMITTED PER OC: (Oral copulation)
   Fellatio: (feh lay shee o) Sexual gratification obtained by sucking the penis; may be practiced by male homosexuals or by female where she introduces penis into her mouth.
   Cunnilingus: (cun ni lin gus) A form of sexual deviation where a person derives excitation by licking the clitoris (kly to ris); it is practiced by female homosexuals (lesbianism) or by a male with a female.
2. CRIMES COMMITTED PER ANUS: (Anal copulation)
   Pederasty: (ped er as ty) A form of sexual intercourse through the anus.
   Carnal copulation of male with male (particularly man with boy) by penetrating anus with penis; also same act with female. This is also referred to as sodomy.
PUNISHMENT: ALL CRIMES AGAINST NATURE (800.01) NOT TO EXCEED TWENTY YEARS IN PRISON.

"Now we're talking. And the photographs? Where are the other photographs? And just so no one accuses us of not being objective, include the other stuff on moral turpitude. Print it."

OTHER FLORIDA LAWS ON SEX OFFENSES
ILLEGAL FORMS OF NATURAL INTERCOURSE:

1. FORNICATION (798.03). Unlawful heterosexual intercourse between two unmarried persons. PUNISHMENT: Three months or a fine not to exceed $30.00.
2. LEWD AND LASCIVIOUS BEHAVIOR (798.02). Any man and woman, not being married to each other, lewdly and lasciviously associate and cohabit together, the offense includes both lewd and lascivious intercourse and/or living or dwelling together. PUNISHMENT: Not more than one year in prison, or one year in the county jail, or a fine not to exceed $300.00.

3. ADULTERY (798.01). Voluntary heterosexual intercourse of a married person with a person other than his spouse. (If either party is married, both shall be deemed guilty.) PUNISHMENT: Not to exceed two years in prison or one year in the county jail or fine not to exceed $500.00.

The glossary of homosexual terms and deviate acts, which concerned citizens, he thought, would find useful, fascinated him: GAY—homosexual; QUEER—a homosexual usually of low class and habits; CHI-CHI—a room or apartment very effeminately decorated, lace works, drapes, etc. BUTCH—homosexual who appears to be very masculine; BITCH—homosexual who is swishy and talks in an effeminate manner, frequently uses "mushy" language; DOG'S LUNCH—a person whose looks and actions are unattractive to the point of non-association; PUPPY'S LUNCH—not as bad as a dog's lunch but still unattractive; BLOW JOB; DINGE QUEEN; SCREAMING BITCH; MASTURBATION; PERVERT

The list went on.

Illustrations of various sexual acts included with the textual descriptions made the publication the defining accomplishment in arousing the citizens to action. And that is exactly what it did. Copies of the pamphlet sold for twenty-five cents, and the committee even provided discounts for bulk purchases. Demand for the pamphlet was extraordinary. Unfortunately, Sloat discovered that the arousal it produced was not the one he had anticipated.

Public reaction was swift and brutal. Sloat was a prisoner in his senate office as dozens of reporters and television anchors camped outside his door. Community groups were outraged at what they regarded as state-sponsored pornography. Even the governor tried now to distance himself from the committee as editorials in newspapers and on television condemned the committee and elected officials who had encouraged or tolerated its activities. Making matters worse, bookstores in gay neighborhoods in New York and Washington sold out of copies immediately. It had become the number-one best seller in high porn.

Then came the calls for Billy Sloat's resignation. He was stunned. He had devoted nine years to this investigation. Nine years! A thankless job. No, he would not capitulate. Surrender was not an option.

But even the new governor backed away.

—◊◊—

THE GOVERNOR'S DESK was bare except for the copy of what now was described as the "Purple Pamphlet of the Sloat Committee."

"Have you read it?" Sloat asked.

"Officially? No." he said. "But it has ignited a firestorm that I'm not willing or prepared to confront. It may be best for other alternatives."

"What alternatives?"

"Resignation," Governor Green said.

"Resignation?" he blurted. "I spent the better part of a decade exposing moral turpitude in this state. I got no desire or reason to resign this committee."

"We're not talking about the committee, Billy."

"Then what?" Sloat demanded.

"A momentum perhaps for impeachment. There is no precedent in this state for impeaching a senator."

Impeachment! His reaction was total disbelief.

"What are you suggestin'? That I resign from the legislature?" Sloat blurted.

Governor Green maintained his usual stoic demeanor when confronted with unpleasant issues, as Sloat unleashed his contempt.

"You hypocritical bastard. Where were you before this broke? You were set to create the database on every queer in this state. Now I'm the one who's left to shoulder the blame. Well I ain't going nowhere without taking plenty of company with me," he shouted, storming from the governor's office.

Hours later, confronting a battery of reporters, with television cameras grinding away, Governor Green was asked about his reaction to the pamphlet.

"Well," he responded, "there is a copy on my desk, or perhaps I should say, in my desk drawer," shaking his head with disapproval.

—◊◊—

ZACK'S DREAM WAS the same dream, but with subtle variations. Never far in the background were Henson and Munjay lurking in the shadows, their voices pronouncing his guilt. Then it was his father lying in the coffin, the eyes opening without warning, lips moving with a silent indictment of the unworthy son. In another variation he was standing alone in a bare room. He could not see the dean, but the voice rang echoes in his ear. Your father—dead. Relief. Only your father, nothing more.

Zack would bolt upright, gasping for air, with David holding him. "You were dreaming again," he would say. "It was just a bad dream."

THE FIRST YEAR in Asheville was exhilarating for David. After eight grueling years of schooling, he was actually opening his clinic. Even with the cash advance from the bank, and his father's financial support, the practice was off to a slow start, but at least it was a start. He could barely afford the receptionist and the one lab assistant, but with eleven-hour days and boundless enthusiasm, word of his competency spread. By the end of the year, he hired his second assistant. Asheville had been a good choice.

But not for Zack. The town was too small for the kind of law practice he had imagined himself in. No challenging courtroom appearances, just routine legal documents, real estate transactions, contracts, petty claim casework, sometimes a divorce settlement. Hardly worth the time and energy he had invested to reach this juncture of his career.

Why here instead of San Francisco? In a city there could be anonymity and separateness. In a town like Asheville, everyone was connected to everyone else. There was no escape from secrets. He had passed up the opportunity as a junior partner in the San Francisco firm to accommodate David's whim in a small Southern town. He was bored. And increasingly resentful. But it was more than that. Since the move to Asheville, a gulf had developed between David and him, and the distance seemed to widen, adding to his uncertainty about their relationship.

Zack gulped down black coffee, grabbed the briefcase, and headed for the office. He tossed the morning paper on the front seat, glanced at his watch and wrestled with the morning traffic. The snowfall during the night had turned to an icy slush, slowing traffic to a crawl. He was running late for the nine o'clock briefing with his client. The lone lawyer in his fledgling practice, he did not have the luxury of a partner. With a half-time secretary who also doubled as his legal aide, he was it.

"Your nine o'clock called. He's running late," the pudgy secretary muttered without looking up. "Coffee?" she asked.

"Not now," he muttered, edging around her desk in the crowded cubicle that doubled for a reception area. There was barely enough room for the small table sandwiched between two easy chairs from Goodwill.

His own space was not much larger. His desk, a couple of easy chairs and a lone bookcase crowded the room, the only relief the myriad diplomas and cheap prints of landscapes against otherwise bare walls.

"I have to leave early. The baby sitter has an appointment after lunch," she said.

"Go," he said briskly.

"Jesus, you're in a pissy mood today," she complained.

"Just my old sweet self," he retorted without looking up.

"You and David at it again," she asked.

He grimaced without answering.

"You guys need a vacation, time out," she offered.

The vacation they needed was from each other. That's what he wanted to tell her. Between his practice and David's clinic, there was little time or money for anything else. Finances were a challenge, especially for David. That rounded off the relationship. Business came first.

He settled behind his desk, tossed the morning paper to the side and sorted through the stack of mail until he found the check from last week's client. Seven hundred and fifty dollars. Not as good as he would like but it did bring the total above last month's take.

THE MEETING WITH his client was brief. The contracts he reviewed were thorough, and when his client left, Zack opened the morning paper to check out the personals, but the headline of a brief article buried on the second page of the national news caught his attention.

FLORIDA SENATOR UNDER POLITICAL FIRE

He was stunned. It took moments for the full impact to register. Sloat was finally feeling the heat. He read the article a second time, then reached for the phone.

"David, you won't believe what I just read."

CHAPTER 31
NEW YORK CITY, DECEMBER 1964

STEPHEN DISLIKED THIS time of year, the time between Thanksgiving and Christmas, and the holiday cheer only deepened his depression. The snowfall had been a welcome change, concealing the angst of the city, but after a few days, the snow had become a dirty slush. He trudged up Sixth Avenue toward Fifty-Ninth. As he approached Fifty-Ninth, a man pulled by a large Afghan hound rounded the corner, and the dog pounced. Stephen's feet slid out from under him on the icy sidewalk, and he fell flat.

"Oh my God," the man exclaimed. Holding the leash with one hand, he reached down to grasp Stephen's arm. "Are you O.K.? Nothing broken?"

"I'm all right," Stephen said. He made an attempt to get up but slipped again on the ice.

"Let me help you. Are you sure you're all right?"

"Positive," Stephen said, this time getting up. The man with the dog fumbled in his coat pocket and retrieved a card.

"Here," the man said, offering the card to Stephen. "Please, if you should need anything. I'm so sorry. Rajah, bad dog!" he said, frowning his disapproval at the animal. "Oh, God. Look. A tear in your sleeve."

"It's all right. Don't worry, I'm not going to sue you or anything."

"Just the same, have it fixed and send me the bill. I'm so sorry!" he kept insisting.

"O.K., sure, I'll send you the bill," he said, hoping that would end the exchange. "Bye now," he said. Walking away, he rounded the corner at Central Park South and entered the bar of the St. Moritz.

He sat at the opposite end of the bar facing the entrance. The double shot of Scotch gave a pleasant warmth as he gulped it down and then ordered another. What a hell of a way to celebrate a birthday, he thought. As he reached for his wallet, he caught a glimpse of a man who had just entered, stopping to speak to the bartender. *The man with the dog. Jesus.* The man noticed Stephen sitting alone, said something to the bartender, and walked briskly toward him.

"Hello again," he said. "Buy you a drink?"

"That's not necessary, but sure, if you want to," Stephen said.

"Fred Bertolli," the man said, extending his hand.

"Stephen. Stephen Smith," he said accepting the introduction.

"New Yorker or just visiting?" Fred asked.

"Live here," he said.

"How long?"

"A few years now."

"Where, if I may ask?"

"Down in the Village. You?"

"Right next door actually. Sixty Central Park South. My family still lives out in Westchester. Typical Italian family. Believe it or not, five sisters and I'm the only brother."

Stephen studied the man's face. He guessed from the lines around the eyes and a slightly sagging chin, that the man was maybe sixty or so.

"And your family?" Fred asked.

"Only child. Just my mother still living in Florida."

So he's from Florida. What brought him to the city? He couldn't be more than twenty-one or two. Has to be at least twenty-one to drink in a bar. Fred toyed with the glass of bourbon. There was a brief lull in the conversation. "So what do you do in the city? I mean what brought you here?" he asked with genuine curiosity, attempting to engage Stephen in conversation.

"What else? Fame, fortune, success. I'm an actor of sorts."

"Of sorts?" he asked. "Either you are or you're not. Which is it?"

"I've done some off-Broadway and some off-off Broadway. It was a dream I chased back in college. That's what brought me to New York. That was before reality set in. Otherwise, I work at a record shop down in the Village, when I want to eat."

240

"You don't sound very optimistic."

"Well, let's put it this way. In spite of the competition," he said, offering a smile now, "I've still got a few years left," and quickly added, "to chase the dream I mean."

"Mind if I ask how old you are?" Fred finally asked.

"Twenty-eight today," he said not making an issue of it.

"In that case, let me buy you another drink. Look, if you don't have anything planned, my sister Marcie is in the city for the weekend. She's making a light dinner. I'm just next door. Why don't you join us?"

"Thanks, but I'd rather be by myself. Nothing personal, but thanks anyway," he said.

"Well, if you change your mind," he said, finishing his bourbon, "You have my card. Just show it to the doorman. Happy birthday, Stephen." He smiled and left Stephen by himself in the bar.

Outside, the snow clouds loomed close. Stephen trudged slowly back down Sixth Avenue, the wind creating a wind-chill factor in the teens. *Was that a come-on or was the guy genuine? If his sister isn't there, I can just leave. Why not? It's my birthday.* He turned back toward Central Park South and reaching number sixty, handed the card to the doorman. Seconds later, he pressed the buzzer to Apartment 6D and was taken by surprise by an attractive young guy who greeted him, his brown eyes accented by an engaging smile.

"Come in, Stephen," he said, as though he was addressing a friend rather than a stranger he was meeting for the first time.

"You're not Marcie," Stephen said at this unexpected encounter.

"She's my mom. Fred's my uncle. I'm Paul. Hope you like Italian," he said. "Mom," he called over his shoulder, "We've got company. Oh," he added, turning back to Stephen, "and happy birthday."

WEEKS LATER, STEPHEN would admit that it was the best birthday he could remember. He also had to acknowledge that he was turning into a dirty old man. Paul Romano was seven years his junior. Most of the guys he had met since settling in the city were his age or older. Most had been heated encounters that, after a couple of weeks, would cool down and then go cold entirely. He had no intention or desire for a permanent bond. But this was somehow different.

Paul's wild enthusiasm and exuberant energy rubbed off on him in spite of his attempts not to let it happen. The kid was as persistent as he was demanding.

Every night, Paul would wait inside the music shop, leaf through bins of recordings until Stephen closed shop, and they would catch a late-night snack, then head to Stephen's small loft apartment on the fourth floor.

Sometimes, when the winter chill relented, they would venture to the building's roof, open a bottle of wine, observe the city's lights, listen to its unrelenting traffic, and finishing the wine, head down to Stephen's loft to make love. What had started for Stephen as a fascination with someone much too energetic for him was turning into something resembling a real relationship. It wasn't love exactly. But what was it? He couldn't say. He just let it happen.

—⁓—

FIVE YEARS HAD gone by quickly for Lee, who had never let on about his anxiety at the prospects of managing a bookstore and beginning an entirely new life in New York. But the venture, which had been challenging, had also been successful. Even Charlie became a fixture, stretched out on the counter top near the register, purring greetings at customers.

Altogether it was satisfying. While he missed teaching and his students—Zack and David in particular—he was surrounded by the books he loved. He welcomed this turning point in his life and the chance to put the university and the committee behind him. Here in the Village, he was his own person, with no need to apologize for who he was.

During all this time, he had resisted the urge to try to contact Stephen, even though David had given him the name of the music shop where he worked. There really was no reason to make a connection. He had even lost touch with David and Zack, having last heard from them soon after their move to Asheville. The inevitable juncture in their lives, moving off into new directions, created the gap in their relationship that none of them had tried to avoid. They had barely escaped the plague that continued to ruin others left behind.

And it was probably for the best. The encounters with the committee, Elmore's suicide, and Chris's death were emotional wounds still raw, memories Lee wanted to put behind him but which came back in spite of himself. Given time, he might attempt to reconnect with David and Zack, but now was not the time. All in all, he was content. Still he wondered—were the boys happy?

AT NINE O'CLOCK, Lee was turning off the lights and getting ready to lock up the bookstore, when the part-time clerk pounded hard against the glass, pointing to a pamphlet he held in his right hand.

"What in hell is this about?" Lee asked beckoning him in.

"Look at this," he exclaimed. "Hot off the press, and we can buy it in bulk."

Lee's eyes widened at the image on the cover of two nude males embraced in a lip-locked kiss, set against a purple background with the title, and below it the caption:

A REPORT OF THE FLORIDA
LEGISLATIVE INVESTIGATION COMMITTEE

"My God," was all he could say in disbelief.

"And just in time for Christmas sales," the part-timer said "Bulk copies for less than a quarter."

"Jesus, dear boy, we can't sell this. We'd be charged with peddling porn," Lee countered.

"And the State of Florida?" the part-timer countered.

He had a point, Lee thought. It was, after all, an official publication of the State of Florida. Yes, he had a point. And bulk sales too. Within two days, five hundred copies sold out at two dollars each.

CHAPTER 32
RELEASE

THE SEASONAL CHANGE was abrupt. Asheville's January snow gave way to a warm spring. There had been other changes as well. David and Zack sat at the breakfast table, eyes glued to the article in the national section of the morning paper:

> FLORIDA SENATOR RETIRES UNDER FIRE
> Amid demands for his resignation after an almost ten-year investigation of communist infiltration and homosexual activity in Florida universities and schools, Senator Billy Sloat entered retirement from the state's senate for what he described as personal reasons.

David read the article again. For six years, he and Zack had suppressed an anxiety they could not shake. They avoided discussing it, but it was always close. Now it was finished. The committee had self-destructed.

"It's over, Zack. Can you believe it?" David said.

"Over?" Zack said in disbelief. "How can it ever be over, David?"

The damage had persisted. The interrogations, the police summons from class, Chris's suicide, the dean announcing his father's death. How could that be over? There was no relief from it. There could never be. The death of a friend, the lives of ordinary people, ruined from public exposure, left scars that would never heal. He and David were still outcasts, hiding behind respectable professions in a small southern town. They were safe as long as they posed no challenge to the public's tolerance of their pretense. What kind of life was it to live such a lie? And their own relationship was unraveling.

DAVID WANTED TO make things better for Zack, but how? Walter Ashton had tried to convince him that their difficulties were just part of a maturing relationship. But in spite of his father's attempts to reassure him, David knew that the issues ran deeper. The last two years had been difficult for them, a long time to begin repairing a troubled relationship, but he had to try.

"We're going to New York," David announced.

"New York? Why?" he asked, but he had his suspicion.

"We need a vacation"

"You go," Zack answered flatly.

"No, *we* go. Time to finish the unfinished," he said insistently. "It's not been easy for you here, I know. I wish I could make it up to you. Don't know if I can, but I have to try. Don't want to lose you."

Zack studied the face, the hair, the hands, contemplating the inner David that still seemed hidden from him. His mind drifted back to a day in the gym, the image of a young man rushing over to rescue him from the heavy weights he so cleverly managed to lose. Truth was they had shared gains and losses. He wanted more than anything to avoid another loss. He reached across the table, touching David's hand, felt the firmness, the confidence of a hand so eager to fix things broken.

"All right then, New York it is," he said. What he didn't let on, however, was a different uneasiness. Stephen.

—w—

BILLY SLOAT RAMBLED through his mother's house. Except for infrequent visits to the nursing home to see his mother, life in the town of Monroe was dull and uneventful. Few people he had known from adolescence still lived there, and among them only a few friends. Each day, he ate alone at what had once been the icehouse that his mother had bought back in the depression and what the new owners had converted to a truck-stop and diner. Other than that, he spent most of the day tracking trends in the stock market or watching television, and at night attempting to find sleep.

The phone call from the woman just passing through was a welcome relief.

"Senator Sloat?" she asked.

"Who is this?" he asked.

"I'm Lisa Chadwick. I'd like a moment of your time. Is that possible?"

A moment? He had all the moments she cared to have. Who was she, though? Another reporter come to harangue him about the committee? No matter. He could handle that. He switched off the television, settled into the Queen Anne chair, and waited for the visitor.

A half-hour later she was standing on the porch. He peered through the lace curtains. She was a frail woman, dark circles under the eyes, thin, tight lips set against a Southern lady's chalk-white skin. No, she was clearly not a reporter. But who? Not a familiar face at all. What could she possibly want?

"Yes?" he asked. "Do we know each other?"

"Are you going to invite me in?"

He motioned her through the door and pointed to the chair, but she ignored the gesture.

"Won't you sit down? Can I get something for you? Cold tea, lemonade, anything?" he asked.

She hesitated, swallowed hard. "No," she answered, offering an empty expression. He noticed something she held close to her side. She held out a photograph.

He studied it, then returned a confused look.

"Who...what?" he hesitated, "I don't understand."

"No, I'm sure you can't," she said. "My son."

He examined the photograph. Was this someone he should recognize?

"A handsome young man. In school?" he asked.

"Was," she told him, "before you came."

He frowned. "Came? Came where? What's this about exactly?" he demanded.

"You're so much like my son's father," she said, evading his question, her smile an accusation that escaped him.

"I asked you a question. Why are you here?" he insisted.

She looked straight at him, her eyes steady, piercing like pins. "To meet you, of course, after all these years, the man who had such an impact on my son's life," her lips forming now a tight grimace. "Yes, you're so alike, the two of you...he admires you, you know."

His agitation subsided. "Your son?" he asked.

"Oh, God no. My husband. My son was at the university."

"The university? You referring to the investigations?" he asked, aware now of her motive for being here.

"Yes, he was there during that awful time."

"It wasn't just an awful time. It was outrageous what went on there. I never saw anything like it."

"But just the same, Senator, you were the warrior come to save it from itself. You sacrificed so much. Where is the gratitude now for your valiant crusade?"

He was calmer now. He had misread her intentions. "Yes, it ain't easy to stand by your convictions, specially in politics. Many are quick to sacrifice their convictions when it suits their purpose."

"Well, you didn't sacrifice your convictions, Senator. No matter the cost. That is precisely why my husband admires you so. Both of you had a calling. A purpose. Me? Just a mother, a wife, a woman minding her place," she whispered, looking blankly at him.

"Well, Mrs.," he paused, "I'm sorry...it's Mrs...?"

"Chadwick. Lisa Chadwick," she said.

"Well, Mrs. Chadwick, that's a noble callin', if you ask me. So many women today have forgotten where their place is."

"Their place, Senator? Just where is that?"

"Why, in the home. Yes indeed, a powerful callin'."

"That's it, isn't it, Senator? It's all about power. The Bible says the meek will inherit the earth. But it's people like you, like my husband, who set the rules, who make sure they're followed to the letter with the power of your convictions. I was content to be a wife and a mother, really—nothing more. But you, Senator, had your principles. You stood by yours, as I did not stand by mine."

He seemed puzzled. "How do you mean?"

"To oppose what you know in your heart is wrong. To keep silent when it's right to speak."

"Well, of course it ain't easy. Lots of people are with you when times is good. It's when times get hard and you're out there alone that your strength is tested."

"As your strength was tested?" she said, her sarcasm lost to him.

"Tested? Yes. Politics can be a messy business. You just cain't know," he assured her.

"Oh, yes, I know just how dirty a business it is."

There was a deafening silence as the two surveyed each other. Sloat felt the uneasiness return, waiting for her to say something more, but she just stood there, as if in a trance.

And then she said, "Can I ask you something personal, Senator? Are you a religious man?"

He was puzzled. Why was she bringing up religion? "Why do you ask me that? What does that have to do with our conversation?" he asked, his voice raspy with agitation.

"It's a terrible thing to lose—your faith, I mean, your religion. I lost mine when I lost my son. They say hate corrodes the vessel that holds it. If that's true, I'm corroded inside and out." Lisa Chadwick moved toward him, her face inches from his. "But if there *is* a just God, you will stand before Him, Senator, as will my husband, as will I," she said, holding the photograph close to his face, "and try to explain how *this* sacrifice, which you demanded, which my husband accepted, and which I tolerated, was justified. Don't you get it, Senator?" She spit the words out like bullets. "This was my son, just the way God made him, your homosexual menace."

Sloat exploded.

"Listen here," his voice was defensive. "I don't get no love out of hurting people. But that situation in the university! I never saw nothing like it in my life. If we saved one boy from being made homosexual, it was justified," he said defiantly.

"You didn't save him, Senator. You killed him."

CHAPTER 33
RESOLUTION

"LEGAL AT LAST," Paul Romano said happily, tearing the wrapper off the box. Buried in the cotton padding was the gold chain he had coveted when they had wandered from window to window among the small shops in Soho. The pendant on the end of the chain had his initials: PR.

"Happy twenty-one, Paul," Stephen said, planting a kiss on his lips.

"You shouldn't," Paul mocked.

"O.K. give it back then," he quipped.

"No," he teased. He slipped the chain around his neck, examining himself in the mirror. "What do you think?" he asked, turning to Stephen. "It's not nelly, is it?"

"You couldn't nelly it if you tried," he said. He glanced at the photo wedged in the corner of the dresser mirror. They had passed a kiosk in Times Square, and Paul insisted on a photo of the two of them. Stephen thought about another photo. Two young guys on a sandy beach, heads together celebrating their exuberant innocence, and for a moment a melancholy surge engulfed him.

"What's wrong?" Paul asked at the sudden change. He edged close to Stephen. "What?" he repeated.

Stephen acknowledged the puzzled expression on the boy's face.

"It's nothing," he said, attempting to pass it off. Paul was persistent.

"Talk to me. Tell me what's bothering you," he pleaded. The silence was heavy. Paul edged closer now.

"I need to show you something," Stephen said finally. He walked over to the dresser and took a photo album from the drawer. There were only a few photos, his mother, his father, two small kids, a youth standing beside a used Chevy, and on the next page two young boys seventeen—eighteen perhaps, outlined against sand dunes on a deserted beach, the color from the Polaroid now faded into a sepia tone of almost black and white.

"Who's the guy with you?" Paul asked.

"Someone long ago," he told him.

"Lovers?" Paul asked cautiously.

"Not quite. Could have been, but no," he assured him. "Someone like you."

"But you loved him," Paul said with directness.

"It's complicated," Stephen said. He wanted Paul to know about the first encounter, that first most exciting, most painful first that he had thrown away, wanted to but couldn't.

"Try, Stephen," he urged.

He studied the faded photograph momentarily, and looking into Paul's troubled eyes, he began the long painful narrative.

When he finished, the room was almost dark from the fading daylight. They sat mulling the room's silence.

"So there it is, ancient history," he said, waiting for Paul's reaction.

Paul gave a reassuring smile. "You talk like you're an old man."

Stephen said: "I feel old."

Paul said: "I like older guys."

Paul took his hand. For the first time since the night in the Okefenokee, Stephen was happy. But still there was the unsettling anticipation of David and a long overdue reunion, which was imminent.

—⁕—

WILLIAM LEE HESITATED outside the Village Music Shop. He peered through the window and caught a glimpse of the handsome blond clerk behind the counter and recognized him instantly: Stephen. Exactly as David had described him in the letter he had sent, except ten years older, no longer a youth but projecting a mature maleness. For a moment, he imagined David and Stephen as they would have been in their innocence. His thoughts shifted quickly to Zack. This was not the reunion he would have anticipated, let alone welcomed.

He sauntered up to the counter and, smiling now, said, "Hello, Stephen. I'm William Lee."

—✺—

IT WAS A perfect early spring day, a clear sky, and the air a pleasant seventy-two. They chose the Tavern on the Green in Central Park for the rendezvous. None of them could afford it, but there was something reassuring, sitting outside in Central Park rather than entombed inside a restaurant down in the Village.

Paul eyed David cautiously. He tried but could not overcome his feelings of both anxiety and jealousy. The best he could manage was a forced civility, which he hoped none of them would pick up.

Zack concealed his uneasiness. He wished Lee had been able to join them to break the tension, but here they were, the four of them making light conversation, skirting the real issue as to why they were together here at all. He glanced toward Paul, offered a closed smile, which the boy returned. Each sensed the other's discomfort.

Zack pushed his chair away from the table and turned to Paul. "What say—this is my first time in the city. Want to show me the park?"

"Sure," Paul quickly agreed, with a breath of relief, and the two walked toward the pond, leaving Stephen and David finally to confront their demons.

Paul and Zack found a spot near the pond and settled on the bench, neither saying anything. They continued to cast uneasy glances at David and Stephen who appeared lost in uninterrupted, intimate conversation. Zack gave a questioning look at Paul. Paul answered it silently.

Zack looked down, diverting his eyes from him and, heaving a sigh, said with resignation, "Whatever the outcome," and he indicated with a nod of the head toward them, "this had to happen." He could read the uncertainty in Paul's face. "Long overdue, kid."

Paul was glad that Zack was here. Whatever would come of this, they would share it.

Zack understood the boy's anxiety. He had a sudden urge to hold him, to let him know that he knew what the fear was like of losing what you had just found. Instead he asked, "First time?"

"Not with guys. First time like this? Yeah. It hurts that it feels so good. Don't want to lose this."

"I know, kid. I know." He reached inside the pocket of his blazer and retrieved a page that had been carefully folded. "Something I want you to know." He unfolded the page. "David and I, we know what loss is. There was a lovely boy, not unlike you. We lost him. We came so close, but we lost him, and then there was the recrimination, self-reproach, regret, even bitterness that we lost him. But even with that loss, he left us something." He handed the page to Paul, who read the lines quietly, in a whisper actually.

Random Thoughts by Chris Chadwick
David and Zack
Night Along the River

> If I must lose you then, give me your hand;
> Remember how we listened to the night
> Intruders from the dark protesting
> While dried oak branches rubbed curiously
> On the roof? We had no rain to lull us
> Into sleep, nor needed rain while stars
> Cold, quiet, distant through the window
> Fixed upon our shyness. The night was cool
> And yet I felt secure and warm beside you
> As we touched. Was that so long ago?
> Again the stars observe, this time a parting;
> Yet look, two stars, cut through the night
> Piercing darkness with their light
> Even as we touch

Paul folded the paper along the creases and handed it back. He was quiet for a long time. In the distance the traffic of the city bridged the immense silence between them. Then Paul asked, "What happened?" and Zack told him about Billy Sloat and the committee.

—⁂—

BILLY SLOAT HAD suffered yet another loss. Annabelle Sloat, whose mind had long since drifted away into oblivion, even as the Parkinson's disease destroyed her body, finally allowed herself to die. This was the one loss he came to accept with gratitude. His other loss, his exile from power and politics, he accepted with regret and bitterness.

But then, as if God had not finished with him, a stroke left him unable to speak or to move, and wholly dependent upon people he did not know in the home where others had looked after his mother. Was this not a vengeful God, he wondered, since the stroke had imprisoned him physically, but left his mind intact, able to hear, to think, but not to speak?

The nurse had rolled him into the brightly painted sitting room, placing him before the television, which blared the evening news. There in the room with him through the glare of the screen were the familiar faces, their voices explaining once again to reporters their utter astonishment at the illicit activities of the committee now far behind them and the senator's total misappropriation of power. Had they only known the extent of the abuse! One by one, the committee's former members denounced the demagogue. Billy Sloat wanted to scream, but the only sound he could make was a gurgle deep in his throat.

Governor Green insisted that something of this magnitude would never happen again. What he avoided explaining was why 30,000 pages of secret documents, condemning over three hundred people, would be sealed off in pasteboard boxes and hidden away from public scrutiny in the senate office building, not to be opened for seventy-two years.

As months passed, Billy Sloat allowed his mind to skip back to the visit from the woman who had confronted him with the photograph of her son. He saw that face, sometimes in sleep, at other times just sitting in that room, staring out into the neatly manicured grounds of the nursing home. Nature or nurture? he would ask himself. Born like that, or made that way? Only God knows. That vengeful, unforgiving God.

—◊—

DAVID TOYED IDLY with his napkin, avoiding direct eye contact. Their conversation had trailed off. After a moment, Stephen forced an end to the uneasy silence. "Go ahead, ask me." He looked up. Their eyes locked for an instant. "Why did I do it?"

David shook his head. Why were they having this encounter after eleven years of rejection? A mistake. Yet here he was dredging up the past. Why hadn't he left the dredging up alone?

"Ask me," Stephen insisted.

You felt it then, but you don't feel it now. Get a life, you said. The words came through again, cutting deep, opening old wounds he thought had healed. *Why did you do this to us?*

"Why, then?" David forced himself to ask.

Stephen paused, searching for words. He owed him this. He owed himself as well.

"At the time, I convinced myself it was to protect you. Truth is, it was to protect me. I never handled rejection well."

David felt a sudden anger, brief but biting. "You rejected me, Stephen. I was the one you walked away from. Me. This is about me. What did I do?"

"It was never about you, David. It was always about me. To lose something, to find it again, only to lose it. That's my life. You were the strong one, willing to move on, no matter what. I was the weak one. I had a long time to think about running away. No more running, David."

FROM THE DISTANCE of the pond, Zack and Paul eyed David and Stephen sitting across from each other, the expression on their faces difficult to read, the exchange apparently over.

David and Stephen cast glances toward Zack and Paul and again fixed their eyes on each other. David nodded, said something. Stephen acknowledged the gesture. They pushed away from the table and moved directly toward the two camped on the bench.

Paul turned away as they approached and set his eyes toward the pond, watching the ducks. Stephen said his name, but Paul kept his attention focused on the ducks.

Abruptly, Zack stood up and edged toward the pond. David moved past the bench, following him. Stephen eased in close to Paul.

"I have to tell you something," Stephen whispered to him, "something that I should have told you weeks ago."

Paul kept his focus on the pond.

"Something I was afraid to say, something I was even afraid to say to David when I had the chance."

Paul turned toward him, capturing the words he had just heard: "I love you."

—⁓—

THE FOUR OF them walked the two-hour distance from Central Park to Greenwich Village, stopping occasionally as they detoured down Broadway to Forty-Seventh. The human traffic competed with the endless stream of yellow cabs, blaring horns. Zack felt fully alive. As they maneuvered through the crowded sidewalk, David brushed against him. It was not an incidental contact. Playfully, he kept nudging him, and Zack knew from the nudges that something broken was made whole again.

When they reached the Village, they found a tree-lined pocket park and, staking out space, propped themselves against the trees, taking in a perfect day without a word between them. Paul's mind replayed Zack's narrative of the inquisition. It was, he thought, like something out of Orwell's novel, when the character—what was his name—at the end had been forced to love Big Brother.

"No, worse than that," David said. "Our country spent four years fighting the Nazis, and all along we had our own Gestapo here."

"Well," Paul said, "at least it's over."

But Zack broke into the conversation. "Don't even think it, Paul. How many Billy Sloats do you think are still out there waiting for the next opportunity? It's a long way from over."

"I have to believe that someday," Paul countered, "we'll have our own day, our own Martin Luther King. I have to believe that," he said adamantly.

Right, kid, Zack thought. That's what twenty-one is all about. But give it a few years. This is 1965.

Stephen squinted at his watch. Five o'clock. "Cocktail time," Stephen announced. "Up, up, everybody. Follow the leader," he said with a mock command.

They ambled toward a hangout around the corner barely able to move after the long trek from Central Park and down the next block, down past the leather shops, nodding at the drag queens headed in the same direction.

Rounding the next corner, they entered the bar jammed with queers just like themselves, the sign over the door with its greeting: *Welcome to the Stonewall Inn.*

—◊—

AFTERWORD

THE SIN WARRIORS was inspired by actual events that spanned almost a decade and represents one of the most brutal attacks on civil liberties in the nation. In 1956, the Florida Legislative Investigation Committee, commonly known as The Johns Committee and chaired by Senator Charley Johns, was formed to investigate the NAACP as a communist front, following the United States Supreme Court ruling overturning segregation in public schools. Unsuccessful in its attack on the NAACP, the committee shifted its focus to homosexuals in the state's universities. The initial interrogations described in the novel were actually conducted without official sanction from the state legislature until 1961, when the targeting of homosexuals was subsequently approved. Consequently, the committee's early activities at the University of Florida were conducted in secrecy, and in locations described in the novel. Because homosexuality was legally a criminal offense or was regarded as a sickness, there was no defense if an individual attempted to challenge the committee with its power of public exposure. Even those merely suspected of homosexual tendencies had no defense, since to challenge the committee would result in public guilt by association—guilty until proven innocent. The public's disdain for any objective discussion of homosexuality allowed the committee unrestricted intrusion into an individual's private life. Those who did challenge the committee, (the account of the reporter in the narrative, for example) risked ruin.

Once the investigation of homosexuals was sanctioned by the legislature in 1961, the witch hunt openly included not merely teachers and students, but gay individuals in all state agencies, especially gay males, branded as "pedophiles recruiting youth into their deviant lifestyles." Toward the end of the committee's existence, with the illicit publication, "The Purple Pamphlet" (described in the novel—the complete text of which can be viewed on the internet, including illustrations), the committee's long-range goal was to create a database on every gay person in the state, and to bar gays from any state employment whatsoever.

By the time the investigations ended, three hundred administrators, teachers and students had been removed from public institutions, and thirty thousand pages of transcripts, along with scores of recorded interrogations, were sealed and kept from public scrutiny, not to be opened for seventy-two years. A public-records challenge resulted in their release in 1994, but during the twenty-nine-year interval from 1965 to 1994, other developments in the gay and lesbian struggle—the Stonewall riots of 1969, Harvey Milk in the seventies, the AIDS pandemic emerging in the eighties—had created an immediacy that overshadowed the earlier assault on gay and lesbian rights, and the history of the Florida inquisition was largely forgotten.

This was the motivation for the novel, which chronicles Senator Billy Sloat's ascendancy as a ruthless political figure and David Ashton's coming-of-age, and coming-out, which places him and his newly acquired extended family on a collision with the committee. But the novel is not intended as a complete narrative of the inquisition. It is about discovery, loss and redemption, about a young man's awakening and acknowledgement of himself in a time and a place not conducive to such honesty and exploration. While the committee's activities frame the novel, the characters—literary creations derived largely from archival records—are portrayed in part as they were or as they might have been. The characters are best viewed as distillations of actual experiences, forming a mosaic of elements stitched together to advance the narrative. Billy Sloat, for instance, is the embodiment of varied personalities defined by their prejudices, phobias, and reactionary vindictiveness. I have taken creative license in creating the characters and the backdrop on which to cast the narrative, a time when gay people, denied legal protection, were seen by many as unfit merely because of their sexual orientation.

Gays and lesbians, however, were not the only targets. The committee set out to investigate any organization or group of individuals deemed a threat to the state, particularly teachers thought to be communist sympathizers, or who included evolution theory in biology classes, or who assigned "radical" books such as *Brave New World*, *The Grapes of Wrath* and *Catcher in the Rye*.

In spite of progress in the gay, lesbian, bisexual and transgender struggle for equality, homophobia, hate crimes and extremists who would drive the community back into the closets are still prevalent, and that is why this piece of history deserves to be remembered. As the philosopher has warned, those who do not know the past are condemned to repeat it.

JULIAN EARL FARRIS
DECEMBER 2011

ACKNOWLEDGEMENTS

I OWE GREAT thanks to Ruth Coe Chambers, Kathy Clower, Belinda Hulin and Howard Denson for the many hours they spent reading the manuscript and suggesting significant changes. Thanks also to Arnold Dolin for his editorial direction and to Art Copleston and other former students at the University of Florida for allowing me to include their experiences during the probes; to Chuck Spence, Burt Peachy, Demetri Polites, Stephen Frost, Jerry Rosenberg, Ronni Sanlo and Scott Cranin for encouragement during the early drafts, and to Steve Berman at Lethe Press for his commitment to the LGBT community. Most of all my thanks and gratitude to my life partner, Jack Montgomery, who refused to gentle me with his critical readings and comments. I dedicate this in memoriam to my mentor, Professor C. P. Lee and to DeVarde whose life and brief time on the earth will not be forgotten.

ADDITIONAL READINGS AND RECOMMENDED SOURCES

State Library and Archives of Florida, Florida Department of State, Tallahassee, Florida.

Schnur, James A. *Cold Warriors in the Hot Sunshine: The Johns Committee's Assault on Civil Liberties in Florida, 1956-1965*. Thesis, University of South Florida, 1995.

Sears, James T. *Lonely Hunters: An Oral History of Lesbian and Gay Southern Life*, Westview Press, 1997.

Stark, Bonnie. *McCarthyism in Florida: Charley Johns and the Florida Legislative Investigation Committee, July 1956-1965*, University of South Florida, 1985.

Beutke, Allyson. "Behind Closed Doors, The Dark Legacy of the Johns Committee," Copyright, 1999 (a half-hour documentary film produced at the University of Florida).

JULIAN EARL FARRIS earned his B.A. in English at Jacksonville University, his M.A. in English at Florida State University and then taught humanities, became an avid sailor, environmentalist and animal rights advocate, wrote and directed video documentaries on the humanities and resides in Jacksonville, Florida with his life partner and their two rescue cats, Bubba and Annie. He is working on his second novel, *Families and Other Strangers.*

—⚹—

CPSIA information can be obtained at www.ICGtesting.com
Printed in the USA
LVOW121429201012

303743LV00002B/23/P